Silence

by

Lyn Miller LaCoursiere

Copyright © 2012 by Lyn Miller LaCoursiere
Printed by Bookmobile
All rights reserved.
No part of this book may be
reproduced without
the written permission of the Publisher.
This is a work of fiction.
Names, characters, places and incidents
are used fictitiously. Any resemblance
to actual persons, events
or locales is entirely coincidental.

Cover photo courtesy of
**Baker Camp on
Lake Sebago, NY.**

Cover design and format
by Genny Kieley

ISBN # 978-1-938990908

SILENCE is a story of sweetness and conflict---

"I see you dead!" An old woman declared when she appears at Lindy's door in Hilton Head and insists she has something very important she must tell her. Lindy is wary of this stranger's insistence and exhausted from loss of sleep, again, after being plagued with the nightmare of the same three men chasing her.

And after hearing what just may be her demise, Lindy panics. Was this it? Had Mario's family won and they finally would kill her too?

Once again Lindy Lewis is in trouble. Her world is in chaos when a stranger predicts her death. And Lindy, not one to be intimated, gathers her wits about her and faces down her adversaries.

Judith Swartz, creator of The Third Age.

Lyn Miller LaCoursiere's ability to create in depth characters draws the reader to want to learn more about each character. Lyn's writing is comparative to Louise Erdrich where Lyn's colorful and creative characters like the heroine, Lindy Lewis, along with staying true to today's culture and the details to the Midwest, causes the reader to not want to put Lyn's book down until completion. Her books are a must have on every reader's list to read. I look forward to Lyn's next novel.

Jennifer Anderson, Fargo, ND

Her characters are a combination of IDEAS, ACTIONS and REACTIONS.

the TRF Times

Lindy is GUTSY, CONNIVING AND STYLISH!

Genny Kieley, Northeast's author of four great historical books.

We all wish sometimes we could be LINDY LEWIS.

Laura Vosika, author of The Blue Bells of Scotland &The Minstral Boy.

Books by Lyn Miller LaCoursiere

Nightmares and Dreams

Tomorrow's Rain

Sunsets

Suddenly Summer

The Early Years

Silence

A note from the author

Someone once asked me if I would ever quit writing, and I didn't have to think twice about an answer. For I have found, that I really need the timely routine of creativeness each day in some form for me to lead a healthy life.

It's going on twenty some years since I first started when Oprah advised us all to start journaling and rushed out to buy my supplies. I bought Pilot pens and yellow legal tablets and then sat down and began to write about my frustrations and firsts.

I had recently become a widow, and my thoughts were scrambled and full of negatives. But, I struggled to sort those feelings of anguish as she advised, and it took many pens and pages of paper, but over time and tears, I arrived at a point where I could put some of those words of discovery into poetry and then prose.

In Nightmares and Dreams, my first book, I used a real life incident about those carpenter ants eating at my home and fences to start my story. As my books have evolved, my characters have become part of my family of friends. They became more endearing as I went along. A lot of Lindy's adventures have been mine, real or imagined, and Reed is a combination of characteristics of persons I've known.

All and all, over time, I've practiced the art of telling a story. And hopefully, I can continue my litany of make-believe for a long time yet.

Thank you again, dear friends for your devoted following. Please feel free to write a review of any of my books and send it to Amazon.com. All my books are available as e-books, and soon Silence will be included.

E-mail me anytime at: lindylewis1@msn.com.

Acknowledgements

I want to thank Judy Ann
and Joyce for their
laborious editing.
Mary M
again for her technical help
and the constant
diligence of my
NIGHTWRITER
friends.

This book is dedicated to
my siblings
Dodie, Edgar,
Dickie, Sharon,
Norman, Judy, Joyce,
Morrie and Gene.
The Miller clan

-1-

"Lindy, I need to tell you this," Reed said as they lay together entwined in the covers in his bed after making love one evening. "You have been cleared of those fraud charges and my company has gotten their million back!"

Lindy sat up stunned. It took several seconds for her to get the words out. Her eyes were large as she whispered, "I am? When, when did this happen?"

Reed hesitated. "Awhile back."

"Well, when?" She persisted.

He hedged, "It was when you took the stand at Mario's trial." He reached over to the bedside table for a cigarette.

Lindy gaped at him, then flung the covers off and stood up in her bikini underwear and yelled, "You knew then?"

Reed groaned and swiped his hair off his forehead. "Lindy, I tried to tell you many times but you always took off and disappeared. How could I tell you?"

"Reed, you could have found a way," she wailed. "What could have been more important than my peace of mind?" She angrily wiped at her tears.

"I knew you wouldn't understand. I even went to Mexico to tell you, but then Murphy's wife disappeared and I had to get back here.

"Well, how long would it have taken you to just say, Lindy you have been exonerated and my company has their million back!"

"I know Lindy, but I just couldn't blurt it out. I needed to explain." Reed threw the bed covers on the floor and stood up to find his boxer shorts.

"Explain what?" Lindy exclaimed, and reached for his blue robe that she had borrowed and worn the last few weeks. She slipped it on.

"Come on, I heard the coffee start perking. It should be ready in a minute," he said and reached for her hand. She trailed along with him to the kitchen and waited, still dazed as he found two mugs and filled them with the steaming brew. "Here," he said then and set hers down on the round oak table and pulled out chairs for them both.

Lindy sat and took a sip of the coffee, then felt it burn its way down into her belly. She set the cup down hard and some hot liquid spilled over the edge and splashed on the tabletop as she exclaimed, "Just when did this happen Reed, when was I cleared of the fraud charges?" She sucked in her breath and gasped, "And just where the hell did the money come from to pay back your company?"

He lit a cigarette and blew a smoke ring as he seemed to be searching for words that could explain this dilemma and finally said, "Goddamn Lindy, I couldn't tell you earlier."

"Couldn't tell me what earlier?" She grabbed for his pack of cigarettes and lit up. But when she inhaled, she choked and coughed.

It was early in the morning on a Monday and the sun streamed in through the three wide windows that faced Birch Lake. Reed watched a pair of mallards glide lazily over the gentle rippling water, then said, "Lindy, I may as well just tell you. I know you're going to be pissed anyway!" He blew another smoke ring. "Remember when you testified for the FBI at the trial?"

"How could I forget!" she wailed now over tears. "That's when I was put behind bars and then forced to sit there in court, just inches from Mario's murderous stare."

"Well, you didn't know this, but I had put together a deal with the Feds, that if, and I said if, you went to court for them, regardless of the outcome, you would be cleared of all charges!" He took another drag of the smoke and she listened shell-shocked as he continued, "And, they would have to pay my company the million dollars!"

"So they gave your company the million dollars which cleared me! How long have you known this? You knew even before the trial, then didn't you?" Lindy gasped.

"I did. But Lindy, I couldn't tell you."

"So you knew even before I took the stand?" She stared at him as all this settled in her thoughts. "Reed, you're telling me that all this time, when I thought I was still being hunted by the FBI, they had cleared me and your company had their damn money back!? She exclaimed again, "You knew this all along?"

"Lindy, I'm so sorry, but I had no choice!" He reached for her hand, but she jerked hers away as if she had been burned.

She was so angry she could feel her face burning. "You said the FBI gave your company the million? Where did they get the money?"

Reed blew another smoke ring. "Goddamn, they've got tons of money. Where do you think the money goes when they confiscate a plane load of weed, or take down a drug bust. Right in their pocket!"

Lindy jumped up out of the chair and yelled again, "Reed, you're saying the FBI used drug money to pay your company the million they say I stole, to clear me of the fraud charges so I would testify for them? Good lord, that's got to be illegal!"

For a minute he almost grinned at the absurdity of it, and her statement. But he knew the great Federal Bureau could do anything they wanted to do.

With tears running down her cheeks, she exclaimed, "Reed, I can't believe you couldn't have found a way to tell me!" She rushed out of his house then, clutching the blue robe and ran down to the dock, tears cascading down her face. She sat by the water and cried hurting tears.

Autumn was broadcasting its last array of colors and wisps of smoke from burning leaves drifted by. After her tears subsided, she watched mesmerized as groups of monarch butterflies fluttered to land on bushes to rest and then dipped for a cool drink of lake water on their journey that would take them, thousands of miles across state lines and over borders to rendezvous at their winter home.

It had been several weeks since she had been kidnapped and then rescued. After a couple of nights in Reed's guestroom, she was back in his bed and had thought they might even stay together. The pain and itching from the bug bites after being left to die in the forest had almost disappeared and the head wound after being shot had healed. He hadn't been too happy when she had walked out of the hospital in Brainerd and arrived by taxi at his door, but he had nursed her back to health. Mario D'Agustino was dead now and her long-lived fear of him and his wrath at her for turning him over to the FBI was finally over.

Reed came out of the house dressed a short time later. He kneeled down by her side and said, "Lindy, I'm so sorry. Goddamn, I didn't mean to hurt you, but you've got to understand, I couldn't tell you about the deal with the feds, it could have influenced your testimony at the trial!"

She sniffed. "That's just the point Reed, I don't understand!"

"Listen, I've got to take off right now and go into town and see the sheriff, but I'll be back at around noon," he said.

"You're leaving now?" Lindy frowned and pressed her lips together in frustration. She swung her legs over the edge of the dock and dipped her toes in the water.

"Look, why don't you relax and I'll bring home lunch and we'll talk." He stood up then in his perfectly pressed jeans and white shirt opened at the throat and sleeves cuffed over, showered and fresh.

She clutched the blue robe closer around herself, knowing she was a total mess. "Okay," she said then and turned away needing time to think. He left the dock and a few minutes later she heard the Corvette roar to life and leave.

When her tears dried, she went back into the house and took a shower and blow dried her blonde hair and put in her brown contacts. Another lump gathered in her throat as she remembered the piles of clothes that Reed had found slashed and torn in his foyer after she had been kidnapped. All those beautiful dresses and summer outfits she had bought in Hilton Head that first summer had been ruined. Cut to pieces by Mario's men when they had taken her. Now, all she had was the pair of black shorts and a tube top, plus a few things she'd had in a bag when she had first come back to Reed's weeks ago.

When she had been left to die in the forest, she had somehow gathered all her psychic energies and sent Reed a message about where to find the million and that he should return it. When she hadn't died after all, she had panicked that it was too late. But thankfully, he hadn't gotten a clear message.

The first thing she did after coming back to his house, after he had settled her in the guestroom was climb back out of the bed. She reached under it to the far corner and pulled out the bag. Her money was safe! She had opened the overnight bag carefully and saw that all the stacks of money were still safe and sound in their bundles.

Yes, she had exclaimed to the walls and ran her hands over the silky greenbacks. She felt better. And it was hers! Not that she hadn't thought it was hers before, but now she didn't have to run and hide to keep it. She had stuffed the bag back under the bed to the far corner. Dressed in her black shorts and tube top, she slipped on her black wedgie flip flops and went back out to Reed's kitchen. He had said to make a pot of coffee, she murmured under her breath looking at the time.

While that was perking, she sat down at the table and let her thoughts ramble. She still couldn't believe that she didn't have to run anymore. That the FBI had paid Reed's insurance company their damn money! That she wasn't wanted by the law any longer.

But she couldn't forgive Reed. Angry and heartsick, she gazed out the window at the lake. How could he have just let her go on like that? Always being afraid, and even having to flee across the border to Mexico.

Not willing to admit that she had committed a crime by burning down her lovely mansion, well- it wasn't up to him to make her suffer for it!

As she fluffed her hair, she suddenly glimpsed a faraway memory and thought, Lordy, I have all my money and the lovely silver Lexis is standing right here in Reed's garage!

-2-

The countryside flew by as Lindy held her foot down hard on the accelerator in the silver Lexus as she sped out of Birch Lake. She blinked back tears as she realized what she had just done, then turned off the cell-phone Reed had bought for her and tossed it in the back seat.

For God's sake, she couldn't have just sat there and waited for him to show up. With another lame excuse, why he hadn't thought she deserved to know the plan he had so carefully worked out with the FBI. It had totally affected her life! Her life, she whispered brokenly.

She took one hand off the steering wheel and reached over and fumbled in her purse for a tissue and wiped her eyes. She had driven for several hours now and was nearing Minneapolis. Glancing at her watch she saw it was close to noon and Reed would have come back with lunch by now, back in Birch Lake.

Well, he just didn't get it, she said out loud as she drove. He just didn't feel I was special enough to treat with respect. Over another sob she remembered it had been so good to be in his arms again and in the safety of his home. But, she had been there long enough to see that he lived his life in an orderly fashion and she had sensed she wouldn't fit into it.

What would she have done with herself when he left for parts unknown to investigate a crime for that insurance company he worked for? Stay there alone in that town? Although it was a nice quaint place, she didn't see or feel the romance he said he felt living there. His house was lovely, but she didn't really feel at home in it. She had grown up in the country, near a small town, but after she got to the big city, she knew that was the life for her.

The traffic had gotten fierce as she neared the twin towns of Minneapolis and Saint Paul and she had both hands glued to the steering wheel as she merged into eight lanes of traffic.

Where would she go in the city? She hadn't lived there since her college days and the last year had been those carefree days of books and young love.

Good lord, decades had passed since then. Her heart skipped as she thought back to those magical years of meeting Reed and falling in love. Although she had come back several times over the years to see him when she had needed help, she had changed tremendously since then.

Did she know anybody who still might be living in the town? She doubted it. But she still had some family who lived out in the country. Did she want to take time and renew the relationships? She thought about that as she drove. The folks were gone but some siblings still resided in the area. It had been quite a few years since she had been back. Did she want to go now? No, she didn't want them to see her in this state. After all the publicized news, as far as they knew she was finally settled safely in Birch Lake with Reed. A good man!

The beat of the city began to excite her then as she soon found herself stuck in traffic in downtown Minneapolis. After long minutes of waiting in line to move, she saw a sign just ahead for the Andrews Hotel. A newly built, "high end experience," it advertised with parking under the huge enterprise.

Now this was what she needed! She guided the silver Lexus onto the right lane and into the parking complex as directed. She took her bags, and then followed the signs into the hotel.

Lordy, the place was beautiful, and it was just the kind of place that would perk her up. Glamour and pampering would help her get over the blues after Reed's failures. Help get my "mojo" back, she remembered it was called and forced a grin on her face.

Shining dark oak floors gleamed and accentuated the lovely greens and blues adorning the plump sofas, chairs and Oriental rugs. Silk shaded lamps sent a soft glow over the casual seating groups. Tinkling background music caressed the ear. The air was cool and dry with a hint of flowers.

She was still wearing the same black shorts and tube top which were wrinkled now and slightly out of place. But she had stopped earlier and reapplied her make-up and fluffed her hair.

"All our rooms are suites," the desk clerk remarked and raised his eyebrows after checking her appearance.

"Really? That's just what I'm looking for!" Lindy answered, with just a little sarcasm to match his and then added, "And I will be staying indefinitely." How do you like that? She thought and signed Lola Lang on the register.

"A credit card?" he asked.

"No thanks, I have the cash!" She quipped and counted out a number of fifty dollar bills, as he stood looking on wide-eyed.

After settling for a week's stay, she said, "And I would like the concierge to come to my room. In an hour, please?"

The desk clerk looked pointedly at her clothes again and remarked dryly, "I will be happy to."

Asshole, she thought to herself, ticked at his snooty attitude.

Finding her rooms, she dropped her things inside the door. The beautifully decorated sitting room again carried on the same theme of greens and blues in the carpet and furniture. The bedroom had a king sized bed, and a dressing table with a three sided mirror. Another framed floor-length mirror took up space. The bathroom was spacious and held a toilet bowl and a bidet in a separate closet. She smiled at that. Then looked for the one thing she had remembered would be offered by this luxury establishment and found the discreet brochure on the desk that declared a safe was offered for valuables, discreetly hidden behind doors in a wall cabinet. She counted out several bundles of bills and locked up the rest.

It didn't take her long to unpack her belongings and she turned on the water in the bathroom. Jars of bubble bath and oils lined a side of the tub and soon the perfumed water edged to the top. She stepped into the flower scented bubbles and groaned with pleasure. Now this was the life, she said to the walls, and raised a foot up and balanced a bubble on her toes. When her doorbell chimed later, she was ready in the white terry robe that the hotel offered.

"Good afternoon, Miss Lang," the concierge said, "How can we enhance your stay with us?"

She greeted the elegantly dressed man and nodded for him to enter and have a seat on the sofa. "Sir," she said with a regal tilt to her head, "I would like you to arrange for a personal shopper from Nordstrom's to come over right away. I need a wardrobe." As she talked she slid several hundred dollar bills across the coffee table to him. "And I also need an immediate appointment in the beauty salon."

"Right away, Miss Lang. Anything else?" He asked.

"Thank you, but I'll decide later," she added.

"I'll make the arrangements immediately and call you." And he walked to the door. "And may I add we are happy to have you with us in our establishment!"

After the door closed she murmured, and my money talks!

Her day was busy and she managed for a time to forget Birch Lake, Reed and the horror of her ordeal with Mario. She spent several hours in the salon getting her hair colored red again, trimmed and styled, then got a manicure and pedicure. She made a stop in the gift shop for one quick, outrageously priced outfit. By late afternoon a personal shopper had been there and taken her measurements and sizes, and laden with her preferences, the woman hurried off to gather a wardrobe for her and promised to be back early the next day.

Now Lindy sat down and caught her breath. She put her elegantly colored toes up on the coffee table and put her head back to rest on the sofa top. She just needed to rest for a minute and then she had to find a restaurant and get some nourishment.

She closed her eyes, blew out her breath and within minutes dropped off. The only sound in the hotel room in downtown Minneapolis after that was the occasional "yes," that she murmured in a dream. She was Lola Lang with a new look. Was it a vision of things to come as she slumbered to the swishing sounds of rolling waves and hot sand tickling her toes?

-3-

Reed parked in his driveway and went into the house. "Lindy," he called out looking around as he walked through the rooms. Going into the kitchen, he put the take-out boxes of lunch on the table.

"I'm back, Lindy. Where are you?' He said loudly and began to unwrap the toasted steak and onion sandwiches and laid out the catsup for the French Fries. Taking milk out of the refrigerator he poured two big glasses and set them on placemats, then laid out the matching napkins.

He stepped back and checked his work then realized the house was awfully quiet. The last few weeks he had grown used to feeling Lindy's presence when he arrived home. He had to admit he rather liked it. Now the place was stone-still.

Goddamn, he muttered as a sick feeling edged down his chest. He turned and in hurried steps crossed the kitchen, the living room, and his boots echoed on the wood floors in the hallway, then on the carpeted bedroom floor. The room was empty and the bed they'd shared for weeks neatly made. He opened closet doors and checked the guest room and that was empty too. In the bathroom, a damp towel was laid over the shower rod and the sink wiped dry and shiny.

He hurried back to the living room, to the windows that looked out on the water to see if she could still be down on the dock. But the only thing he saw were the monarch butterflies bounding on the water here and there.

Now that sick feeling hit him for real. But he had one more thing to check and he hurried to the garage. His heart lurched abruptly when he saw the silver Lexus was gone!

He stood still as loneliness swept through his thoughts and uprooted his emotions. But he immediately swept them away and got pissed. Why would she leave now? Goddamn, she didn't have to hide anymore!

He swiped at his hair that had fallen down on his forehead as he stood by the windows. He had thought that they could have stayed together this time. Had even contemplated marriage. But apparently he'd

Silence

been whistling in the wind. She wasn't serious. And like before, just ran out and away!

He dialed her number on the cell-phone he'd insisted she have. It rang and rang.

"Pick up, Lindy," he said into the receiver, "Where are you?" But after about twenty rings and nothing, he gave up.

He went back into the kitchen and sat at the empty table and ate the cold sandwich and fries. Then he sat for a long time at the table and gazed out at the lake. He lit a cigarette and blew smoke rings. Goddamn, he said out loud, but I just couldn't find a good time to tell her! Then growled, but I should have known she would be pissed when she found out that I knew all along that she had been cleared.

After the ruckus with the D'Agustino family, the two men drowning and Mario's death, Birch Lake had settled down. Manny had gone back to Dallas and the FBI had faded back into the horizon. Things had started to look good but still Reed sat. He felt alone after all the action.

Then he thought, maybe she just went for a ride and will be back soon and breeze in the house with a smile. But then he had to admit that why would she take all her jars and bottles of make up along if she was coming back! He'd checked and they were all gone.

Getting up from the table, he forced himself to clear the dishes and wipe up the crumbs. He filled the dishwasher and turned off the coffee pot.

Well hell, he muttered and grabbed his keys and dark glasses and went back out to the Corvette. He wasn't hungry so he didn't go to the Woodman Café, but went to the Legion, the next best meeting place in town.

Jesse Montes, the sheriff, was there and waved at him as he came in.

"Join us, Conners. I put my deputy in charge today. I'm taking Sue here to the casino to play some blackjack and have dinner," Jesse said.

"Hey thanks, I will," Reed took the stool next to Sue, who glared at him, but he just smiled at her.

Susan Montes was seldom seen around town and most residents stayed at arm's length from her. Her family had lived in Birch Lake for generations and had originated from Norway. Her grandfather had started a mining business in the northern parts of the country and the business was carried down through several generations and was still operating under a conglomerate with a board of directors. Sue was an only child and the last remaining member of the family. Reed knew she got a handsome check each year from the business. Her father, a widower, had some terse words with Jesse before he died, and Jesse had no choice but to nod and promise again, never to divulge their agreement. Then the old man kicked off, much to his relief. And Sue never knew that her father had traded her to Jesse. In that exchange, if Jesse took Sue, a spoiled brat, off his hands and married her, an official position could be arranged for him as sheriff in the township. And Jesse being a young Mexican, full of testosterone, jumped at the chance. And he had been bought and jerked around by that cantankerous ass-hole ever since. And Sue, being pampered and spoiled rotten growing up, used her pedigree and made his life miserable. But Jesse liked his position, even the pretentious home on the lake after the hovel he'd come from in his homeland. And so for years he had shut up and had his own daydream. But one night after the mess in Birch had been cleared, Reed had joined Jesse for a drink, and they both had gotten totally blitzed and had divulged some of their inner secrets.

Sue was middle-aged now, and had a definite Norwegian look about her. Her hair was gray and her blue eyes crinkled with lines around them when she smiled. Not that she did that often with the town-folk of Birch. Her life was centered around the golf club of Brainerd and the movers and shakers of that community.

Reed smiled at her now even though he knew her actions were mostly for show.

"Where is your houseguest?" She asked now leaning over Jesse. Her dangling earrings flashed in the late afternoon sunshine that blazed in through the windows.

Reed tossed a bill on the bar and reached for the Crown Royal and stalled for time. "Lindy is doing her thing at the moment," he declared not wanting to divulge any more than that. Aside from being a pretentious snob, Sue was a terrible gossip.

Reed looked around the bar and nodded to a number of friends. Actually he knew most of the customers, except for several groups of strangers who were apparently visiting the area. Some of the lake summer homes were rented out for the season and that brought in extra revenue for the businesses.

He nodded again now to Jesse and Sue Montes after finishing his whiskey. "Hey, thanks for the company, I've got to run and take care of some things." He stood up. "Good to see you again Sue," he said, "and take good care of my friend!"

He did not like her, and tolerated her only because she was married to Jesse. Several years ago, she had made advances toward him at a party which he had immediately refused and she'd been pissed ever since. And today he was just not in the mood to make nice to her.

He went back out to the Corvette and took off. And instead of turning off highway 371 again at his crossing, he sailed right by, the Corvette's well-oiled parts purring contentedly as he shifted gears.

Silence

After minutes of concentrating on the speed and performance of his vehicle, Reed slowed down and let his thoughts roam freely.

Now what would he do? He had to admit this whole episode, this whole upheaval of Lindy coming back into his life, and the repercussions, had left a mark on him.

Goddamn, he smacked a hand on the steering wheel. He'd only done what he had because he was watching out for her. But, like the words of that old country tear-jerker, he felt used and abused.

He lit a cigarette as he sped along, but where the hell was he going anyway? He slid into a U-turn and headed back to Birch Lake.

The telephone was ringing as he came into his kitchen and when he picked up, the familiar voice of Ed, his boss from the First Federated Insurance Company boomed in his ear.

"Conners, I heard about your tangle with the boys from south of the border. You took care of the fuckers?"

"We did. I had help!"

"Good riddance of garbage. Hey, are you about ready to come back to work?" Ed's voice echoed over the phone. "I need you on a big one!"

"Well hell, what's up?" Reed asked. He pulled out a chair from the table and sat down.

"I've got a twenty-five million dollar claim that needs looking into. Something looks fishy."

"Where at?" Reed listened. Goddamn, he was just in the right mood to get on someone's case and make them bleed.

"Stillbrook," Ed said, "close to Minneapolis. Some old dude keeled over an upstairs railing, no apparent illness the medical examiner says. He'd been living with a daughter and has two sons that are running the family's business."

"What's their business?" Reed asked now.

"Builders. You've heard of Hovland Homes? That's them. They own most of the small town." Phones rang in the background in Ed's office as he talked.

"Yeah, I've heard of the company. Don't they build those custom palaces out in the north suburbs down there?" Reed blew a smoke ring as he thought over what Ed was saying.

"That's them! I need you on this, Conners. Call me back by the end of the day!" Ed hung up abruptly as usual.

Reed went out and stood and looked at the lake. After what had happened out on it, he just wasn't enthused enough to go out and fish or just cruise over the water. He went over and got in the boat, checked switches and anchors, then tucked the cover over the top. In the house he packed a suitcase with underclothes and toiletries and put his jeans, trousers and jackets in a zippered bag. He went to the phone and called his neighbor Abby.

"Are you leaving again so soon?" She asked.

"A new case," he said. "Abby, I'm wondering if you could call my cleaning lady and give her the key to come in. I figure I'll be gone a few weeks, but you know my cell number."

"Oh sure, Reed," she said. "We'll keep an eye on your place."

"Thanks Abby. Tell Joe he can take the boat out anytime if he wants. It's full of gas."

It was dark by now and going on ten o'clock. Wanting to get on the road to Minneapolis early, Reed went to bed and fell asleep, almost instantly.

After several hours something woke him up. He sat up dazed, and glanced around his bedroom. Nothing seemed out of place, but then out of the corner of his eye, he was sure a shadow had moved just outside his shade-less window. Pissed, he threw the covers off and opened the drawer in his bedside table and took out the .38 which was loaded and always ready. Then he slipped through the darkened house and quietly opened the back door, the gun ready to blast who or whatever was out there!

.

-4-

Lindy awoke from her nap on the couch in her hotel room, momentarily dazed. The pink and orange floral patterned dress and the strappy pink high-heeled sandals she was wearing were new. She hurried to the big floor length mirror and gawked at herself. And, she was a redhead! The last she remembered, she was a blonde! Now her hair was short and arranged in a short cap of wispy fringes. She turned this way and that way and did like it. Then she groaned and remembered; she had left Reed in Birch Lake. She swallowed a sudden sob.

But he just did not take my feelings seriously, she wailed and sat down and furiously wiped at tears as all the raw feelings surfaced again that she had fought with on the drive to Minneapolis. But after a few more minutes of painful sobbing, she determinedly blew out a breath and dried the tears.

After repairing her make-up, she gathered up her purse and room key and locked up. Downstairs in the lobby, she saw several eating places were advertised; a coffee shop, a five-star dining room and the Hideaway. And she chose the Hideaway, which she saw was located on the roof top. Back in the elevator, she punched the stop for the place and saw it was up a floor from her suite on twelve. It came to a smooth stop and she stepped out and into a large open air room, with white linen covered tables and glowing candles. Booths lined along two sides, and a dance floor was off to another, then a long marble bar with people three deep lined another wall. Music purred from speakers and dancers swayed to Beyoncé as she crooned a romantic ballad.

"Good evening," a host at the door announced and then pointedly asked, "Do you have a reservation?"

He too was puffed-up. She would have liked to tell him she was very familiar with the business and being snobbish wasn't one that drew customers.

"No, I'm alone and I don't have a reservation. But I would like a table and have dinner." And after he checked the amount on the bill she slipped in his hand, he suddenly did become very friendly.

Silence

"Certainly," he said now. "Follow me madam." And he led her past the packed bar and the sea of tables and people to a booth.

Lindy walked with a practiced sway in her stride and her red head held high. As he waited for her to get settled, she said, "Would you be so kind and tell my server to bring me a glass of your best champagne, please?"

"Certainly madam," the man said and began to walk away.

"Excuse me please, sir?" she said then. "My name is Ms. Lang, please don't call me madam!"

"So sorry," he said.

Lindy studied the menu as she waited for her champagne. She was tired of burgers and roasts and the fattening wholesome foods of the Midwest. Starting now, she was going to eat light and get back into shape. When she was being measured for the new clothes, she had been horrified at the extra inch that had sneaked onto her waistline. An inch there and four pounds of fat, that is. Of course, while she had been recuperating at Reed's house, she hadn't done any exercising. And Reed had been intent on getting her back on her feet by feeding her all the goodies which she ate with gusto. But no more! Good lord, if she had stayed in that small town, she would have turned into a fat middle-aged old lady. It was bad enough getting to middle-age, but to be overweight and old, well, this sent shivers through her just thinking about it.

After the first taste of the bubbly wine, she fumbled in her purse and found the silver cigarette holder and slipped a Marlboro in it. Then remembered the "No smoking" signs in the hotel, except here in the open air Hideaway.

How did they expect you to enjoy champagne without a smoke? She mumbled. No wonder the place up here is packed.

Now she had time as she sat in the elegant rooftop room in the hotel in the new Andrews hotel to work on her plan. She had over a million dollars sitting in the safe in her room. She had gotten lucky way back when she had been in Newport, Rhode Island and invested it in stocks and within days the market had exploded. Then her investment broker had wisely reinvested her money and in the end her original investment had almost doubled. She'd been outrageously lucky this last year at keeping her million plus intact, but now she had to get serious. It was over with Reed and she didn't have anyone she cared about in this part of the country. She sipped at the champagne. She had signed in the hotel as Lola Lang and was a red-head again. She had liked the distinctiveness she'd felt it gave her in Mexico and wanted that feeling again.

But what would she do now, and where would she go?

She had loved the landscaped, colorful vistas of flowers and trees when she had lived in Monterrey, Mexico. But Lordy, she couldn't go back to that country where the D'Agustino family lived. Even though Mario was dead, his cousin Rio Prada was still alive and would certainly find her and do her in too. Her lips curved in a smile as she remembered running into her friend Monica who lived in Monterrey, and the fun times they'd had together.

Taking the new cell phone Reed had convinced her she needed out of her purse, she turned it back on and dialed Monica's house in Monterrey.

"Hey girlfriend," Lindy said. "How are you?

"Lola Lindy, where the hell are you?" Monica's voice was clear as a bell over the miles. "How are you?"

Lindy laughed. "First of all, I'm fine now. I know you talked to Reed a few times and he filled you in on all the action. Birch Lake has settled down now, but I left."

"You left? I wondered how long you would be content to stay there, even though you had someone there who wanted you," Monica said.

"Well, I tried, but I need to come first with the guy I love. I didn't with Reed." And for a moment, even though she appeared to be a classy well-dressed woman of means as she sat in the elegant restaurant drinking their most expensive wine, Lindy felt like a lonely uncertain little girl at heart.

"So, are you coming back to Monterrey?" Monica asked.

Lindy hesitated for a minute, then said, "No, I don't dare come back, with Mario's cousin living there with the families. But I'm thinking of coming close."

"Okay, girlfriend let me know and hurry. It's party time here in the south!"

-5-

With the .38 clasped in his hand, Reed crept silently out the back door of his house. At the corner of the building, he stuck his head around it for a quick look. It was one of those black nights, so dark you could barely see your hand in front of your face.

He blinked hard and strained to get a clearer look. Now he could make out a dark form standing in front of his bedroom window. It didn't move, just stood there. Since all the commotion in Birch lately he was still worried about more repercussions from the D'Agustino family.

He took a quick step and rounded the corner. From what he could make out now through the blackness whatever it was looked to be tall and burly. Tall as the window! That meant over six feet.

Sweat glistened on his forehead. A fucking giant, he groaned inwardly.

"You got one minute!" he yelled then, pissed at the nerve of some asshole to come on his property and snoop at his window.

His finger burned to pull the trigger as he stood, legs braced.

Then to his astonishment the trespasser dropped down and let out a piercing growl. Reed raised the gun and fired, toward the sky to scare him off. And just then a shaft of moonlight spread over the back yard, and, he saw it was a bear. A huge brown bear!

His heart lurched in his chest and he fired in the air again. But now to his horror the animal charged straight at him. Reed fired the .38 a third time, this time just over its head. And suddenly and finally, it veered off toward the woods which edged up to the back yard. Then he saw two small bundles of fur scramble out of the bushes and take off after the fleeing animal.

Goddamn, he said again to the night as it gathered its velvet darkness around him. He lowered the gun and stood by the side of his house and listened. He could hear the mother bear still grumbling to her babies as they charged back into the forest. It was common during the summer for bears to venture out of the woods and scrounge for food. They were extremely curious about humans and it had happened that they could break into a house and completely demolish it in their search for anything edible.

He went back into the house and saw it was four o'clock in the morning. His legs were shaking so badly he sat down quickly at the table. Sweat ran off his face as he tried to calm down. He realized his mistake of not grabbing his rifle instead of the .38 on his way out there. But how was he to know it was a bear out there at the window. But he knew mother bears were especially dangerous and could tear a person to pieces if they had their youngsters with them and thought you were going to harm them. He could have been clawed to death! He lit a cigarette with a shaking hand.

It was a late summer Saturday coming up, and the countryside was ablaze with clover and its various wild flowers and scents. Soon the leaves and grain fields would be turning color and the hum of machines would rumble over the land and gather the bounty of another season. Autumn was great, but the start of winter always depressed him. But after it settled in, he liked the coziness of his fireplace and his books and of course his snowmobile and skis that stood in the garage. But now, he had a lot of summer left to enjoy and he intended to do just that when he got to Minneapolis.

After drinking a pot of coffee, he locked up the house and garage and got on the road. The sun was just coming up and the traffic was sparse on the highway. He slid a new Norah Jones CD in the player and sat back as he sped over the roads. Then thoughts of Lindy crept back again to haunt him.

Where the hell had she gone? Why didn't she answer her cell-phone? He had left at least a dozen messages by now. He sank into a funk.

Maybe he should have pursued those thoughts of matrimony! But was he good marriage material? He was closing in on the big 50 and had never been married. He didn't have kids but thought about being a father. He had always thought he would be one sometime. Was it too late? He pictured teaching a son to walk, to ride a bike, shoot a gun and telling him about the birds and bees. Maybe having a little girl, a little Lindy. He thought about that and smiled. How would Lindy raise a miniature of herself? His mind wandered over the pictures as he drove and Norah sang her love songs.

Suddenly depressed, he tossed the CD in the back seat and slipped Willie Nelson's latest in the player. He began to feel better as the skyline of the twin towns of Minneapolis and Saint Paul soon came into view. He was driving at seventy-five, going on eighty miles an hour to keep up with the rush. He swore at the rude aggressiveness of some highway drivers.

In the city, he swung into the parking ramp under the huge First Federated Insurance Company building which was located in the heart of downtown

Silence

Minneapolis. Locking the Corvette, he grabbed his briefcase and hurried to the elevator. When it stopped on the executive floor he was greeted by a receptionist who ushered him in to the inner office where Mona, Ed's secretary, sat at her usual desk.

"Reed Conners!" she exclaimed and flew into his arms.

After a hug they stepped back and sized each other up.

"Mona, you are looking so good!" Reed said then and smiled for the first time all day. "I didn't know you were back at work already."

"I couldn't stay home any longer. I'm done with all the treatments and need to keep busy." She had worked for Ed for years. She was somewhere in her fifties, Reed knew, but looked to be in the forties. Her black hair had started to grow out after the chemo treatments and curled in wispy tendrils, and the pallor in her cheeks had disappeared.

"Is your sister still staying with you now and then?" Reed asked as he put an arm around her waist.

"No, I convinced her that I'm okay and for her to stay at home and take care of her own family." Mona smiled up at him.

"Does that mean I can come over soon?" Reed joked.

Mona laughed, "Maybe."

"I'm sorry about not keeping in better touch with you. Your sister did tell you I called quite a few times though, didn't she?"

"She did, and I heard about all the events going on up in Birch on the news. I'm just glad you didn't get hurt!"

"Me too." Reed laughed.

"Can I ask where the wandering Lindy Lewis is?" Mona asked.

"She left. And, I don't know where she is." Reed shrugged his shoulders.

Nonchalantly Mona remarked, "I thought after being left to die in the woods up there in your country, she would have settled in and taken up housekeeping with you."

"Not happening," he remarked dryly.

"Did you want her to?" Mona asked curiously.

"Honest to God, I thought about it," Reed confessed. And then added, "But she apparently found my life much too boring!"

"You really think so?" Mona looked at him strangely. "I would think she would have wanted your stability in her life."

"Who knows! Listen I'm starved, do you have plans for dinner tonight?"

"I do now," Mona smiled. "But Ed is waiting for you. Come on," she said and led the way to the double doors leading into the CEO's office.

-6-

While sitting in the rooftop Hideaway restaurant in the Andrews Hotel in downtown Minneapolis, Lindy ordered a shrimp salad with a raspberry dressing and rye crisp crackers to start her "get in shape" program. She sipped her champagne and then took her time as she picked daintily at her dinner. A plan had begun to take place as she sat demurely enjoying the ambiance and the elegant atmosphere. Now, this was what she had given up in Monterrey, Mexico when she had to abruptly leave the city because of the unscrupulous D'Agustino families. She had loved having the rich and famous artist and prominent resident Marguerite Ames as a dear friend. Loved being sought out as a psychic and having her own business and especially loved having her old friend Monica there. Belonging to the elegant country club had been another exciting adventure. Now she had nothing left of that life that she had striven so hard to achieve. An empty ache reared in her chest.

Would being with Reed have been enough to make her happy? She had thought so, at times.

Well, now that wasn't going to happen either.

When she had signed Lola Lang to the hotel register as she had checked in, she had, had a vague idea of the change she needed to make. But Lordy, she needed much more money to live in the style she deserved now.

First however, she had to bank the million plus dollars she already had for safety. No more carrying all that cash around. She could get robbed like that time in Dallas when that bandana clad thug had stolen her BMW. Luckily, she had beaten him at his own game, and stolen it back with her money untouched in its hiding place.

Taking her telephone book out of her purse, she looked up several numbers. One was to financial banker, James Burns in Newport, Rhode Island, the man who had invested her million previously, when it had almost doubled in value for her. He answered on the first ring and Lindy poured on the charm.

"Mr. Burns," she said, "remember me, Lola Lang?"

"My dear, it's so good to hear from you. Have you come to Newport?"

"I wish, but I'm stuck in the Midwest for now. How are you?" She asked.

"Working late again as you can see."

"James," she said sweetly, "I'm wondering if you can look at some "for sure" investments for me. I need something short term."

"I can do that. Give me your number and thirty minutes and I'll call you back." The man had been all business when she had met him months ago, and she had felt a certain magnetism between them and could have acted on it, but didn't have time then, or now, to pursue a romantic interlude. But she had trusted him previously and needed his expertise right now to increase her financial worth.

"Thanks, I'll wait for your call." Lindy clicked off her cell-phone and finished her salad and then sipped at the second glass of champagne as she sat. Just then a stranger edged his way through the crowd of dancers and came over to her table.

"Hello," he said, "You look pretty lonesome sitting over here by yourself. Would you like to dance?" He was young, blonde and had the bluest eyes she had ever seen!

Lindy smiled. "Thank you," she said, "But I'm waiting for a call."

"Well, let me wait with you," he exclaimed and began to slide into the booth.

"Excuse me. I said I'm waiting for an important telephone call!"

He no doubt didn't get turned down that often, and stood for a minute as her reply sunk in. "But you will later?" He continued.

Lordy, he was so cute. Young and cute!

"Maybe," Lindy said, not wanting to completely turn him down in case she changed her mind. He turned and disappeared into the crowd. Well, she did have to admit she felt somewhat flattered that a young stud like that would find her attractive enough to want to dance with, but for heaven's sake, he should have seen that she was old enough to be his mother! What was his plan anyway?

She nibbled on her rye crisp as she thought about that. Then the haunting memory of being in Reed's bed came back to haunt her again. The warmth of his body under the covers, with his arm thrown protectively over her hip when she awoke was heavenly. She thought about that for a while, but then grimaced as she remembered how he had gone and blown it.

Well, she had to admit, she hadn't been in any hurry either to tell him that she had a lot of that insurance money left, that he probably assumed she'd spent recklessly. But that was beside the point! Her cell rang then.

"Ms. Lang," James Burns, the financial banker from Newport, RI was on the line again.

Silence

"Hello James. Have you got some good investments for me?"

"Here's what I have, Ms. Lang, I'll express them to you tonight. Look them over and get back to me ASAP. Several of these, which I've marked, are immediate purchases, and you would need to get to these tonight!"

Lindy smiled into the cell. "James, you are a sweetheart. Here's my address at the hotel."

"I'll get you set up immediately from this end, Lola," he replied. Of course, he would make a goodly amount of money on her investments too!

That done, Lindy put in another call, and this time back to Mexico. But instead of calling her friend Monica, she dialed the number of the real estate company that was handling the sale of her house in Monterrey.

"Miss Lang, I've been trying to reach you," the realtor said. "I sold your house the first day it was on the market, and have a check waiting here for you!"

"Hey, good job! They did come up with the full price, didn't they?" Lindy asked.

"You bet. Five hundred thousand. They loved it, especially with it being fully furnished, and leaving the tea-pot collection for them to enjoy was the final selling point!"

"The place was turn-key, so they should have," Lindy replied. "Take out your fee and express the check to me here at this address," she added. She smiled then. She had doubled her original investment.

Lindy was through with dinner and got up to leave. She stopped at the front desk in the hotel and informed them that she was expecting important papers and that she wanted immediate delivery that night. And, of course, she put a bill into the hands of the clerk.

Going back to her room, she slid between the silken sheets in her bed, and only a few hours later she awoke to the telephone ringing. When she answered, the desk clerk said a currier was there with a delivery for her.

"Send him up," She replied, sleepily.

With just enough time to locate the white robe supplied by the hotel, she fluffed her hair. And after slipping another bill in the hands of the delivery man, she said, "Could you please wait downstairs as I'll need to send this back right away?"

She went to the desk in her suite and laid out the sheets listing the investments James Burns had expressed to her. She studied the names of the companies he had suggested she should put her money in.

It was two o'clock in the morning on a Monday. Since yesterday, she had left Reed's house in Birch Lake, driven hours to Minneapolis and settled into a hotel, had a new identity and a new look. Sitting at that table on the roof, alone last night, she had decided she would not waste any more time worrying about "what could have been." She was indeed moving forward.

Now in her hotel room, in the middle of the night, still half- asleep, she suddenly felt her fingertips began to tingle as her hand lay on the top of the listing of investments she'd gotten. She ran a hand over each enterprise and checked the ones that made her fingertips hum. Simple as that, and she was done! She sent her selections back to James Burns, confident her selections were hot commodities.

She went back to bed and slept soundly the rest of the night, but awoke again when the telephone on her bedside table rang in her ear to announce she had another letter. It was nine o'clock in the morning and time to get up anyway.

"I would like breakfast and a pot of coffee too." She told the clerk. She had scads of things to do.

The concierge knocked on her door shortly after with papers for her from the realtor in Mexico. He also was trailed by a server who pulled in a table and set out her breakfast. She'd had several minutes to refresh after getting up from a sound sleep and stood now in her new white dressing gown and the high heeled backless slippers with the pom-poms over her toes that the sales lady from Nordstrom's had insisted she needed. The hotel employees scrambled to please and of course she slipped some more bills in their out-stretched hands.

After she had fortified herself with a sumptuous breakfast, she called James Burns again at the Newport, Rhode Island bank.

"Ms. Lang," James Burn's voice oozed over the telephone line. "I have your preferences right before me and as soon as I get your capital, I will buy in."

"Thank you, James. I'm on the way now to see my banker. You will have the funds within the hour."

With that done, Lindy dressed in one of her new dresses, a black and white figured A-line that stopped just short of her knees. Black sling back Robert Haan shoes and a matching big Coach purse completed her look. She fluffed her red hair and added a bright lipstick, then twirled in front of the floor-length mirror.

Lordy, I look good! She giggled. And what a change from the shorts and jeans she had habitually worn in Birch Lake. A sudden pang shot though her heart again at the haunting memory. But, she swallowed hard and hesitated only a minute this time. Then tossed her head and hurried outside the hotel and got in taxi.

"Union State Bank, please," she told the driver and after a short ride got out and walked into the grandiose establishment. To her, banks always smelled of money and she loved it! She hadn't been in this one since college, decades ago

"I'd like to see the president," she exclaimed to a receptionist. And after seeing several of the tellers raise an eyebrow at her apparent audacity, she was led into an office where a gray-haired man sat at a desk with a phone in his ear.

"I'm Jack Winter," he said then after setting the phone down. He stood up and curiously looked her over from head to toe. "What can I do for you? " He asked, then extended a hand.

"Mr. Winter," she said, "My name is Lola Lang. I grew up and went to college here." She said.

"Welcome and have a seat. Should I call you Miss or Ms.?" he asked.

Lindy smiled. "Ms. is just fine."

"May I ask how long since you resided here? Can't be more than a few years," he commented with a twinkle in his eye.

"Thank you. You are a charmer, and I'll admit to a few." She adjusted the hem line of her dress after sitting down.

"Are you in town to stay, Ms. Lang?" He asked.

"Well, I'm not sure. I'm thinking of looking into some real estate," Lindy went on smoothly. Actually she was, but not in this part of the country.

"Good idea. We can give you good rates on mortgages right now. What type of business are you interested in doing with us today?" He asked then.

"Mr. Winter." She smiled sweetly. "I need two things. First, I'll need a bank draft."

"Okay." He said and took out some papers. "What amount do you want it for?"

"Five hundred thousand dollars!" She said and opened her Coach bag and began laying out the bills on his desk.

Mr. Winter watched with an amazed look on his face, then stood up from his desk and hurriedly went to close his door.

"Did you win the lottery or something?" He exclaimed looking on as she piled the bills on his desk.

"No," she said, "I won it at the casino!" Although her million was clear now, she worried if he might recognize her as the one and same woman who had been involved with drug lord Mario D'Agustino, and the shooting in Birch Lake. And, perhaps think she was trying to clean up tainted money.

"Well, I'll be dammed," he murmured. "I just might take up gambling."

"It was my lucky day. This was in Chicago," she added, in case he might check on her.

"Wow," Mr. Winter said shaking his head.

"I want to invest this amount today. It's exactly five hundred thousand dollars!"

Mr. Winter cleared his throat twice, as he looked at the pile of cash.

"This will cover the cost of the bank note." Lindy directed, and moved the money closer to him. "Also," she went on, "I would like to open an account, and taking the check out of her purse handed it to him.

Silence

"And this is from the sale of my house in Monterrey, Mexico," she added.

Mr. Winter cleared his throat again as he studied it, while apparently dazed at this redheads bold business sense. But this could be just what he needed. Things were tough in the banking community lately and these transactions would look good to his board of directors, even though, something about this woman seemed a little off key.

But he said smoothly, "Ms. Lang, it might take a few days to clear this check with the Bank in Mexico but I'll be happy to take care of things for you!"

"Of course," Lindy smiled. "One more thing, I'll need a safe-deposit box for my papers. I'm staying at the Andrews Hotel," she added.

"I'm pleased to do business with you. Ms. Lang."

The banker then laid out the papers for her to sign and asked for her identification card, Social Security number, and two corresponding identification cards which she had ready, all of which, she had bought and paid for, some time ago.

After shuffling papers, he finally said, "Well, Ms. Lang, here is the bank note. Do you want me to express it for you to your investment house?"

"Yes please, I would," she said, "to the First Newport Bank in Newport, RI in care of James Burns."

After an hour, she also had a checking account and a safe deposit box ready for her papers and of course, the rest of her million. Having completed her business, Lindy strolled around downtown Minneapolis and shopped.

The day slid by and it was soon late afternoon and she was starving. There was a restaurant across the street that looked vaguely familiar, and then remembered she had gone there with Reed for their college graduation celebration, years ago. Now, she recognized the life-size bronze statue of the nude woman out front. And, the sign on the door that said Gina's.

-7-

"Morning, Conners," Ed, the CEO of First Federated Insurance exclaimed and stood up from his desk. He reached over a hand.

Reed smiled at the man. Although Ed was a few years older, they were good friends and had met at a cocktail party where the host had been a mutual acquaintance. Ed had also enjoyed several week-ends fishing at Birch Lake.

"Morning. Good to see you," Reed said after shaking hands. For some years now he had worked for the insurance company as an investigator, whenever Ed came across a questionable case. And knowing he did not waste too much time on pleasantries, Reed sat ready to get down to business.

Opening a thick file Ed said, "Reed, let me remind you, we're talking about a twenty-five million dollar insurance policy here." He went on then reading some of the notes for Reed, "Jonas Hovland was eighty-four years old when he died. He has two sons, Aaron and Nigel, and Rena, a daughter. His wife Lina died many years ago and was from California. I heard she was originally from the Middle East. It is estimated the family's entire worth is around four hundred million, counting the properties in which they live. And I might add," Ed said, "there's talk that Hovland Homes might be experiencing some hard times with the slowdown of new building contracts."

Ed closed the file and slid the thick folders over to Reed and sat back.

"Do you know the family?" Reed asked.

"I've seen them around at various occasions, but not personally."

Reed swiped a hand over his forehead as he leafed through the sheets again.

Jonas Hovland had lived alone for years in the family mansion with the help of a housekeeper. He had started his business as a carpenter contractor in his twenties and ran it with an iron hand until a year ago when he had had a stroke. Rena, his unmarried daughter and youngest child had taken him in to live with her in her home in a wing of her huge house. She had also hired a companion to cater to his needs, which had increased lately.

"Did you ever meet Rena, the daughter?" Reed asked Ed curiously.

"Yeah, couple of times. Good looking dame. We have a mutual friend, and I heard she went to work every day in the business offices in downtown St. Paul. That she started out as a receptionist in their small office years ago and was never promoted out of that position as the business grew. I guess her father stubbornly believed a woman's job in life was to marry and have children. But she still took her seat in the outer offices at the Hovland Homes offices, and recently, she has demanded to sit in on the daily morning meetings. Even has gotten her own corporate investigators to see that she has equal partnership in the business.

"Okay, Ed," Reed said then closing the files, "I need to get a room, and I'll get back to you in a day or two with a plan."

"Good," Ed replied. "I want to wind this up by the Labor Day holiday."

That didn't give him a lot of time, Reed thought to himself. But he knew Ed well; he always pushed for a speedy resolution.

On the way out of the offices Reed stopped at Mona's desk. "Could you meet me at Gina's at about five o'clock?" He asked.

"That works for me!" Mona said, "I've got a stack of calls to make and mail to send out." She blew a kiss and waved him out.

He drove a few blocks to the downtown Mayflower hotel and booked a room for a week, with the option of an each week renewal. He had no idea how long this case would go, and of course the company would be picking up the tab for his stay.

The Mayflower had been a downtown fixture for years. The restaurants were gourmet and the sheets Egyptian cotton. He had stayed with them occasionally over the years and knew the owner.

The lobby of the hotel was ultra- modern, having just gone through a complete renovation since he had stayed there awhile back. Now the colors were various shades of reds and oranges, with black and white accents in the art and furnishings. The lighting was low and flattering and the floors shimmering oak. Even the uniforms of the employees were black and white, trim and fresh.

His room held a king-sized bed, a large desk and chair and a couch and a matching easy chair arranged in a circle to form a sitting area. A compact bathroom opened up to a shower and tub. Fluffy white towels hung on a warmer.

He hung his clothes in the closet and put his underwear in the chest of drawers. Then put his toiletries in the bathroom and ordered up a pot of coffee from room service. He sat down in the easy chair and began to study the case file.

Jonas Hovland's oldest son Nigel, was in his fifties, married with six children and lived in the Royal Oaks area. A picture showed he was a handsome man, with graying hair and brown eyes and an olive shade to his skin. He was a big man at six two and weighed two hundred and ten pounds, and drove a black Lincoln Navigator.

A note described the snobbish Royal Oaks as an area of luxury homes built by the Hovland Company with at least a two million dollar price tag. It had started with Nigel's house and over time the company had bought up all the land and built the showpieces that attracted buyers from all over the states.

Nigel Hovland was a church deacon and head of the gated association. His wife, Lilly, was a homemaker and never set foot in the offices.

Aaron, the second son, lived on Main Street in St Paul, in a co-op in the new residential high-rise in the heart of downtown. There the homes started in the millions too. Aaron was blonde with blue eyes and Scandinavian features like his father, whereas Nigel took after his mother with dark eyes. Aaron's suntanned good looks were well known around town as he drove a Silver Porsche and never did get serious about women. However, the brothers were thick as thieves in the family business.

Reed laid out the two pictures of the Hovland men on the desk and studied their features until he was sure he could recognize them in a crowd. And just then the room service order came. By now it was late afternoon and he needed caffeine. And as he drank the strong coffee, he continued to read.

Rena, the daughter, was in her forties, single and beautiful. A full length snapshot showed her as a slim woman with dark hair and eyes and fashionably dressed. The picture taker had caught her walking down a sidewalk and when Reed looked closer, he could see what she had been doing. She had been hastily trying to slide her right hand in a pocket to hide the fact that she had several fingers missing on that hand.

Then he came to the pictures of the death scene. It showed the Rena Hovland house and the cat-walk that connected the two wings of her home. A long railed area that was fifty feet long separated the upstairs bedroom suites. It looked down, ten feet below to a marbled foyer where Jonas Hovland had met his death. The pictures showed a part of railing missing, and Mr. Hovland sprawled grotesquely on the floor below. As Reed drank his coffee he studied the position of the body. The man was thin. The medical examiner's report listed him as grossly dehydrated and found evidence of starvation. He also had found some early signs of Alzheimer's or dementia and high blood pressure. Nothing else yet, but debilitating for a

Silence

man his age. However, the medical examiner was not able to discern absolutely, just yet, the cause of the bruising on the side of his head just above the ear. And whether it happened, before or after the fall. The report also said that according to the caretakers, the man had refused food and water in a demand to go back to his own home.

Reed rubbed his eyes and left the papers on the desk and went over and settled in the easy chair for a cigarette break, even though it was a non-smoking hotel. And he didn't notice that immediately a smoke eater came on and sucked up the smoke with a low purr. He glanced up curiously at the apparatus, and then recalled he'd read that to still attract the amount of foreign trade the hotels catered to, if the establishments could afford to pay the high premium to by-pass the no-smoking bill, hotels could allow smoking in the privacy of their rooms.

He sat fascinated, and watched that action for a few minutes and mumbled; if you got the bucks you can buy most anything!

Sitting down again at the desk to resume studying the notes, the next pages were written by the detective in charge of the investigation. That was a Marty O'Brian from the St. Paul Police Department. He had ended his report by writing; tests are inconclusive whether or not this is a natural death.

So that was it. Ed, his boss, the CEO from First Federated Insurance had growled at him, "Find out what the hell is going on!"

-8-

Lindy's new pink high-heeled sandals were killing her feet as she walked the last block to Gina's restaurant. She had spent the morning at the Union State Bank with Jack Winter, the president. She had exchanged her five hundred thousand dollars to buy a bank note for the investments her financial whiz in the Newport Bank had advised.

She felt her investments choices were sure and right on. Now as soon as her check for the sale of her house cleared she would invest in something else. And, she would deposit the rest of her capital over time. When all was done, she'd sit back and count her assets and go on with her plans now that she had established credibility with the banks.

She opened the door into Gina's and stepped into the aroma of mouth-watering steaks being cooked on an open grill and fresh baking bread. A middle aged blond that resembled Mae West in both looks and dress greeted her.

"Good evening sweetie," the hostess greeted her and smiled, then asked, "Are you joining someone?"

Lindy returned her smile. "No, I'm alone," she said.

"Not for long, I'm sure. Follow me," the woman said and smiled again, then led her to a booth.

Lindy put her packages on the vacant seat and sat down with a groan. Lordy, she had walked miles today and her feet felt like they were on fire from her new sandals.

A few minutes later a waiter stood ready to take her order.

"I would like a glass of your best champagne, please," she said and studied the menu. On her second glass of wine, the pain in her feet had subsided and she felt much better. She had bought some accessories and some replacement make-up at the department stores, but she'd wait for her personal shopper's return, before she bought anything else.

She ordered a petite steak and an extra order of vegetables. 'Low salt and no butter,' she emphasized. As Lindy sat sipping her wine and thinking over the accomplishments she had completed that day, she had a clear view of the bar, which was jam-packed with early evening customers.

When she glanced over a second time, she suddenly gasped and sucked in her breath. On the other side of the bar, and seeming to be looking right at her, was Reed! And he was with a woman!

She swallowed hard over her shock and blinked her eyes. Sure, that was him! She could see that now. And, he definitely was with the woman. A beautiful one with short black hair. Then she saw them touch glasses and smile at each other.

For a minute she didn't know if she should cry or what! Well, he sure didn't waste any time, she thought sadly as tears pricked her eyes. Now all her positive feelings went down the tubes. She had just left Birch Lake yesterday and here he was in Minneapolis, with another woman. Jealously stabbed her in the heart. How could he do that?

Her hand shook as she picked up her glass of expensive champagne and took a big swallow to clear those tears, but now it left a sour taste.

Lordy, what should she do? She certainly couldn't just go over and say hi. As she sat amidst her tumultuous emotions, she noticed he would dart a look in her direction from time to time. Would he even acknowledge her if she did go over to them? To do what? Yell and make a scene? Did he even recognize her with her new look?

She took another sip of the champagne and it still didn't taste any better, but it did soothe her bruised feelings, and then, peaked them in outrage!

How could he go from saving her life, and spending all that time with her in his bed, and in one day be sweet-talking someone else?

Hadn't she meant anything to him? She looked for a cigarette in her purse. Then groaned when she remembered the non-smoking signs, and instead slathered a piece of bread with real butter. To hell with dieting!

When her dinner came, she asked that it be boxed up and laid out some bills.

"I need to go," she explained to the waiter. Then she stood up, breathing fire in her thoughts and marched right over to the bar and tapped Reed on the shoulder.

"Hey, lover," she managed to say coolly. "You sure don't waste time, do you?"

Reed turned from the bar to look at her with a look of total surprise on his face, then a moment later, recognition.

"Lindy," he said, "it is you!"

"It sure didn't take you long to replace me!" Lindy said with daggers in her eyes as she gave Mona the once over.

A look of frustration came over his face; then something between embarrassment and sorrow.

"Lindy," he said then, "this is Mona. She works at my insurance company."

"Hello, Mona," Lindy said nodding at her. "I'm sorry to interrupt your evening but, keep in mind I just got out of his bed yesterday!" Lindy said pointedly.

Poor Mona just sat demurely, not saying a word.

"But Lindy, you left!" Reed muttered and then added, "Which you usually do!"

Lindy snapped back, "And I will again!" and she marched off. On the way out of Gina's, she put a sway in her hips.

Lordy, what was he doing with Mona? She was much older, but Lindy had to admit, very classy looking and well dressed. But surely, he hadn't been in her bed too!

She hurried out of the restaurant and fortunately found a taxi waiting outside the door. Finally back at the Andrews hotel and in her room, she tossed her shoes in a corner and pulled her dress over her head. Then slipped on her robe, and sat down.

Should she cry more tears over this man? She thought about that for a while. Then decided, no, she had spent enough of those on him. The cheating jerk! She dug out her cigarettes and lit up even though the place was non-smoking.

***

Several days went by, and Lindy stayed close to the hotel. Her personal shopper came back again with an armload of things and out of those she picked several dresses and a couple pairs of designer jeans with silk shirts. Her Newport banker called to say he had invested her money as she had directed and everything was moving along grandly.

She had been spending money like a drunken sailor lately, and had begun to worry that it would soon run out before she could replenish it. But now, she knew her lovely dollars would make more for her and that helped in her sorrow over Reed.

She had told Monica, who lived Monterrey that she was thinking of moving close to her soon. But of course, not in Mexico, and she began to think of other places in the south and one place interested her.

Hilton Head Island, South Carolina kept coming back to her. Lordy, she had loved that island, and the ocean. She had gotten up early many times to watch the awesome sight as the sun rose up over the water. She thought of the other fascinating cities she had traveled to, but none of them excited her anymore.

She decided then. It would be Hilton Head Island.

-9-

There was a lot of information in the Hovland report, but the number one issue that piqued Reed's interest as he studied the files he'd gotten from Ed at First Federated Insurance Company was, the three family members, Nigel, Aaron and Rena. They all claimed to have been together that whole day that their father died. And conveniently, were each other's alibi. But Ed had declared, "Conners check it out, "Something feels fishy!"

Reed stood up and stretched. He glanced at a side view of himself in a mirror across the room and at the slight roll around his middle. He worked the kinks out of his back, thinking, goddamn, I was just getting myself in shape! Then, remembered seeing the amenities the hotel offered, having a work-out room "fit for a king".

Well great, I'll check it out first thing tomorrow, he growled to the walls in his room. Then deciding he was though reading about death and destruction, dropped his clothes on the bed and went in and stood under the shower and let the hot water drum on his tight shoulders. His stomach ached for food, a good steak as he hadn't eaten anything except that BLT he had stopped for on the way down to Minneapolis that morning. Now the sun had started its decline in the afternoon and it was time to meet Mona at Gina's.

He thought of Mona and how well she had looked when he'd seen her at the office that morning. Had she really whipped the cancer with all the treatments she had undergone? He had known her for a good five years now, ever since coming to work for Ed. Their easy friendship had evolved into an occasional tryst in bed which they both enjoyed and which they never complicated with promises.

He thought of Lindy again then as he stepped out of the shower. These past weeks in Birch Lake he'd felt good having her in his house. At times previously, he'd get so pissed at her for the commotion she would bring to his life, when all he wanted to do was spend time on his boat and fish. He'd just get settled into it and hell, here she'd come again and wreak havoc. But, he had to admit that he still had some feelings for her.

Yeah, he growled to the tiled walls in the bathroom, and let that grind on his thoughts for a few minutes. As he stood contemplating those feelings, he remembered that she'd left again. No more, no matter what, he just wouldn't let her get to him anymore! And so with that determination in mind, he dressed in pair of pressed jeans, an Italian knit sweater and Tony Lama boots and was off to Gina's for a Crown Royal on the rocks and one of her mouth-watering steaks.

Mona was already there and sat with knees tucked in at the bar. She'd taken off her red business suit jacket and laid it over her lap. Now the lacy low cut shirt allowed a peek at her bust-line. Her short black hair lay tousled perfectly.

"Hey, beautiful," Reed said and slid on the next stool, "Am I late?"

Mona smiled. "I'm early. My taxi got me here a few minutes ago. Ed left so I didn't see any reason for me to stay."

Reed laughed and said jokingly, "Sometimes you two act like an old married couple."

She raised an eyebrow. "I've just worked for him long enough to know what I can get away with!"

Just then Gina came over.

"Reed Conners, I missed you at the door," she said. He stood up and pulled her close in a bear-hug.

Standing back now he said, "Gina, good to see you."

"And I might add, Reed Conners, it's about time you came back to town!" She motioned the bartender over. "Are you still drinking Crown Royal?" She asked.

"Still," Reed answered.

"Paul, start a tab for Reed and don't take his money," she instructed the bartender. "Listen kids, have a good time and I'll check with you later." As she hurried out to her post, her blonde hair and diamonds sparkled in her haste to greet more of her adored customers.

Reed laughed as she left them and said, "You know, Mona, I've known Gina since college. She worked at a casino back home, then left to come to Minneapolis and waitressed around town for years. I used to work for her when I was in college back then, when she finally rounded up enough money to buy this place, a run-down joint then.

"I didn't know you two went way back," Mona said.

Picking up the iced Crown Royal, Reed tasted the smooth whiskey, then said, "Oh yeah, way back, and she's one of the best!"

"Reed," Mona said then and paused to take a sip of her martini, "Tell me what went on in Birch, when you shot that big-time drug dealer?" She studied his face.

Silence

Reed felt for his cigarettes in a pocket, and then swore silently at the no-smoking policy. And that frustration gave his words a hard emphasis. "I had no choice. He was going to kill an innocent woman!"

"You mean Lindy Lewis, don't you?"

Reed reached for his whiskey again. "Yeah," he said. And then something directed his gaze across the dimly lit room to the booth where a lone woman was sitting. He did a double take. Goddamn, the woman sitting just across the room looked something like Lindy. But it couldn't be her. What would she be doing here in Minneapolis? She had to be far away by now.

"Well, you saved her life, Reed." Mona reached over and touched his hand. And then seeing anguish momentarily cross his face, she raised her martini and clinked their glasses, then said, "Let's talk about something else, should we?"

It took a minute for Reed to change courses, and then he smiled at her. "Tell me Mona, are you feeling good enough to come up north soon?"

"I am," she said. "Let me know when you wind up this case. It would be great to go back with you and see all the autumn colors."

They had just resumed their conversation when someone tapped him on the shoulder. He turned and there stood Lindy! So it was her after all!

"Hey lover," she said.

He groaned inwardly, caught between guilt and surprise, and, also with just a little feeling of regret. He had never seen her looking quite like this. At the lake she would usually slip on shorts and a t-shirt. Now her hair was red instead of blonde, her face beautifully made up with make-up and her dress very fashionable. Taking it all in a quick glance, he noticed the pink spike heels she had on were definitely pick-up bait. His heart lurched.

After her outburst, and as she marched away, he recognized that extra swing in her stride she put in whenever she was pissed.

Mona had sat quietly through all this and she said now, "Reed, do you want to go after her?"

He was silent as his emotions played havoc with his intentions. "No," he said then, shaking his head, "It's okay."

Just then Gina came back. "I've got a nice table ready for you two. Come on." And she led them into the dining room to a table covered in white, topped with a glowing candle and a vase of pink roses. A group called the "Golden Strings" were serenading the diners with their violins. The ambience of the room finally calmed Reed as he sat. "I just need a thick steak," he said.

"Your friend Gina does a fine job here, doesn't she?" Mona commented.

"She does. Do you come here often?" Reed asked.

"Sure, this is one of the nicest places in town, you know," Mona said closing her menu. "And, you can order me another martini, and then, I'd like the fresh salmon and asparagus."

Gina only employed waiters in her restaurant, believing a man would work harder for his money. They were trim and efficient, mannerly and well-groomed. Reed remembered her saying, one complaint and they're out the door! But, he knew she thought of her help as family and treated them all as such.

One stood ready now, and took their order. And within minutes the waiter brought crisp salads and hot baked popovers for them to start with. Their dinner was outstanding and their coffee and liquor wonderful.

Reed left a hefty tip for their waiter and held Mona's chair as she got up. "I'll have the boys bring my car around, and I'll take you home," he said as they made their way out of the dining room and into the lobby.

"Thanks," Mona said and winked at him, "And maybe you can come in for a nightcap."

"Yeah?" Reed smiled. He stepped outside and handed the valet a bill, and within minutes the second valet brought his shining Corvette around to the door. "Thanks, guys," he said to them. Mona stepped out then and expertly slid into the confines of the car as both valets stood by and admired her sleek lines, too.

At her condo, an elevator took them up to the fourth floor, and she took out her keys and opened up her door.

"Come on in," she said then.

Reed had spent time quite a few times in her home, which he saw was as beautiful as ever.

"While I was lying around sicker than a dog, I had a decorator come in and redo some things. Do you like it?" She asked now as they stood in her living room.

"Beautiful," he said glancing at the elegant room done in all white with black accessories.

"Sit down, and I'll get us a nightcap," She said then and went to a liquor cabinet where she poured brandy in two crystal snifters.

As they sat on the new feather soft, white leather couch drinking the brandy, Mona slid over close and leaned in and found his lips.

And, Reed didn't have a choice but to succumb to her advances!

-10-

After lying in a funk for days in the luxury hotel room, Lindy finally climbed out and declared she was not ever going to cry over Reed Conners again!

A call to Newport, RI helped tremendously when James Burns reassured her that the five hundred thousand she had invested was steadily growing in value.

"James," she said, "I will not be at this address any longer, but you can reach me anytime on my cell."

"Miss Lang," he exclaimed, "You are leaving Minneapolis?"

"Yes. And James, call me immediately if the markets even start to take a dive!"

"Certainly," Burns cleared his throat. "But Miss Lang, may I ask where you're going?"

Wary of his questions she answered evasively. "I'm not sure, somewhere in the south."

"Well, this is a coincidence; I am going to Charleston, South Carolina soon."

"Really?" Lindy commented.

"Yes, I have a winter home there," Burns said. "Maybe we can get together sometime," he urged.

"I will look forward to that!" Lindy gushed, although she had no intention of doing it. And you better not be leaving anytime soon as long as you have my money, she thought to herself as she closed her phone.

She also called the desk and told them she was checking out.

She was going to South Carolina too, but to Hilton Head the island she loved. And this time she would be very careful and not get involved with some shady character who could mess up her life. She showered and got ready for the road trip. Thank God, she had her Lexus back. It would take her three days of driving to reach Hilton Head, she figured. But it all depended on how much time she would spend to rest along the way.

She packed her make-up and underclothes and slid her new dresses in traveling bags. Then she dressed in jeans, a bright pink shirt and put on her sneakers for driving. But took her pink strappy high heels along to slip on later when she stopped along the way.

It was noon before she got on the road out of Minneapolis. Rex, her stuffed black Labrador dog, sat proudly on the front seat with her, guarding against any devious predator who thought a redhead traveling alone could provide some dalliance.

As she sped through Chicago the first day and its jam-packed freeways, her hands were clamped tightly on the steering wheel as she got stuck between the semi- trucks and bikers. Finally, out of the nerve wracking traffic she wound her way through Indiana and the next day into the blue hills of Kentucky. The sun had set in the west as she turned off the freeway and onto a side road leading into a small town, and to a motel that had been advertised on signs. As she drove up to park, she laid Rex down again on the floor in the front seat, and said, "Sorry, old pal," to her stuffed traveling companion.

The Landers Hotel had just opened for business several weeks ago and the new landscape was lush. The décor was contemporary, sleek and modern. Colors were varied hues of blacks and gray, accented by startling white. She had always loved the smell of new wood and even the odor of fresh paint. And for a minute she stood startled, as it suddenly reminded her of the renovation of the house she and her husband had worked on. Which, she had never allowed herself to dwell on since the fire. Ever!

She had driven hundreds of miles again today and was dead on her feet. And as she checked in she hadn't noticed a man sitting in the lobby reading a newspaper. She didn't notice that behind the paper he listened to her arrangements with the desk clerk with interest. Or that he folded his paper and nonchalantly followed her at a discreet distance as she found her room.

While just inside, Lindy dropped her things on a chair and lay down on the bed fully clothed, and immediately fell asleep.

Sometime later, her eyes flew open as sudden danger woke her out of a sound slumber. And right at that moment in the darkened room, she had a vision of a man just outside her door and she knew his intent. As she lay stiffened in fear, she heard the door open quietly over the carpeted floor, and in that split second she screamed. And, as her shrieks echoed through the halls of the Landers Hotel, the intruder stopped in his tracks. In the melee that followed, Lindy jumped out of bed and grabbed the first thing her hand fell on which was the Gideon Bible that lay on the bed-side table. She waved it wildly at him and yelled again. Totally surprised, the man turned and darted back out her door. She ran out in the hall and screamed help!

Soon doors opened as people peeked curiously out at the disturbance.

"What kind of place is this?" Lindy yelled again at a white-faced desk clerk who came running.

"What happened?" he gasped out of breath.

"Someone broke into my room!" she said, her voice shaking.

"I called 911," the young man declared. "Come down to the desk with me, they'll be here shortly."

"Wait a minute," Lindy said and hurried back in her room and not only grabbed her purse, but all her things as well. Thank God, she still was fully clothed.

Within several minutes, a black and white police sedan sped to the curb and two men came inside.

"You reported a disturbance?" The taller of the two asked; his right hand ready over the handgun on his waist.

"A break-in, into an occupied room." The desk clerk promptly said.

"And you are the occupant?" The policeman asked and looked at Lindy.

All the while Lindy stood in silence, terror-stricken at what she had just seen in the vision. The man was a killer and she knew what he had planned for her. And, it was ugly.

She turned from the gathering of people in the lobby and sank into a chair, all the while clinging to all her belongings.

For God's sake, she couldn't start babbling about seeing things and that she had seen a vision and there was a killer on the loose in their town? That, in that split second vision, she had read the man's intentions; that he was a serial killer who played a deadly game with his victims.

How the hell could she explain knowing that to these two young ambitious cops? They'd definitely keep her around for a while.

"Yes," she said, "I was sleeping and then heard someone open my door." Not daring to tell them what she'd seen. And, then too, maybe she was totally off base. Maybe it was all a bad nightmare.

"Your name please, Miss?" The shorter of the two asked now taking out a notebook.

"Lola Lang," Lindy said.

"Where are you from?" he asked with pen ready.

"I'm just traveling through." She didn't have to tell them her life story, she decided. She shrugged her shoulders up and down to relieve tension.

"From where and going to?" he continued dryly.

When she hesitated, he gave her a quick once over. "Miss Lang?"

"I'm from the Midwest and on my way to South Carolina." Lindy said.

"Any idea who was at your door?" He barked then.

"None. How could I know that?" she demanded.

"Was someone following you? A boyfriend or a husband?" The tall cop asked, stepping in closer and breathing his bad breath in her face.

"Are you running from someone?" Shorty shouted in her face.

Lindy sat up in the chair, and realized she had to get the hell out of this small town before they arrested her! And gathering all her gusto, she stood up and declared; "Gentlemen," she said, "you have my statement, and now I want an escort out to my car, and then out of your town. If you refuse, I shall call your attorney general and report I was unfairly detained."

The two policemen stood stone-faced as she gathered her things and glared at them expectantly. They looked at each other dumbfounded at her apparent audacity and then followed her out of the Landers Hotel.

"But we can only go to the city limits," Shorty said as they stood aside, as she got in her Lexus.

"Just be sure that I've not been followed that far!" She demanded firmly and slammed the car door.

It was just past three in the morning as Lindy drove out of the town in Kentucky, and as she passed by the city limits sign she saw the black and white turn off.

So that was Kentucky! Instead of her imagined impressions of white board fences and show horses and beautiful people drinking mint juleps, her first contact had been being a killer's selected victim, and then meeting the pair of buffoons.

She had managed to get a few hours of sleep before being so frightfully awakened and now thoughts of finding another place for more rest was not an option. After the scare she'd just had, she was wide awake and decided to get back on the road again. She reached for Rex and set him up next to her in the passenger seat. Glancing at him she remarked, "Too bad you're not real Rex, you would have made mincemeat out of that psycho!"

She drove on into the black night, where the gnarly oak trees graced the side of the highway, where colonies of insects, spiders and rodents dwelled in the lacy hanging moss. Where the alligators spread out on the banks of the wetlands, still now; but their bugged eyes were wide open in the dark watching the activity going by on the road.

-11-

Reed untangled himself from Mona's silk sheets and gazed down at her sleeping form. She was lying sprawled on top of the covers, with a smile curving the corners of her lips. Still awake after their rendezvous, he gently moved her into his arms and then he too, fell into contented sleep.

The sun was up when he opened his eyes again and found Mona had left the bed. He went into the bathroom and turned the shower on and let the water sluice over his body. First hot, and then cold. He found the extra toothbrush and brushed his teeth, then the brush for his hair. He used the mouthwash and deodorant, and refreshed, went to the kitchen where he found her engrossed in the daily paper.

"Good morning sweetheart," he said and bent to brush a kiss over her lips.

"Hmmm--, you smell and taste good. Did you find everything okay?" She asked.

"Just where you always keep them." He remarked about the necessities she kept for him when he stayed over.

"Have some coffee and the toast is ready." Mona said. She sat perfectly at ease in a see through black robe, her face devoid of make-up except for a pale gloss shining on her lips. A pair of small red-framed reader glasses perched on the tip of her nose. And today her short black hair, wet from the shower lay tousled in a pixie look.

"How are you?" Reed asked as he took a seat at the table. Mona was just getting back on her feet after completing weeks of grueling chemo for the cancer she'd been diagnosed with months earlier.

"Reed Conners," she joked, "you were just what I needed. I feel good!"

"Thank God, for that," he said as he searched her face. "Are you going into work today?" He stirred his coffee.

"Absolutely!" she replied. "That place couldn't run without me!"

"I'm sure, you're right." Reed laughed. They drank their coffee and ate their toast in the breakfast nook of her up-scale kitchen. The early morning sun gleamed on the stainless steel appliances and granite counter tops.

Back at his hotel by eight o'clock, he lit a cigarette and opened the Hovland files again. Reading over the reports, he decided his first contact was going to be Rena Hovland. And, he wanted to catch her at home in her own environment.

Rena lived in Restlesswaters, on the banks of the Saint Croix River. Reed put her address in the new GPS he'd had installed in the Corvette and it listed the streets and highways right to her door. It took thirty minutes to get there and as the last few miles flew by, he gazed at the limestone walls that the roads had been carved out of. Driving through the main street of Restlesswaters, at the outskirts he followed through a tunnel of huge trees and bushes which finally ended in a clearing of landscaped grounds that sloped down to the flowing river. Flowers and grasses swayed in the gentle breeze as he parked in a circular driveway. As he got out, he stood for a minute and gazed at the beauty of the place. The house was a two-story contemporary of gray brick. The driveway; a shade of a darker cobblestone. Worth millions.

He went to the handsome carved wood double doors and pressed the bell. The picture perfect surroundings were totally silent, and as he gazed amongst the splendor, he thought of his own paradise in Birch Lake, and how he liked it much better then all this stiff opulence.

He turned back to the door as it opened and a young man with an Italian accent asked, "Who are you and what do you want?"

Reed had his card ready and handed it to the guy.

"My name is Reed Conners and I would like to see Miss Hovland, please?"

"Miss Hovland doesn't have time today. I'll give her your card and she will contact you." And he started to close the door in dismissal.

"No, you don't understand," Reed said and slid his foot in the door. "I suggest you find Miss Hovland right now. I'll wait." And he stepped in the foyer.

"You can't do this." The man was dressed in a white shirt and black tie and trousers. "I will call the authorities!" He exclaimed and put his hands on his hips, then turned to the voice coming from behind.

"Fenmore, what is going on?" A woman stepped into the foyer and glared at Reed.

"Who are you?" She demanded.

He recognized Rena Hovland and reached out a hand. "My name is Reed Conners; your man here has my card."

Rena Hovland took it from Fenmore and studied it for a minute. "So you're from the insurance company. What's the problem?"

Reed had read in the files, that Rena Hovland was fifty two years old. He saw she looked much better in real life then in her picture. She'd never been married and didn't have any children. Her features were dark like her mother's Eastern heritage. She was beautiful, slim and trim. Today she was dressed in a white silk suit and as she held his card, her dark eyes seemed to send sparks flying toward him.

He stood relaxed, just inside her door and said, "Miss Hovland, First Federated Insurance has decided they need a little more information into your father's death."

An irritated look came over her face. "We've given our statements to the company. Months ago!" She reached out to hand his card back to him.

He ignored her attempt. "Miss Hovland," he said, "I'm a special investigator for the insurance company and I need a few minutes of your time to go over some vital information."

"Oh, for God's sake. I don't have time! Fenmore take care of this," she ordered her minion.

Fenmore puffed up his shoulders and Reed saw then he was in perfect shape. Evidently, Miss Hovland kept her man buffed. What was that about, he wondered!

"Fine," Reed countered then. "I can wait until you are through with your meeting."

She glared at him, then turned and walked away and slammed a door.

Fenmore stood defiantly. "You can leave now, the boss says get out!" Unperturbed, Reed walked down the steps and the cobblestone sidewalk. The lovely Rena was a bitch, and he could see she would not be a willing participant to deal with in his investigation.

He got in the Corvette and lit a cigarette. Should he wait and follow her into Saint Paul to the Hovland offices? Nah, he grumbled and drove off. I can find her there. He knew she drove a Mercedes, and he headed back to the city.

It was going on ten thirty in the morning and his stomach was howling for more food. The piece of toast he eaten at Mona's was just an appetizer. In the city he stopped at the place he had noticed on the way out and parked the car. Dick's Diner, it was called. Inside he took a stool at the counter and immediately a cup of steaming coffee was set before him.

"Cream or me," a feminine voice whispered in his ear.

Coming out of his reverie, Reed looked up at the smiling waitress standing in front of him.

"You don't remember me, do you?" She asked.

He had raised the cup for a drink of the coffee, but now before he could taste it, she said again, "Reed Conners, you saved my life!"

He put the coffee cup down and studied her openly. She looked familiar, but from where? When? Then he got it. He recognized her sparkling brown eyes. This was the girl he had been engaged to marry years ago. The girl from his home town of Willeston.

Silence

"Georgia," he said then. "You live here?" He asked, still surprised. Now he tasted his coffee.

"I have for years," she said then.

"What do you mean I saved your life?" Reed asked.

"Well, if we had married I probably would still be living in that one horse town."

Taken aback for a minute, he didn't respond, and then mumbled "There's that."

"After I called off our wedding Reed, I packed up and left. I met a great guy here in town and got married. We own this place!"

"Well, congratulations are in order then!" He added cream and sugar to his coffee. But suddenly he wasn't hungry anymore. After another few sips of his coffee, he stood and waved to her as she was busy across the room.

Small world, he mumbled as he walked to his car. He wouldn't have recognized her in a million years. Now decades later, she had gone from a slim beautiful redhead to a buxom blonde. For a few minutes he wondered how their life together would have been. Still living in Willeston he was sure of and probably would have had a houseful of kids. He thought about that, and, also remembered the feeling of relief he had when she had broken their engagement.

Goddamn, he didn't want to deal with the "what ifs" in his life. He got in the Corvette, lit a cigarette, then slipped a new CD in the player and listened as the Bare Naked Ladies told the world how to drink tequila.

It took a few minutes for Reed to get his thoughts back on the purpose of his day. But he still hadn't gotten something to eat and guessed he might as well wait a few hours and call it lunch. Right now he wanted to meet the Hovland's.

He found the Hovland offices right off using the GPS directions. Located right in downtown Saint Paul, he saw the capital building was just a few blocks over as he drove into a parking ramp located right under the six story brick building. As he got on an elevator, a plaque on a wall declared the place had been built in 1995 and owned by the Hovland Company, which was located on the top floor.

So besides being the contractor for million dollar homes, Hovland owned this piece of real estate; a real money maker with the leased businesses on the bottom five floors. Then the elevator stopped on sixth and the doors whisked open.

He stepped out and into a foyer of the Hovland Homes Offices where a large desk sat inside the elegantly decorated room. A green plaid couch and cream colored easy chairs sat invitingly on the lush carpet. The tables were a shining mahogany and lamps illuminated the art on the walls. After the already muggy weather outside, it felt wonderfully cool and dry and even seemed to have a perfumed scent in the air.

"Hello," Reed said as he stood at the desk and waited for someone to come out through the inner doors and acknowledge him.

"Hello," he repeated again after a few more minutes of silence, and then, he heard the scream.

-12-

Lindy gazed at the beauty as she drove onto the causeway that connected Savannah, Georgia and Hilton Head Island, South Carolina. The huge arching bridge was a fourth of a mile long. Oyster beds gleamed in the marsh lands all along the way. At the top of the bridge, the Atlantic Ocean was a line of blue as far as the eye could see.

All the fatigue of the long drive and the lasting vestiges of horror of the last weeks left her body and thoughts as she drove on. The traffic here was heavy now and it would take another thirty minutes to get to the tip of the island where she was going to be staying.

As she drove through the familiar streets, she saw new shops and also a gated community had sprung up in the year that she had been gone. She turned down the window in the Lexus even though it was still hot outside, as she wanted to catch the scent of the sea.

As she drove by the Shelter Cove complex of condos, shops and restaurants she remembered when she'd met Mitzi there and where they'd had so much fun last summer. But it was also where they'd met Mario and his brother Andre right there in the Oasis Patio Club. She blew out a breath when she recalled how that had changed things. Lindy drove on and finally got to her destination, The Yacht and Tennis Club; which was an older, but up to date resort that hugged the tip of the island. After she drove up and parked, she ran into the main office building and found her friend Yolanda in her office.

"Hey girlfriend, I'm here," Lindy greeted her.

"Lindy, I didn't expect you until tomorrow!"

Lindy grimaced. "I left early, actually in the middle of last night."

"Good lord girl, you've been on the road since?" She asked.

"I stopped for a sandwich somewhere, but yes." Lindy limped over to a chair, but instead of falling into it, she grabbed the top and held on as she shrugged the ache out of her shoulders and back. Her jeans were wrinkled and the shirt she was wearing was one she'd slept in the night before. But she had repaired her make-up and fluffed her hair awhile back.

"I've got your condo ready; it's the same one you always have. The owners are glad to have you for a renter since you're alone and don't trash the place. And Lindy, they are not coming down anytime soon due to sickness, so you can stay as long as you like.

"Great," Lindy exclaimed and took out some bills. "Here's for the first month, and a deposit on the next. And Yolanda, ask them if I could have an option of an open lease, please?"

Yolanda smiled. "Okay. Are you planning on staying with us then?" She asked.

"Maybe," Lindy straightened up and went to the desk and filled out the papers. That done, they agreed to get together later in the week for dinner. Lindy got back in the Lexus and drove through the gates that kept the uninvited out and found the familiar parking spot.

The exclusive complex had five rectangular buildings that sat with one end facing the water and were ridiculously over-priced. Some were individually owned and some owned and leased out by the company. The buildings were three stories, all two-bedroom apartments except the end units that faced the water, which were single units. During the times she had been in Hilton Head, she had stayed at different resorts and always came back to the Yacht Club. The one bedroom condo she loved the best was on the second floor and just yards from the water. She had sat out on that balcony and watched the sun come up over the water many times and would even set the alarm to be sure to wake up early.

She scrambled up the stairway now with her things and opened the door to the condo. Right inside the door was a foyer and a closet, and the bedroom and then a hallway opened into the living room with a full kitchen off to one side. She saw the place had been renovated and redecorated with wooden floors and top-end furniture. The wall and window that had faced the water had been taken out and replaced with wide French doors that opened out to the balcony. Lindy opened them and sucked in her breath as she stepped out and gazed out at the ocean that went as far as the eye could see. Two rattan chaise loungers with pillows of orange, cream and pink stripes stood ready and she sank down in one and put her feet up and her head back.

She watched now enthralled as the sunset cast its glorious brilliant rays over the constant moving waves in the ocean. And when twilight settled over the water, she went inside and turned on the shower in the bathroom, and felt the water soften the aches and pains from the long journey. She dried her red hair and fluffed it into a carefree spiky look and dressed in one of her new Nordstrom dresses, a black and white floral. She slipped on another pair of strappy high-heeled sandals; this time silver to match her silver trimmed Coach purse.

Back in the Lexus she drove to Main Street again and followed it down to the gated complex where all the locals went to escape the tourists. Here she had been introduced by friends over the years and was always welcomed. The place was called Gloria after the owner and was a classy, expensive dining and dancing club that offered the best fresh seafood and fine wines and cocktails.

Lindy parked her car and as she walked up to the building she noticed the outside walls were almost covered now with a vine called kudzu that was such a nuisance in the south that you couldn't kill even with an axe.

She opened the door into the club and stepped into a sitting area where a tuxedo clad man stood greeting newcomers. Soft sounds of flamenco guitar floated over from a stage where a girl sat on a high stool entertaining.

"Hello Johnny," she said and threw her arms around the man.

"Lindy Lewis," he replied and laughed. "You're back!"

"I'm here for a while." Lindy stood back and straightened her dress.

"Are you alone tonight?" Johnny asked.

"I am. Are any of the gang here?" She looked around the bar and tables.

"I haven't seen anyone yet. But they usually stop in about now. Take a stool and I'll send them over." Johnny nodded toward the bar and winked at her, then walked back to his post at the door.

Lindy sat down at the bar and looked around. It seemed like it had been ages since she had been there, but actually it had been only about a year. Lordy, she'd been to the east coast, to Mexico, and then back to the north.

She ordered a Manhattan from the bartender and opened her purse. Thank God, the non-smoking laws had not reached this state yet and she took out a cigarette and fitted it in the long silver holder. When the drink came, she took a sip of the wonderful concoction and sat back.

Lordy, here she was back where she had started from. But now, thank God, she was smarter she hoped. And of course, much richer than she had been then! Which, reminded her, she had to call James Burns and see how her investments were coming along. By now, she had him on speed-dial on her cell, but she saw that she had accidentally turned the phone off. She panicked at what she may have missed.

When he answered her frantic call, he said "Lola Lang, I've been trying to call you. You won't believe what happened!"

"Oh my God," she gasped, "You didn't lose my money did you?"

"Miss Lang, you realize I don't actually have your money, don't you?" he sounded miffed at her accusation.

"I know, James," she said, "I'm sorry. But what's up?"

James Burns cleared his throat. "Miss Lang," he said again, "I've been trying to tell you, your investments have increased amazingly in value since the market opened this morning!"

Lindys heart picked up its beat. "James, have I doubled my investments?"

"Not quite yet, Miss Lang, but you have a remarkable knowledge as to when a product on the market is ready to buy into. Again, all your selections abounded with amazing momentum!"

Lindy hid a smile and inhaled on the Marlboro, then stared off into space for a few seconds. Her investment of five hundred thousand dollars had begun to make more money in just a few days. She thought happily about that. But suddenly her fingertips begin to tingle. It was a sign! Lordy, it was time to get out!

"Mr. Burns," she said urgently. "You are such a miracle worker. But right now. I want to sell!"

"You want me to do what? Miss Lang, your investments are just beginning to grow!"

But she was adamant. "No James, I won't take the chance." She knew her luck had waned, and she knew the signs. "You can send the check to this address," and she directed him to send her check by courier.

That done, Lindy drank to her good luck. Then she smiled at the bartender and asked, "By any chance have you see Mitzi around lately?"

Coming over to her he said, "No, I haven't seen her for a long time. But where have you been?"

"Here and there," she replied.

"Lindy, I just remembered, someone has been in a few times asking about you!" He wiped the bar and gave her a clean ashtray.

Lindy's blood ran cold as she frantically looked around the room.

Was a killer still out there waiting to get her?

-13-

The scream resonated against the walls and to the outer area where Reed stood waiting for someone to acknowledge his presence at the Hovland Home Offices.

He stood for a minute and listened. There was nothing else, only silence, and then a door closed somewhere. He took off on a run through the doorway to the back offices and as he ran he glanced into the rooms, but the place seemed to be empty.

Where was everybody? The doors out in front were open and Rena had said she was on her way into work. It was now 10:30 in the morning.

What the hell was that scream about? And who went out a door?

As he rushed into what looked like a conference room with a long table and numerous chairs, he stumbled against something on the floor. He caught himself from falling against a chair and looked down to see a body lying sprawled grotesquely on the plush carpet, a pool of blood already soaking the front of the person's shirt.

Right away, he recognized Rena Hovland. He recognized the cream colored silk suit she'd been wearing just a short time ago when he'd been at her house. A knife protruded from her chest as she lay on the floor, and as she saw Reed stand over her, she gasped, "Take it out!" Blood bubbled to her lips.

He kneeled down by her side, found his cell phone and dialed 911.

"Lie still," he said after calling for paramedics. "Help will be here in a minute." He put a hand on her shoulder to comfort her. "Rena, who did this to you?"

"Take it out," Rena whispered again. "Please," she begged hoarsely while gasping for breath.

Reed knew that if he did the flow of blood might be worse.

"Please," she moaned faintly.

He knew better than to touch anything in a homicide case. But he couldn't stand her pitiful pleas. Her cries! Goddamn, how would he feel with a knife stuck in his chest? He shuddered.

He looked around and saw a bunch of cloth napkins on a coffee bar in the corner of the room and ran over and grabbed some, kneeled down again and quickly pulled the knife out of Rena's chest. Immediately blood gushed out and he quickly put the napkins over the wound and applied pressure with both hands. She moaned again, and now, became still.

Had he killed her? With one hand holding the make shift bandage, he felt for a pulse in her neck. He found it, but it was faint.

The minutes dragged as he held the napkins on her chest, and he could see they were rapidly becoming soaked with her blood. Where the hell were the medics?

"Rena, open your eyes and wake up! Who did this to you?" He said again.

Her eyes fluttered and she moaned. Then she was still again.

"Rena, it's me, Reed Conners. Can you tell me who did this to you?" The sweat on his forehead trickled down over his face and into his eyes. He swiped it with the sleeve of his sweater. Now as he talked, he finally heard sirens in the distance.

"Rena, help will be here in a minute, hold on!" He put a hand on her neck for her pulse again, then blood began to seep out of her mouth and she began to choke.

"Rena," he whispered franticly and gently turned her over on her side. Just then the paramedics charged into the room, the police right behind.

Reed moved from her side as the medics flew in ready to do their work. Then, suddenly he was grabbed in a choke hold and pulled to his feet. Before he realized what was happening his arms were yanked behind his back and handcuffs snapped on.

"You're under arrest," a cop said and pulled him out the door and into a hallway.

"Read him his rights," he said to his partner and the partner, a younger man stepped up and recited the Miranda.

"Wait, wait, I didn't do it!" Reed managed to say. Then looking down at himself and at the blood on his hands and his clothes, he knew he was in trouble!

"Listen," he talked fast, "I'm an attorney. I just walked into the office and heard her scream. I ran in back to see what was going on and found her on the floor." They stood outside the Hovland Offices, waiting for the elevator, one cop on each side of him.

"Save your story for the judge!" One of the policemen said.

"Believe me," Reed said, "Just check my wallet."

"Nah, we saw you. We got the knife and your prints will be on it." Just then the elevator purred to a stop and the two policemen shoved him inside.

A cold sweat broke out on Reed's forehead. Now he realized how the situation looked and he knew he was in deep trouble. They put him in a patrol car that sat at the curb, one of three cars there with their lights flashing. He sat behind the screened partition in the car and heard them call into headquarters.

"Victim stabbed and unconscious is on the way to a trauma center. We're bringing in the perp! We're four minutes out."

Pissed and frustrated, Reed tried to sit back in the seat in the patrol car, but his handcuffed hands were in the way.

"Listen," he said again to the guys in the front of the patrol car. "I didn't do it! You're wasting valuable time on me while the real killer is getting away. My name is Reed Conners, I'm an attorney. Just look in my wallet and check my identification."

"Save it, asshole. We don't give a rat's ass who you say you are." The two patrolmen laughed. "We got you with the evidence!"

"The nerve of this creep, thinking he could get away with this!" The older of the two men said as he lit a Camel. Blue smoke curled around his head as he sucked hard on the unfiltered smoke.

"Fucking A," his young partner remarked. "The bloody knife was right there where he dropped it. I think he was getting his kicks watching her croak!"

"Takes all kinds, buddy," the older cop said. They started off then with the sirens blasting through the morning.

Reed couldn't believe the situation he was in as the car careened through the Saint Paul streets. It was no use trying to communicate with these flunkys. Goddamn, how the hell could the city employ such imbeciles? Couldn't they see right off he was innocent? He fumed as his thoughts flew.

At the Police Department he was taken to a dinky room and told to take a seat.

"I need to make a phone call," he exclaimed but he was quickly shackled to a table.

"You'll get you chance when we tell you, you can!" A burley red-face clerk told him.

Reed sat and waited. All the while cussing at the predicament he was in. Several hours later, the arresting officers and a new man entered the foul smelling room they had left him in.

"My name is Detective Stone," the plain clothes man said.

By now Reed was furious and hot and sweaty, and had a hard time trying to keep from swearing a blue streak. He swallowed hard. He had been searched when the cops had handcuffed him at the scene, and they had taken his .38 and his cell-phone along with his wallet.

"Reed Conners," Detective Stone said now and held the picture on Reed's driver's license up and compared images. The he studied Reed's other identification cards.

Silence

"We'll need to run you through the process," he said then and stood up. "Jesus, it's cooking in here. Let's get the hell out of here," he said to the two cops, who smirked back at Reed at they were leaving.

"Excuse me, Detective Stone" Reed managed to say without swearing. "I get to make a call!"

"You can, but not until we tell you, you can!" Detective Stone was a tall and muscled Afro-American man. Dressed in a blue tailor made pin-striped suit that fit perfectly, French cuffs with gold links peeked out of the sleeves. His hair was steel gray and his face lined.

"Wait a minute, call the Minneapolis Police Station and ask for Detective John Murphy over there!" Reed shouted as they left him still shackled to the metal table that was bolted to the floor.

By god, he grumbled, if he ever got out of this hell-hole he'd sue the hell out of the whole goddamn Saint Paul Minnesota Police Department! He banged his unfettered hand on the table-top and time dragged as he waited.

He knew that as soon as the department got a hold of Murphy, he would straighten out the confusion, wouldn't he? But the thing was, these ass-holes here would let him sweat behind bars as long as they could. Goddamn it, he swore to the grimy green walls.

But, then a horrible though crossed his mind. What if it wouldn't be as simple as a phone call to

Murphy, and his reference being able to get him out of this? Reed's breath caught. Who then could get him out of this predicament?

Goddamn, this wasn't happening! And to take his mind of the circumstances he found himself in, he forced his thoughts back to the case.

Who had stabbed Rena Hovland just as he had come into the office? Who had wanted her out of the way?

Had it been one of her brothers, Aaron or Nigel? Or both? Did they want to stop her from suddenly horning into how they run the family business? Up until his death, she had been forced by her father to sit placidly on the edges for decades as a lowly receptionist.

Reed sat in the hot stuffy room, one hand shackled to the bolted down table. The fingers on his other hand drummed on the scarred and dented metal top in his frustration. Sweat ran down his forehead, and his Italian knit sweater was soaked. And then suddenly, his thoughts flew to Lindy and how she must have felt sitting in prison not so long ago. How frightened she must have been!

Now he wondered where she might have gone.

His thoughts went back to their time together at his home in Birch Lake after the kidnapping and Mario's death.

Damn, Reed grumbled to the dingy walls in the jail, that had been good, and then it was over.

-14-

Lindy had arrived in Hilton head just hours ago and had settled in, then went out to find her friends. Now she sat in Gloria's anxious to see them again, especially Mitzi.

When the bartender mentioned that someone had been in several times asking about her, she whispered, not again and shivered.

"Reggie," she said, "do you know who it was asking about me?"

The bartender shook his head. "Sorry Lindy, both times I was busy with a full house." He looked around now as a new crowd arrived in high spirits and lined up for service. "Jesus, catch you later," he said and turned his attention to these new money-makers.

Lindy looked around and saw some familiar faces, but no one she thought would be interested enough in her to ask questions. She sipped on a Manhattan and tried hard to relax, but worried, could there still be someone from Mario's family looking to even the score again?

The only living relative was Rio Prada, a cousin who resided in Monterrey Mexico and he had been escorted out of the US by the FBI, along, with the bodies of his nephews, Sam and Pedro and his cousin Mario D'Agustino. Could someone from that major dynasty be still out looking to get her after the huge murder investigation had gone on in Birch Lake?

She sat huddled at the bar as she contemplated that thought. After some time thinking about all the emotional fears she had gone through back then, she reminded herself she'd had enough. She had survived jail, kidnapping, and getting shot. And now, she was not going to live in fear here on her special island. She was here to relax and get a tan, if nothing else.

She turned her attention to the woman on the stage as she started singing a familiar song. The bar curved around the stage and now Lindy could see her clearly as she sat on a stool on the raised stage. She remembered a sign in the foyer advertised stage and screen entertainer, Mere Lyn would be there at Gloria's for a special engagement. Now her voice and guitar strings mesmerized the crowd as she began the familiar all-time favorite song, Patsy Kline's Crazy.

Lindy sat riveted as the words and music engulfed her memories. For the second time now in the last days, thoughts of her wonderful marriage and then the loss of her husband managed to sneak through her resolves to absolutely shut out the pain of those feelings. And she had been successful all this time.

Now as she sat listening to that song, a picture of her husband suddenly flashed across her thoughts. This was one of his favorites and he had had it in his vehicle's CD player for years. They had owned a flourishing trucking business in Minneapolis then when times had been so good, and she had just thought it would go on forever. Unable now to shut down all those memories, the time slid back to the day all this craziness had started. All this rushing around, running scared over the last few years.

She had had chili simmering on the stove and bread baking in the oven in the beautiful renovated kitchen in that mausoleum of a house, waiting for him to come home. He'd had his annual physical scheduled for late in the day and she expected him to walk in the door any minute declaring his good health and swoon over the aroma of the mouth-watering supper she was cooking.

Instead, after several hours had gone by, the telephone finally rang and it was him calling.

"Lindy," he had whispered brokenly, "I'm still here at the clinic. I've got a spot on one lung and now after a CT scan, they're sure its cancer!"

She still remembered sinking down on a chair at the table. Still remembered the sudden pain in her heart.

She unconsciously put a hand over her chest now, over the beautiful Nordstrom dress as she sat on the stool at the bar in South Carolina. The music soared through the room as the woman whispered those soul searching words in the song, and Lindy felt the same hurt again that she had gone through those months as her husband's illness had progressed.

She grabbed her purse and fumbled for her cigarettes, found the long silver holder and the lighter. She busied herself for a few minutes and tried to shut out the pain-filled memories. Now the song was finally over and the customers clamored for more. And Mere Lyn took her bow and went on to another of her special renditions that had made her millions in the music business.

After Lindy got her cigarette going, she sat with her head bowed as sorrow set in, absolutely taking her down the dark alley of hurt and anger, the thing she had fought tirelessly to escape. She reached for an ashtray and put the smoke out, as tears threatened to escape over her brown contacts, and as she wiped at them, she brushed her burnished red hair off her face.

Silence

If someone from her past had been sitting next to her now, they would not have recognized her from the brown-haired, blue eyed middle aged woman from the past. Not that she had been dowdy, but she'd had an altogether different look about her. More relaxed in carriage and manner. Now, some might call her edgy and bold.

As she sat there on the bar-stool with the Manhattan, a drink she'd never tasted before until lately, she looked around the place at the strangers. Who were they? What the hell was she doing here?

Then a vision flashed across her thoughts. So poignant and clear, she almost cried out. The exact image again, of her husband as he had shouted while in the depths of despair, "why me!" And it had guiltily haunted her for the eight months they had valiantly struggled with the debilitating disease, that she was the survivor.

By now, all the starch had gone out of Lindy and she slid off her stool and hurried out the door of Gloria's. She found the Lexus and drove back to the condo. There she took off her beautiful dress and carefully hung it up. Slid out of the silver sandals and perched them on the dresser. In the bathroom, she took out the contacts and her make-up, all the while totally concentrating on the tasks to keep herself busy.

What was happening to her, she wondered, her thoughts bordering on hysteria. She fought to control them. She couldn't let go, she wouldn't! She'd been okay and able to be happy she thought, until lately. Now she was afraid, afraid that if she did let go, she'd fall down a dark abyss of frightening pain and loneliness.

She sucked in her breath as she put on a robe and went out on the balcony of the condo. Maybe if she concentrated on the moonlight as it played on the waves of the ocean, she could crowd those feelings. Skip over and forget them like she had successfully done all this time.

She swiped at her eyes as she sat in the orange and pink striped chaise lounge. Lordy, she wouldn't think about those things and cry. For God's sake, it had been well over a year or two since her husband had been gone, and she had gotten along just fine without letting herself fall apart. She lit a cigarette and blew smoke into the night air. The sky was brilliant with stars and the air cool.

Maybe she could call Reed, maybe talking to him might take her mind off these thoughts. But no, that didn't seem to be something she wanted to do. Then she remembered that she had left him too. And that whole thing hurt.

She put her head back on the chaise and closed her eyes. Tears sprang out then and cascaded down her cheeks, and her heart opened up and let go of all the anguish she had tried so desperately to escape.

Silence

And she was back to the time that had changed her life so drastically.

Her husband had lain in a coma for days in hospice, and terribly anguished, she had asked a nurse, "How long can this go on?"

And the kindly nurse had replied, "Maybe not too much longer. Sometimes they worry about having to leave their loved ones behind."

A night or two later, as Lindy sat at his bedside, she just couldn't stand hearing his labored breathing and seeing him wincing in pain as he struggled, she made a decision.

She bravely slipped off her shoes and crawled up into his bed. She gathered him in her arms. "It's okay sweetheart," she whispered, "we'll all be okay here, you can let go and go to God." Then, within minutes, as she held him, she felt him draw his last breath.

She stayed there for long minutes holding him in her arms, realizing what had just happened. Then she kissed his still lips and gently laid him down and got up and called for help, all the while in shock at what she had done.

She had stoically gone through the final arrangements, and thought she had coped gracefully with the twists of fate. She was learning to live alone and face the inevitable silence in the house. She learned to sleep in the middle of the bed and survived the demons of the night.

Then strange things began happening in that beautiful house they had worked so hard to renovate; their mini-mansion, as they called it.

A huge mirror fell off the wall, with a vengeance she thought. And pictures would continuously move out of place. Then she would catch a whiff of his cologne as she walked through the rooms. One night, she awoke out of a sound sleep and saw him standing by her bed. He didn't say a word.

Lindy lay there frozen in shock. Then the image had faded and after a few minutes, she jumped out of bed and put the bedside light on. She looked around but saw nothing out of order in the bedroom, then ran through the house snapping on all the lights as she went. From that time on, she had been afraid in the lovely place they had slaved over together.

Then she had found the ants, large black carpenter ones crawling in the attic, just over her head and that was the last straw. She had panicked.

She shivered now as she remembered seeing the mass of moving creatures devouring the structure of her home. As Lindy sat out on the balcony in Hilton Head Island, a streak of lightning suddenly flashed across the sky, startling her out of the depths of hurt. She sat up then, aware again of her surroundings and wiped her eyes. And after some time, the dregs of despair finally left and she fluffed her red hair out of her eyes.

Now maybe, she was going to be okay!

-15-

Reed sat in the Saint Paul jail for four hours before John Murphy came charging into the smelly room he had been in forever it seemed.

"What the hell is going on?" he asked now.

"Goddamn, it's good to see you, Murph. Get me out of here. They won't listen to one word I say."

"Wait a minute, my friend. It's not that easy." Murphy wiped his brow with a white handkerchief that he took out of a breast pocket. "You were arrested!"

Reed tried to stand but the shackle was still holding him down. Pissed again he said, "Listen, I just started working on the Hovland insurance case and met Rena Hovland. I was waiting in their office to see her when I heard this scream and I went to investigate. I found her lying on the floor with a knife stuck in her chest. I called the paramedics and when they finally showed up, I had pulled the knife out of her and was trying to stop her from bleeding to death."

"Jesus, buddy, it was a mistake by you to even touch the weapon!"

"Mistake, for Christ's sake, don't I know it!" Reed growled.

"I came as soon as I got the message. How long have you been sitting in this sweat box?" Murphy loosened his tie and opened his shirt collar.

"For about four hours, I think. I don't even have my watch, for Christ's sake." Reed swiped at his hair.

"Okay, I'll go out front and see what they've got." Murphy went to the door.

"Tell those fuckers, to get in here and unlock me. I'm no goddamn criminal!"

Reed growled.

"Hang in there buddy. I'll be back shortly!" And Murphy left.

Reed sat in the holding room as he knew it was called. If he had his cell, he could call up another of his buddies to come get him out of there, but hell no, he was stranded.

Murphy came back a short time later." Here's what they got. They arrested you on suspicion. Listen to this, the victim survived and is out of surgery and is expected to be okay. The knife did not puncture a major organ."

Reed blew out a relieved breath. "That's good news."

"Yeah, I'll say." Murphy took a seat on one of the rickety chairs. "Now I can't get you out on my say so alone, so who can I call? Too bad, Tanner is gone. He'd blow in here and raise hell and you'd be out in no time flat."

"I hear you. Murph, can you call Ed over at the insurance company? Tell him what's going on and ask him to send some of our attorneys over here."

"Sure, I'll get on it right now. And it'll take a few minutes but I'll get you out of this hellish place." Murphy went out again.

Later in the day, Reed was released after Murphy went to see Rena and she cleared him of the charge. She admitted it was her old boyfriend who was jealous of her sudden change in lifestyle, who had been stalking her lately and he had followed her to the office that morning.

Reed had spent the rest of the day dealing with the repercussions of those morning episodes and when he finally got back to his hotel room and stood in the shower, he tried to belt out one of his ballads to change his thoughts, but his voice cracked and faltered.

Goddamn he muttered. One whole day had been shot to hell and he had accomplished nothing. But if you called getting arrested on suspicion of murder, and getting cleared of it in one day, that was something, he muttered to the walls. But he was in a foul mood.

After drying off, he checked the time. It was after nine o'clock in the evening and he hadn't eaten anything all day except for a bologna sandwich at around noon as he had sat in that dingy room in the jail. He hadn't even eaten breakfast in that café he had stopped at that morning when he had run into Georgia, his old fiancée from Williston.

That experience had totally dashed his appetite.

He lit a cigarette as he stood naked and finally thought to hell with it and climbed into bed. As he puffed away, the smoke eater in the ceiling started purring and sucked the smoke up into its whirling fans. He punched the pillows and stacked them up behind his head.

Swearing again that the day had been a bust, he made plans for the next. First thing he would do in the morning was to go see Rena Hovland in the hospital and find out what the hell her boyfriend was all about. And after different scenarios had crossed his mind, he crushed his cigarette out and soon was sound asleep.

Hunger pangs rattled around in his belly as the first rays of sun dazzled across his face. He awoke and blinked his eyes at the glare and remembered it had been daylight when he'd crashed the night before and hadn't pulled the drapes in the room.

Reed turned on the shower again and let the water wake him fully, then dressed and went down to the main floor in the hotel and to the busy coffee shop. The wonderful aroma of fresh ground coffee awakened his senses and within minutes he raised the steaming cup of goodness to his lips and savored the flavor. He ordered eggs, bacon, home fries and toast.

"And a tall glass of tomato juice," Reed added to the list his waitress had jotted down.

After a breakfast that he would have to admit "was one of his best," he found the Corvette in the ramp and drove to the huge hospital complex in downtown Saint Paul. The minute he opened the first door into the building, he was hit with the all familiar scents of sickness. A reminder, of former incidences, in which had resulted in someone being hurt and hospitalized.

At the information desk, he asked for Rena Hovland's room and was told to take the elevator to the fifth floor. A guard was posted at her door and as Reed approached he stood up.

"You can't go in, sir," he said and promptly stepped on front of Reed.

Reed took out his identification. "I'm the one who found her!"

"Sir, unless you are a doctor, I've got orders to stop everyone." The guard shrugged his shoulders.

"Guard," a quavering voice drifted out then from the room. "You can let him in."

As Reed looked, he saw Rena was awake, but looking pale and drawn.

"Good morning, Miss Hovland," he said stepping in. "Are you feeling strong enough to talk?"

She studied him silently.

"Should I come back later?" Reed asked. "I don't want to tire you out."

She turned pain-filled eyes to him and whispered. "I remember you. I don't like you, but I need to thank you for taking that knife out of me."

Rena looked to be around fifty some, Reed saw and he stepped closer. "Tell me about this person who did this to you, Rena."

"Why? This doesn't have anything to do with your investigation of my father's death." She put a hand over her chest and winced as she inhaled.

"Well, that remains to be seen." Reed stepped closer to her bed. "I understand you cleared me of the stabbing, and named your boyfriend as your assailant. Who is he? How long have you known him?"

Rena moved in the bed and then groaned in pain. Then he saw she pushed a button on a remote and lay back and closed her eyes.

After a few minutes of silence, he thought she must have dosed off from the pain medicine she had just gotten from the machine. Then she whispered, "The fucker has been stalking me. I am lucky that knife just slipped between my ribs and didn't get in high enough to cut up my lungs," she whispered again.

"Rena, tell me his name, where he lives and a description." Reed took out a notebook and a pen.

She took a shaky breath and whispered, "What the hell. His name is Bobby Wilson, and I can't remember where he lives." Rena stopped talking and took another steadying breath. She lay quietly and a tear slipped down one cheek.

"Will he go to jail?" Rena asked then.

"If he is charged," Reed said. "It depends if the prosecutor wants to charge him, then too, if you want to press charges."

Rena closed her eyes again, and then said, "I'll need to think about this," then murmured, "Please leave."

Reed nodded and said, "I'll stop in later." He turned and left the hospital, the fresh air outside a welcome relief. He got in the Corvette and roared off back toward the Hovland offices.

Back at the place of Rena's stabbing; a pert secretary was sitting in the outer offices and greeted him with a smile. Apparently she didn't have a clue he'd been there before.

"How can I help you?" she asked pleasantly.

"I would like to see either Aaron or Nigel Hovland please," Reed said as she gave him a quick once-over.

Today, he had dressed very conservatively and was wearing an Italian cut charcoal gray pin-striped suit with a pristine white shirt and a black and white silk figured tie. His shoes were a gleaming black tasseled Cole Haan loafer. He'd even changed his gold Rolex to a white gold watch to go with his attire. Even he had to admit he looked pretty good, especially since he'd taken time to stop in and see his favorite and expensive hair stylist and gotten his hair shaped and cut after coming to Minneapolis.

"And whom shall I say would like to see them?" She slipped on cheater glasses then to check him out better.

He grinned at her apparent appraisal. "Reed Conners from the First Federated Insurance Company."

"Mr. Conners, if you'll be seated, I'll check with them." And she sailed through the same doors he had run through yesterday when he had head Rena scream.

Reed set his black briefcase down and found a seat. Soft music purred from hidden speakers and the air conditioner cooled the rooms from the soggy outside atmosphere. He reached for a magazine, and then put it back on the coffee table as the secretary rushed back.

"Mr. Conners, Nigel Hovland will see you at once." And she held the door and preceded him down a hallway and stopped outside a door and knocked.

"Mr. Hovland," she said after opening it. "This is Mr. Conners."

"Come in Mr. Conners," Nigel Hovland said extending his hand. "First off, I have to thank you for getting to Rena in time."

Reed stepped up and they shook hands.

"Have a seat, Mr. Conners, now what can I do for you?"

Reed sat, and then said, "Mr. Hovland, tell me how Bobby Wilson fits in this picture?"

-16-

Lindy wiped her eyes on the bottom edge of her robe. Her face and eyes were a swollen mess she saw as she looked in the vanity mirror, but now, a feeling of calm had come over her and she slid between the covers. She closed her eyes and in several minutes she was asleep.

Then in the midst of all that calm, the dream came back. The same one she'd had and feared months ago while living in Monterrey and the same one she had tried to tell Reed about. The same faceless men! She was running fast to get away, so fast her breath was coming in bursts.

But she awoke in the morning and not remembering the vivid video that had been circling around in her thoughts as she slept, she dressed in a sweat shirt and pants and hurried down to the ocean and the water's edge. The tide had been in and left behind a glorious assortment of shells, and now the gulls were happily breakfasting on fresh seafood.

Lindy sucked in the fresh sea air, and savored the beauty of the water as far to the left and the right and out across as far as she could. She marveled that over on that side of the water, Morocco lay in all its mystery.

She started walking to the right, the same way she had gone countless times before. And today, just after sunrise she was in high spirits; happy to be back in her special place.

The sandy beach went on and around a great part of the island and as she walked, she gazed at the many homes and businesses along the way. All of them were set back from the dunes with long planked boardwalks that led over them and the deep sand. The homes varied from huge mansions to cozy little houses set among the palm trees, along with condos and flourishing businesses. Tall oats and wild native grasses and yucca plants grew in a perfusion of texture and color.

As Lindy strolled along, the beach became busy with new arrivals, some residents and some tourists. It was breezy as always this late summer day down by

Silence

the water and you could tell who the locals were as they were bundled in light jackets. The tourists were still in skimpy shorts and t-shirts and Lindy smiled, remembering how she used to dress when she first arrived from the frozen north. As the sun reached higher in the sky during the day, the southern temperature would escalate.

She stopped from time to time and picked up a shell and stuffed it in a pocket. She'd been doing this each time she came to the island and had a beautiful collection of the sea's gifts that someday she would display when she had a home again. As she walked on, the beach had numbered markers posted for emergencies, and when she got to a certain one she ran up the boardwalk to a familiar condo.

"Hey, Mila," she called out to a friend who lived on the beach.

Mila, a woman from Peru, had come to live on the island some ten years ago.

Lindy had met her on one of her walks and had been a guest in her home many times in the past.

"Lindee, my friend from the north," Mila greeted her in her broken English as she flung the door open and pulled her into a hug.

"Mila, I'm so happy to see you." Lindy managed to say as she gasped for air in the woman's exuberant greeting. Then Lindy stepped back and gazed at her friend.

Mila was somewhere around fifty or sixty, she wasn't sure. She had long dark curly hair that she wore in a pony-tail, out of which tendrils sprung every which way. She had a gypsy look about her as she wore dangling earrings and bangle bracelets and long skirts and always smiled.

"Lindee," she said again punctuating the last syllable of Lindy's name. "Have you come back to leeve?"

Lindy smiled at her friend. "Well Mila, I'm thinking about staying here. But I just got here yesterday."

"Pardon Lindee, my friend. I spoke ahead of myself. I'm so happy to see you now!" She took Lindy's hand and gently pulled her inside her air-conditioned home. "Come in and have a tea."

Lindy stepped inside her house, which from the beach side, you were immediately inside her living room.

"You are looking good, but your hair! Eet is so bright!" Mila said and gestured to Lindy's red color.

Lindy smiled. "I had it done a while ago!"

As they talked Mila motioned her to a seat at a small dining room table. Within minutes, Mila had a pot of tea ready and they were sipping something that tasted fruity and decadent.

"How was your trip back to Peru?" Lindy asked.

"Lovely," Mila said. "I see my family and friends, and ate too much good food."

Silence

Lindy held the china cup up then after a few swallows of the tea and asked, "Mila, what is this?"

Mila smiled. "Eet is my best recipe. I grow the leaves in my garden at home."

"Wow," Lindy exclaimed. "I think I like this!" And suddenly the two women were smiling and chatting again like old buddies.

"I like what you've done with your place," Lindy said then after looking around Mila's home and seeing it was altogether different from her last visit.

"Gracias Lindee, I have mucho pesos to buy pretty things." Mila smiled and straightened her bracelets.

Mila's living room was done in a mellow mustard gold, with red accents. The walls and wood floors were gold. Matching couches of red linen and red and gold plaid chairs formed a conversation square, centered with a hanging chandelier over a dark chocolate stained coffee table. Lovely silk shaded lamps adorned the matching end tables. Oil paintings depicting landscapes and mountains of her home country of Peru adorned the walls in beautifully framed artwork.

After finishing several cups of tea, Lindy stood up, and suddenly, sank back down. She put a hand over her forehead and realized she felt slightly drunk.

"Lordy, Mila what the hell is in this tea?" She didn't know if she should be mad at her friend or what?

Mila smiled proudly. "My goodness Lindee, eets my new recipe. It's very good in my country, and I sold mucho."

After Lindy sat for a minute, she shook her head to clear it. "It's some strange stuff you've concocted my friend." She stood up.

"You don't like it?" Mila asked with a concerned frown.

"Well, I'm not sure. But I hope I can find my way home!" Lindy joked, and then smiled. "I'm just teasing Mila, but I have to get going." And she got up, waving and smiling as she went back out to the beach.

Lordy, she thought, that was some witches brew! And it took some time for her body and mind to work harmoniously, and when they did, Lindy promptly forgot about it and continued her walk.

Further down the way, an overturned small boat lay on its side and apparently was used as a place to sit and rest. It had been there every time Lindy had gone this far on her walk and now she went over and sat down on the top. It felt good to rest her legs as she wasn't used to walking this much, but after a few more days at it she would be a pro.

The tide was slowly marching in, she saw and remembered it would crest again during the night when the moon was at its highest, and leave the beaches strewn with an assortment of sea beings.

Lordy, it felt good to be back. She sat for a while and savored the feeling and let her thoughts roam.

She wondered then if her husband would have liked this place. He had been a hunter, a fisherman, and a professional bowler. He'd never had the chance to experience the beauty of the ocean, and now she felt sorry that they had never found this together. But today, she didn't have that feeling of fear she'd always tamped down on when she thought of him. And today it didn't frighten her to let the feelings flow and feel the loneliness. She had faced his departure and she hadn't fallen into that dark hole of pain that she had feared.

It was okay.

-17-

Nigel Hovland's face darkened when Reed asked, "How does Bobby Wilson fit in this picture?" Reed had come back to the Hovland offices to get some answers from one of Rena's brothers.

The man sputtered, "That bastard has been trying like hell to get into this family. He wanted to marry Rena! Marry her for Christ's sake!" He laughed.

"Why not?" Reed asked.

"Well, she never has had much to offer, except her being a Hovland."

Reed ran a hand over his tie as he listened to Nigel run down his sister.

For Christ's sake, he'd met Rena, and the woman was beautiful! But he knew the Hovland history; that her father had only allowed her to work as a receptionist in the business. That after the old man died, she had promptly promoted herself and demanded equal rights.

Apparently the Hovland son was just as much of an asshole as his father, Reed thought and forced down the urge to punch him. "What do you know about this Bobby Wilson?" he repeated.

"Not much," Nigel answered. "He's of questionable heritage. Something dark, maybe from the Middle East." Nigel sat down at his desk and motioned Reed to take a chair.

"What's the man do?" Reed asked.

"He passes himself off as a financial adviser, but I can't find the company he says he is affiliated with."

"Does he appear to have money?" Reed asked again as he studied the man's actions.

Nigel smirked. "Oh yeah, and he lets it be known that he comes from a long line of genteel ancestors from the fiefdom of King Orca of Malaysia, or some such outrageous place."

Reed laughed out loud. "Far enough away, and the story far out enough not to be able to check."

"You got it," Nigel said. "My brother has been against him all along too, says he's a lying thief, but Rena wouldn't believe a word of it.

"What does the man look like?" Reed asked then.

Nigel grimaced. "I guess you could call him good looking. Six feet, close to one hundred and ninety pounds. Brown eyes and curly black hair. Dresses in Brooks Brother's suits and tailor-made shoes."

"Got an address?" Reed had taken out a notebook and was jotting down the information.

Nigel blew out a disgusted breath. "I was able to trace him to the Marquette Inn in downtown Minneapolis. Then he disappeared or, paid someone to keep his occupancy quiet." As Hovland talked, he bounced a pencil up and down on the top of his desk.

"He use a rental car?" Reed asked and looked up.

"Yeah, he had a Hummer one time I saw, and then he cruised around later in a Mercedes CS2. Dark blue or black."

"How long has he been on the scene?" Reed asked.

"Fuck, I don't know," Nigel said irritated. "Close to a year maybe."

"Mr. Hovland, let me ask you this, do the three of you children of Angus Hovland inherit equally?" Reed asked then and studied the man's face; he saw him hesitate for an instant as he searched for an answer.

"We are working on that." Nigel Hovland finally said.

Right away, Reed sensed something else going on and took a shot. "By any chance, do you three have some legal action taking place too?" He saw the man suddenly freeze up and decided that was all he would probably get today. And he got up and extended his hand again.

"I'll let you get back to your work, Mr. Hovland." As he walked out to the Corvette, he had found out several important things. The man portrayed the look of an intelligent contented family man, but Reed had sensed that underneath his polished image, lived a controlling narcisstic bigot. And without a doubt, he knew there had to be some legal action going on. More than likely, Rena had brought it suing her brothers for equal rights to inherit the Hovland millions.

Reed left the Hovland offices in downtown Saint Paul, and now slid into the late afternoon traffic that cruised at seventy five miles an hour in the eight lane exodus to get out of the city.

"Goddamn," Reed swore at the break-neck speed and the passion that seemed to overtake these road warriors. He liked to take his Corvette out on the road, but not in the midst of this knot of insanity, but he flew along with the masses into Minneapolis.

Next on his list was finding Aaron Hovland. The address listed him as a resident in the old/new renovated Hawthorn Hotel in downtown. This old cornerstone had been brought up in style and sold as a co-op. That meaning you bought a unit, but you were actually buying a piece of the property as a whole also. Reed had heard each apartment went for a million five, and its address being the latest swank abode in the cities to reside in.

12th and Hawthorne was the address and he had heard the original owner was a rich old dude who lived part-time in one of the penthouses on top floor. Now as he approached the street, he saw a large area for guest parking had been made accessible in view of a doorman who stood just inside the building on guard at what appeared to be the main entrance.

Reed swung in and locked up, then saw the underground parking entrance for its owners.

Stepping under a blue awning, he approached the building and rang the doorbell. When the man answered through an intercom, Reed said, "I would like to see Aaron Hovland,"

The doorman took his time sizing him up, taking in his sleek suit, and silk tie.

"And whom shall I say is calling?" He asked.

Reed took out his cards. "My name is Reed Conners, and I'm from the First Federated Insurance Company."

"Is he expecting you?" The doorman was attired in a dark blue suit with a lot of brass buttons and a brimmed cap that matched the blue of the awnings on the four-storied building.

"No," Reed answered.

The doorman pulled his cap brim down firmly. "Well," he said, "you can't just walk in here expecting to be welcomed."

Reed ran an irritated hand over his forehead and brushed at his hair. "Well, would you ring him and see if he could welcome me?"

"Well, if you say so," and after that weird conversation the doorman went to his desk all the while leaving Reed to stand outside. After nodding his head and a few moments on a telephone, he opened the door and motioned Reed to the elevators. "Third floor, number 310," he said.

Irritated at this wait, Reed grumbled a clipped thanks and stepped in and rode up to third. He stepped out into a hallway that was beautifully decorated in a theme of blue again. Carpets were thick piled, tables with silk flowers and lamps gleamed amongst the hushed tones of luxurious blues and gray.

Reed found 310 and rang the doorbell. As he stood, he straightened his tie again, yanked at his belt. Even though he had paid a fortune for the Cole Haan shoes, they hurt like hell! Goddamn, he growled, what had possessed him to drag out the big guns today?

Just as he was standing with a pissed off look on his face, the door opened and a young woman stood there. His eyes popped, when he realized all she had on was a white frilly apron and high heels but she had a big smile on her face.

"Welcome home," she gushed and stepped up to him to throw her arms around his neck, then drew him into a deep kiss.

Well, Reed was caught off guard and could do nothing but stand and take this abuse. Her lips were soft and full and as she stood close, her breasts pressed delightfully against his chest.

He reached his arms around her and enjoyed the moment, then really had to force himself to step back. "Sorry, to break this up but I think you've got the wrong homeowner." Then added, "Not that I don't like this kind of greeting!"

The young woman looked askew, and then murmured, "I'm sorry, I thought you were Mr. Hovland. The maid let me in to get ready for his arrival."

Reed laughed. "The man knows how to live." He swiped at his hair. "Okay, I'll come back tomorrow. Have fun!" He turned and left and found his way downstairs and back out to this Corvette.

Goddamn, suddenly he was lonely and it seemed like it was happening to him more often. As he drove, he thought of Lindy again and wondered where in the hell she had gone to? Wherever she was, he wondered if she missed him. If she could just turn off her feelings like this and go on to someone else?

He thought of all those years she had been married and he'd never heard from her. He'd never met her old man, but he knew from what she had told him that she had been totally happy with the guy. As he drove through downtown Minneapolis, dusk had set in and the street lights were beginning to come on. Even though the city was alive with action, there was a SILENCE among the activity as everyone hastened to their destined places of belonging.

Reed lit a cigarette as he drove and then thought, where the hell am I going. Where do I belong?

-18-

As Lindy perched on the top of the abandoned blue row-boat on the sands of the beach, a calm feeling had finally settled over her. She had faced her dreaded demons head on last night as she sat on her balcony and shed all those pent-up tears she'd been running away from all this time.

Could it have only been several years since her husband had died and left her? Lordy, it seemed so much longer. She had traveled miles in and out of the country since then. And met a lot of people, both good and bad! She shook her head and fluffed her red hair. Well, here I am in my favorite place and today I am going to start really enjoying it.

She slid off the boat and resumed her stroll back to her condo. Her body felt and looked slim and trim today and as she walked, and even in her loose sweats and wind-blown hair she still attracted looks from some of the male population.

Yes, she said as she walked along feeling wonderful and free. But then she also remembered being tied up and helpless, left in the forest to die just a few months ago and those feelings of desperation.

She hurried over the boardwalk and the dunes that led to her place. She opened the doors and in the kitchen immediately got the coffee going, then stripped and turned on the shower. After getting dressed, she sat down with her coffee and got out her friend Mitzi's telephone number. It had been a long time since they had talked, way before Mario's trial. At that time she had left Hilton Head in a panic after seeing Mario shoot that FBI agent, and hurried back to beg Reed to help her. She had never dared call Mitzi fearing it would have involved her in the murder investigation. Now the phone rang and rang at that number and finally a woman answered.

"I'm calling for Mitzi," Lindy said.

"Who?" The woman asked.

"Mitzi Grover," Lindy repeated.

"Sorry, I don't know her. This is my number."

Lindy sat puzzled. "Would you know where she has moved to?" She asked now.

"No, I don't, and don't call here again!" And the stranger hung up.

Lindy put the telephone down and checked her phone numbers. It was the same one she had called Mitzi on many times earlier. And after checking with the telephone information, the operator had no listing for her.

What was going on? Where had Mitzi gone?"

She made some wheat toast and slathered it with almond butter, then took her toast and coffee and went out on the balcony.

Was Mitzi still on the island? Reggie, the bartender at Gloria's bar seemed vague when he said he hadn't seen her for a long time. Well, one thing she could do was go over to the house Mitzi had lived in. Maybe someone there could tell her something. So after getting dressed, she got in her silver Lexus and drove over to the address where Mitzi had lived.

It was a gated community of houses and condos and of course Lindy was stopped at the gate.

Thinking ahead, before leaving her condo, she had searched the telephone book for a name of a resident that lived in the same complex to use when questioned.

Now the man who operated the gate opened a window and eyed her expectantly.

"I'm coming in to see my friend Mitzi Grover," Lindy said leaning out the car window.

"Sorry," the man said. "I don't have anyone by that name living here."

Lindy expected this, and then said, "Could you try Ted Brown?" She smiled then and took off her sun glasses and fluttered her eyelashes at the man.

He gave her an interested second look, and then checked his books. Ted Brown was listed, and was having a party for friends that afternoon and had directed him to send over all the females that showed up at the gate.

"You want to go to this shindig he's having today?" the gate-keeper asked.

"Absolutely, and I hope you will be there, too!" Lindy flirted.

The man beamed. "I just might drop in to look the place over." And he opened the gate and Lindy rolled right on through.

The community was beautifully landscaped with trees and bushes and a pond here and there. The drive led through curves and hills, to an area of condos. Lindy remembered Mitzi's place and immediately parked and went to the door of her old condo.

Six steps up to a wooden deck led to her door. She rang the doorbell and waited.

And within minutes a young woman came to the door.

"I'm here looking for my friend, Mitzi Gardner. Did you know her?" Lindy asked anxiously.

"No, you must be the one who called. Who is she anyway?" As she talked, the woman shook her head. "I'm so tired of people coming over here looking for that woman!" She turned to close the door.

"Wait, please," Lindy said and stepped up closer on the deck. "She's my best friend and I've been gone for a while. Do you have any idea of where she moved to?"

"No, I don't!"

"May I ask how long you have lived here then?" Lindy's voice trembled.

"About two months now. And I rented this through an agency," the woman added kindly then. She looked to be about forty years old, wearing shorts and a halter top.

Lindy stood silently now as she thought about what she could do. Then the woman offered, "Why don't you check with the Police Department, they could probably track down your friend." And she closed the door before Lindy could ask about those other people who had been looking for Mitzi.

She drove out of the gated community and waved at the gatekeeper as she exited through the out driveway. Now she was really worried. Mitzi was not listed in the telephone directory and she wasn't at her previous address. She drove back through main street and to Gloria's, the bar and restaurant where she and her group of friends used to go. It was now early afternoon and the place was clearing out after the noon rush. Reggie was behind the bar and greeted Lindy as she slid up on a padded stool.

"You're back, good to see you," he greeted her.

Lindy smiled at him and picked up some nuts from a dish. She needed a minute.

"Your usual?" Reggie asked.

"Lordy no, it's way too early for a Manhattan, but I'll have a glass of Pinot Grigio."

"Right," he said and turned to fill her order. When he came back to her with the wine, she asked, "Reggie, where are my other friends, the ones Mitzi and I used to come in with?"

"It's been awhile, Lindy," He answered evasively and walked off to take care of another customer.

"Wait a minute Reggie," Lindy said when he came back. "Something's not right here. By any chance, were they being questioned about me?"

Reggie hesitated for a minute, and then said, "Lindy, Mitzi and the rest of those guys were being hassled by some assholes who passed themselves of as detectives. But we all thought they were on the wrong side of the law."

"You mean thugs?" Lindy asked. A chill shuddered down her arms.

"Looked like it. Jesus Lindy, about that time, your friends scattered." He ran a hand over his mustache.

"Reggie, "I'm trying to find Mitzi," Lindy said. "Do you have any idea where she is?"

"I don't know. I haven't seen any of them for months."

Lindy leaned in closer and pleaded tearfully, "Reggie, if you know anything tell me!"

He walked away and poured a beer for a lone customer and then came back. "Now when I think about it Lindy, she did mention once she thought she was being followed. I don't think I saw her after that."

Now Lindy's thoughts turned fearful. It must have become known that Mitzi had dated Andre, one of the D'Agustino brothers.

Had the brother's henchmen caught up with her?

Lindy finally gave up and drove back to her condo, but was deep in thought. Maybe the idea of contacting the Police Department did have some merit. She had met a woman once who worked as a detective for the department. Did she dare call this person and ask her to look around for Mitzi? Well, maybe not today. She'd have to think about it more first. The evening wore on and Lindy put on shorts, a tee shirt and flip flops and ventured down to a beachfront bistro for a cocktail and a sandwich.

The setting sun was turning the clouds into a kaleidoscope of colors and shapes as she found a table in amongst the tanned clientele. A combo was tuning up their guitars for the evening's entertainment and the aromas of burgers and fries wafted in the air from the kitchens.

A light breeze tousled Lindy's red hair as she glanced around at the people, then found her smokes and put a cigarette in her long silver holder. As she reached for a lighter from her purse, a man reached over and said, "Lady, like the song, let me light your fire!"

Lindy looked up and saw a man holding a slim gold lighter, with a smile on his handsome face.

She took his offer of a light and said "thanks" as she blew smoke toward the darkening sky.

"Are you with someone?" he asked.

"No," Lindy remarked flippantly.

"Can I be that someone?"

"I'll have to think about it," was her snappy reply. This evening Lindy didn't have the energy to play the games of single life. She just wanted to be alone, but still wanted people around her. She needed to think about Mitzi.

Mitzi had been living with her mother and she had a son. She was a nurse and she used to work at the hospital here in Hilton Head. For sure, that's where she would still be, as she didn't move around that much with her boy being in school. First thing tomorrow, I will go over and certainly find her there, Lindy planned.

But later that night, while she was sleeping a vision slipped through her dreams. She hadn't had any clairvoyant experiences for weeks and thought perhaps they had left her for good. But no, here they were again and this time she saw Mitzi.

But oh no, Mitzi, her dear friend looked like she was dead!

-19-

Reed drove back to his hotel in downtown Minneapolis and parked the Corvette in the underground lot furnished by the place. As he took the elevator up to his sixth floor room, he was in a depressed mood. Here he was on another case, stuck in the beginning of another long period here in the city, when he should be home at the lake enjoying the last days of summer. Now the dew filled mornings there had added crispness, and when the country side warmed up with the sunshine later, the delicate scents of the harvested fields and wildflowers laced the breeze and spread over the land.

In his room, he hung up his suit and tie and sat down in an easy chair and turned on the television. But the six o'clock news was full of sadness and strife here in the city and it bummed him out even more.

Goddamn, he grumbled to the walls of the room as he sat in his boxers. He had spent the day working intently on the Hovland case, and now he was exhausted. But it was too early to spend the evening sitting alone in this room and he went in the bathroom and turned on the shower. As he soaped up and shampooed his hair, he thought of the times Lindy would join him in his shower back home in Birch.

Yeah, the woman could get to him, and then trying to forget, he tried out a few tunes. He'd heard Rod Stewart had put out a CD of the standards and he hummed a few now that came to mind. After drying off, he used his Armani deodorant and cologne liberally, brushed his hair and slipped back into the same tailored suit he'd worn that day, but now with a new white silk shirt that he left open at the throat. Glancing in the mirror he studied the lines in his face, checked his teeth, and thought he still looked pretty good for being almost half a century old soon. He went back down to the garage and got in the Corvette and roared through the car filled space with a purpose. He was going to Gina's and catch up with his old friends.

Silence

As he drove up to the familiar restaurant, the two brothers were still there after years busily greeting customers, opening doors and parking cars.

"Evening, Conners," one said and opened the door of the Corvette.

"Hey buddy," Reed exclaimed as he jumped out and shook hands.

The other brother ran up and offered his hand.

"Looking fine," he said and stepped into the car and sped away to park.

Reed walked into the restaurant, where the luscious aromas of grilling aged beef and baking bread greeted him. Gina was busily taking dinner reservations on the phone and eyeing a growing crowd of customers waiting in the foyer. When she saw Reed saunter in, she hung up the phone.

"Hello beautiful," he said detouring the people and pulling her into a hug.

"It's about time, my dear!" She said and kissed his cheek, then asked, "How are you after all that ruckus up there in Birch?"

Reed grimaced. "I'm trying to forget. It was goddamn awful! We had both the FBI and the mafia up there."

Gina checked him over and said, "I kept up with the drowning and then that woman's kidnapping!" She stepped back and looked him over.

Reed had known Gina since he was in college and had worked for her in that hamburger joint on campus. Where he and Tanner had met as cooks and where he had met Lindy, when she worked as a waitress. Now decades later, still looking like a million somewhere in her seventies, she was beautifully decked out in a black dress with a shimmering purple and silver jacket. Her shoes were spike heeled black suede and her nylons black silk. Silver and diamond jewelry adorned her ears, neck, wrists and fingers. She always said; if you got it honey, wear it, and tonight she had it all on.

"You heard then that I had to shoot that asshole in defense?" Reed's voice shook a little as he said that.

"Yes baby, I'm sorry you had to do that, but you had no choice." She reached out and put her arm around his shoulders and hugged him again.

"I'm having a hard time with this," he finally admitted to Gina as she led him into the bar area.

"Listen my dear friend," she said, "that whole D'Agustino, Mercado and Prada family is a dangerous bunch of drug dealers and killers. I know I've met them all!"

Reed looked at her surprised. "You've met them?"

"Oh yes," Gina exclaimed, "They would slip in and out town often." She brought him over to the bar. "Paul, look who just came in!" She said to the bartender. "Now, I want you to just sit and relax. You're among friends, Reed!" She sat him down and kissed him on the cheek, "I'll be back as soon as I get my lovely customers taken care of." And she bustled back to her devoted following.

"Hello Paul," Reed said, reaching out a hand to another old friend.

"Good to see you," Paul exclaimed as they shook hands. "You okay after all that notoriety up there in your town?" As Paul talked, he reached up to the top shelf of the bar and got the bottle of Crown Royal whiskey.

"I'm not over the hell, but I had to get out of town for a while." Reed took out a cigarette, then remembered the non-smoking laws now all around the country and stuffed the pack back in his pocket.

"Sorry buddy," Paul offered seeing the irritated look come over his face.

Reed shook his head. "Not your fault."

"You in town for a while now?" Paul asked as he wiped down the bar. The evening crowd had started to filter in as Gina directed her waiting customers to relax and have a seat in the bar until she could get them into the crowded dining room.

"Yeah, the boss is after me to clear up a case. Looks like I'll be here for a while again." Reed took a drink of the whiskey and waited for the warmth to hit his belly.

"Will you have time to catch some games?" Paul asked.

"Hope so." Reed ran a hand through his hair.

"How about this week-end? The Green Bay Packers will be here," Paul said, and then hurried off to take care of some new arrivals at the bar.

As Reed sat mulling over taking time off to get in some games, Gina came by.

"As soon as I get things simmered down, sweetie, I'll join you." She said and sailed back in to her dining room like a mother hen watching her chicks. And after an hour or so, she turned her dining room over to her assistant to run.

"Okay my darlings," she said then to Paul and Reed and settled on a stool at the bar. Paul put a glass of her special top shelf brandy down for her.

"You've got a good night going, I see," Reed commented.

"I'm so lucky," Gina said. "Having home games has tripled my business."

"Good for you." Reed blew out a breath, and then shrugged his shoulders to relax his tense muscles.

Gina saw his apparent stress and reached over and rubbed his back. "My dear, you've let all this bizarre business get to you. Let me know which hotel you're at and I'm going to send my massage therapist over to see you. "

"Sounds good to me," Reed said, "And sometime tell me what you know about that outfit across the border. Right now, I've got someone else I want to ask you about."

He raised his glass of Crown Royal and took a hefty drink

Gina joined in and for a few minutes they sat in companiable silence and listened to the soft strains of the guitar trio as three guys entertained on stage near an intimate dance floor off to the side of the bar.

"Great sounds there," Reed nodded towards them.

"Brothers, I found here in town. They've been doing gigs together for years; Del, Bill and Jeff."

"Talented guys." Reed nodded his head to the beat for a minute, then turned his attention back to Gina and asked, "What do you know about the Hovland family?"

She gazed at him for some seconds. "Is that what you're working on?" She asked.

"Yeah," He said. "Old man Hovland died and his insurance policy is worth twenty five big ones."

"I heard he croaked," Gina said and as usual too, didn't mince words. "Sure, Angus used to come around in his hay-day." She laughed, and went on, "He was quite the pussy-hound, as he liked to be referred as. When he and his groupies came around, he did spend money!"

"Do you know his kids?" Reed asked.

"I know them, not well of course."

"How well?" Reed persisted.

"Aaron, the youngest comes in most often." Gina straightened a diamond bauble on her hand as she talked.

"Do you know any of his friends?" Reed asked.

"Some," Gina blew out a breath. "He travels with the rich and beautiful people of this town."

"How about Nigel Hovland, what do you know about him?" Reed swiped a hand over his forehead and through his hair.

"Well, he's got a good looking wife and a bunch of kids and to prove he's a dedicated family man, he brings them in often." Gina smiled.

"What aren't you telling me?" Reed grinned at his old friend.

"Reed, my darling, you know I don't tell tales on my customers."

"And I wouldn't expect you to," He returned, but went on, "But might he have something to hide?"

Gina smiled then murmured, "He gets around, but he is careful!"

"Aaron Hovland is the black sheep in the family then, huh?" Reed went on.

"Well, yes, but Rena is the one to watch!" Gina smiled at him.

"Okay, what do you know about the daughter?" Reed asked. His cell-phone rang then but instead of answering it or checking the caller, he let it go to messages.

"Reed my dear, Rena grew up being a dowdy nobody. The father kept her in the company but only in a lowly position. The fucker didn't believe a female had brains enough to be a credit to his company."

"I read that in the files. And now she has her own office and sits in on all the decisions! I met her today and she is a good looking woman."

Gina laughed. "Good for the old gal."

"What about this Bobby Wilson character, where did he come from?" Reed sat back on the bar stool and put his foot over an ankle.

Gina's laughter stopped and she shook her head. "Now here's where the mystery starts; out of the blue, a few months ago, she came strolling in all dolled up on the arm of this dark-skinned stranger."

"Bobby Wilson, huh?" Reed took a drink of his whiskey.

"That's the guy!" Gina said.

"Do you know where he came from?"

Gina laughed again. "He claims he's a financial broker from Malaysia. But then again some say he's from South Saint Paul."

"Does he have money?" Reed wanted to know.

"He dresses and spends like he does, but then again some say it's all hers."

"Asshole," Reed muttered to himself.

-20-

Lindy's eyelids fluttered in her sleep, at the clairvoyant vision she had just had. She had seen Mitzi her best friend, who she had been searching for, lying cold and alone somewhere.

She awoke instantly and jumped out of bed, tossing her covers on the floor. Her eyes were wide now in shock as she ran from room to room in the small condo, trying to find some semblance of direction.

Where are you, Mitzi? She wailed to the walls as she grabbed a robe and hastily buttoned up. She refused to dwell on the thought that she might be dead. It just couldn't be true.

Should she call the police, the FBI, or somebody? But who? What could she say, that she'd seen Mitzi in a dream and she looked like she was dead?

She sat down and forced herself to take some calming breaths. That's it, she murmured as her shuttered breathing slowed. Then she closed her eyes and willed the vision to come back and show her where Mitzi was. She waited patiently but after long minutes and nothing happening, she sadly gave up on the idea.

She had decided the day before to check out the Hilton Head Hospital to see if by any chance Mitzi might still be working there as a nurse, or if not, if she had left a forwarding address. Maybe it was a wild goose chase but one she had to check out.

The hospital was a huge complex of upscale medical offices and rooms, having been built and completed several years ago. Since the island had an average of one million people coming through a year, plus a permanent residence for about ten thousand, it had drastically needed its own facility instead of having to send patients to Savannah, which was thirty minutes away.

Lindy parked her Lexus in the ramp and found the main lobby. When she came to the information desk, she hesitated, and then asked how she should go about finding Mitzi.

"She's a registered nurse," She stated.

Silence

The lady in attendance studied her. "I'm sorry we don't give out that information."

"But you see she's my best friend. I've been gone and now she's disappeared," Lindy answered.

"But she must have left a forwarding address," the woman said.

Lindy tried to still her impatience. "She didn't. I've been to her last address, and new people are living there. Please, would there be anyone here who would talk to me?" Lindy insisted. "I need to find her."

The woman picked up a phone, then told her to take a seat. "Someone will come from Human Resources, but it'll be a few minutes."

Lindy went over to an area of couches and chairs and sat. She had no idea who she was waiting for. A good thirty minutes went by and finally two people came up to her, a security guard in a brown uniform and a lady dressed in a business suit. Lindy looked at them questioningly.

"Are you an acquaintance of Mitzi Grover?" The lady asked.

Lindy stood up, "Yes," she said. "My name is Lindy Lewis. She's a good friend and I've been gone for a while. Now she's moved with no forwarding address."

"Have you checked for a new listing with the phone company? The woman asked kindly.

"I haven't found anything. Can you tell me if she still works here?" Lindy asked then. "I remember how excited she was when she started here."

The security guard said then, "I can only tell you this. She is no longer employed here." Lindy turned forlorn eyes to him. Then he added, "Miss Lewis, I have a good friend down at the police department. Give him a call, maybe he can help you."

Lindy's breath caught. "Has something happened?" She asked the couple.

"No, not that we know of, but give him a call." And he gave Lindy his card with a telephone number on it.

Lindy thanked them and went back and found her car. Should she really go that far and finally talk to the police? Maybe she should look around Hilton Head some more. But as she drove over the streets and passed the familiar haunts, her heart was in her throat. And again, that same vision of Mitzi lying somewhere, alone and cold, flashed through her thoughts. And she made a U-turn right in the middle of town square and headed for the Police Department.

It was a small building wedged in between the fire hall and a Subway restaurant. Lindy parallel parked along the street and went in. It was the first time she had been in this one, and was surprised at how small the place was. A young man in uniform sat in front at a desk. The room had a smattering of hard back chairs lining the walls.

Silence

Lindy took out the card she'd gotten and read, "Is Mike Mann here?" She stood back and looked expectantly at him.

"May I ask why you want to see the chief?" He asked.

"I'm wondering if he would help me find someone." Lindy answered.

Just then she looked up and saw another man come into the room.

"You want to see me? " He asked and caught her by surprise. She sucked in her breath. He stood handsomely attired in blue pin-stripe suit. He looked to be in his mid-fifties; with graying hair, steel blue eyes and physically fit.

He walked up to her and she was glad she had taken the time to put on her make-up, and wear one of her new day-time dresses and matching high-heeled sandals.

She reached out her hand. "My name is Lindy Lewis. I'm staying here on the island and I'm looking for a friend."

He looked her over and then took her hand which was calloused and hard. "Mike Mann," he said. "Come on into my office, Miss Lewis," he said and indicated she should follow him. "Have a seat," he said, sitting down at a cluttered and busy looking desk.

Lindy followed, wondering what was coming.

"Miss Lewis," he said, "Can I see some identification please?"

She looked at him surprised and asked "why?"

"It's a usual request. I need to know to whom I'm talking to."

Lindy took her cards out of her Gucci purse and put them on his desk.

He spent a few minutes studying them, especially her picture on her driver's license.

"You're from Minnesota. I see. How long will you be here?" Mike Mann asked.

"I'm not sure," Lindy answered. Truthfully, if her friend wasn't there, how long would she stay? "I'm renting a condo over at the Adventure Inn." She said.

"Nice place." He said. "Tell me, what is your friend's name?"

"Mitzi Grover," Lindy said.

"When did you last see her?" She felt his steel blue eyes study her as he waited for an answer.

She hastily thought back and realized it was over a year since she had raced out of Hilton Head. After Mario had shot that agent they had spoken briefly on the telephone, and Mitzi had worried that she might be dragged into something being she had dated Andre' D'Agustino, Mario's brother. They hadn't spoken since and she never did appear as a witness. Lindy hadn't dared contact her either in case her calls were being traced. And now after all this time, she felt total remorse at not keeping in touch with her.

Silence

"It's been a long time," Lindy said now. "Some things happened and I guess it's been almost a year." She had truly felt SILENCE was necessary to keep Mitzi out of the D'Agustino mess.

"Tell me about Mitzi Grover. I need her age and description." Detective Mann asked.

Worriedly, Lindy stared at him and her face paled. She did manage to whisper, "why?"

"Usual request," Chief Mann said.

Lindy looked down at her shoes as she thought about Mitzi's description and whispered, "She is in her late forties, probably five foot four and about 130 pounds." Her breath shuttered and continued. "Her hair is blonde and she has brown eyes."

"Does she have any identifying scars or birthmarks that you know of?" He asked then.

Lindy sucked in her breath as she remembered. "Yes," she exclaimed, "She has a tiny crescent shaped scar on her left cheek on her face.

Chief Mann sat engrossed in a file for a few minutes and then looked at Lindy. "I have an unsolved case. A cold case if you will. Miss Lewis, would you be willing to look at some photos of our Jane Doe?"

Lindy started shaking and she clasped her hands together at his question and gasped, "Are you saying my friend is dead?"

"Hopefully not. But it wouldn't hurt to check."

She looked into his eyes and saw kindness in the blue depths. She sat up straighter in the chair and whispered bravely, "I will try."

Chief Mann took out some pictures, which looked to be 8x10 black and whites. He shuffled through them and laid several out for her to see.

"Just take your time, Miss Lewis." He said gently.

Lindy leaned closer, and then chills swept up her back. It was her. Mitzi!

Of course her eyes were closed and she was without make-up, but the moon shaped scar stood out on her cheek plain as day.

"Oh my God, it is Mitzi!" She gaped at Chief Mann.

"This woman was found dead with no identification. And no one fitting that description has ever been filed with the missing person bureau. Are you sure this is Mitzi Grover?" Chief Mann asked.

Lindy fought back tears. "Yes, it's her. But where is she now?" she finally managed to ask.

"She's buried in the cemetery over at the Lutheran Church on First Street. I can take you there," he said, and then took a hanky from his suit pocket and handed it to her when he saw her tears.

-21-

Reed sat with his friends and savored the whiskey that cooled his throat and warmed his stomach. Gina had taken a break from her dining room and Paul, the bartender, stood behind the bar.

"Do you know where I might find this Bobby Wilson now?" Reed asked.

"I'd say follow Rena Hovland and you'll see where he hangs his hat." Gina remarked dryly and lifted her crystal cocktail snifter and took a hefty sip of her brandy.

"I've seen the guy operate and he's pretty slick," Paul said as he wiped the bar.

"He'll largely buy drinks for the house and flash his platinum, but it always had Rena's name on the charge card!"

"One of those," Reed swore. "And he's hooked himself up with this Rena. I met her houseboy, could he be one and the same?"

"If he's dark and younger, that sounds like him," Gina huffed.

Reed filled them in then on Rena's stabbing, and that he'd spent the day in jail after finding her, and being taken into custody on suspicion. "But she finally confessed her boyfriend had done it and I was released."

"You mean this character, her boy-toy, tried to kill her?" Gina exclaimed. "Why the hell would Wilson do something like that to his cash cow?"

Reed ran a hand through his hair, and shook his head. "I don't know as yet, but I'm going to find out. Goddamn, I sat in jail for helping her!"

"Jesus," Paul growled, "You got in touch with Murphy didn't you?"

"Oh yeah, I did but it took time. He went to see Rena Hovland in the hospital and she finally admitted to him it was this Bobby Wilson who stuck the knife in her."

"Murphy's a good man." Gina commented.

"Oh yeah, I'm going to hook up with him tomorrow and in the meantime he's going to dig into this guy's background. See where in the hell he comes from." Reed finished his Crown Royal whiskey and Paul slid a fresh one over to him.

"How old is Rena Hovland?" Gina asked.

"In the report it lists her as being forty one and born in between her brothers. Nigel the oldest is fifty and Aaron the youngest is thirty five." Reed took a taste of his drink. "Rena is a good looking woman."

"Their housekeeper raised her, I heard. I'm not sure when it happened that she came out in all her glory, but it was before the old man died, which must be going on six months now." Gina added.

Reed nodded his head. "Going on that, has anyone seen Wilson around with anyone else?"

"Not here," Paul answered, "But I'll keep my ear to the ground."

Reed left Gina's after another hour and went back to his room at the nearby hotel. He had the strangest feeling however, when he came back into his room that someone had been in there. Not that it was messed up or anything out of place but just a feeling. He checked through his clothes and everything was there, and he had all his files and papers in his briefcase which he never left out of sight. He undressed and sat down and light up a cigarette, then thought over the situation. Now who the hell was spying on him, the Hovland family or this Wilson character?

The next day, after showering Reed dressed in his usual pressed jeans, boots and brown leather bomber jacket, and after breakfast in the hotel dining room he swung down to the Police Department to join up with Murphy. But using an old trick, he hung his "do not disturb" card on his outside doorknob, then stuck a piece of scotch tape over the door and frame on the bottom of the door. He'd be curious to see if someone entered his room again.

"Conners, good to see you buddy," Murphy said as he came into the detectives office.

"Morning," Reed said and took a seat at Murphy's desk. "Did you find anything on Wilson?"

"Ah-ha, we picked him up at a bar in Restless Waters last night and listen to this, we ran his name Robert Elmer Wilson with the social security number he gave us, and this number belongs to some poor soul who has been dead for eighteen years."

"Do his prints match up with anyone in our database?" Reed asked.

"Nope, but we're doing an international search now. But we had to let him go after twenty-four hours. That was a couple of hours ago."

"Too bad. I'm going over to the hospital to see Rena Hovland. Do you want to come along?" Reed wanted to know.

"Wish I could, but I've got to be in court at ten. But, I'll catch up with you later today." Murphy stacked a bunch of files together as he spoke.

Reed got up. "Call me on my cell," he said and left the downtown Minneapolis Police Department.

On the way over to the hospital in Saint Paul, he turned on country radio and Faith Hill whispered her famous love song called Breathe.

This morning Rena Hovland was sitting up in a chair by her bed in the room. The tubes and bottles had been removed and only a bandage braced her chest.

She looked at Reed with irritation. "What the hell do you want now?" She asked. Her face was pale and her hands shook as she adjusted a blanket over her knees.

Despite her rude greeting, Reed smiled at her this morning. "How are you today Rena?" he asked.

"I need to get out of this hell-hole!" She exclaimed.

"What does your doctor say?" Reed opened his jacket as he stood by her side.

"I haven't seen the fucker yet today. I've got things to do!" She glared at him.

"Anything I can do to help?" He asked.

"Just get out of my face." Rena said to him.

"Soon, Rena," he said patiently. "But not before I get some questions answered. Like where and when did you meet your lover, Bobby Wilson? And is he the boy-toy that answered the door at your house when I came over yesterday?"

She glared at him, and then was silent.

"What's the matter Rena? The man stabbed you. Don't you want him to pay?"

When she still didn't say anything he said, "You are going to press charges aren't you?"

Then she finally said, "I will not say anything until I've talked to my attorney!"

Knowing he probably wouldn't get anything more from her, Reed said goodbye and left the hospital.

On a hunch, he drove back to Restless Waters to Rena's house. He wanted to get another look at her place, get a feel of her neighborhood. Driving up her street in the late morning he parked a few houses down and thought he'd sit for a while and see if there was any movement around her home. And just to make it look as if he was checking a map for directions, he held one up in plain view.

The day was sunny and brisk, frost had dusted the area over night and now the leaves on trees and bushes curled at the edges. Wood smoke from fireplaces perfumed the area and crept in the open window of Reed's classic Corvette. He turned off the country radio station and slipped on a CD of a new recording he'd gotten in the mail from a friend some time ago and had never had time to listen to. Dick Milner was the artist's name. Now the soft strains of an accordion mellowed the morning as Reed kept an eye on the house.

After an hour or so, by God, he was sure he saw movement by one window! Could it be someone in cleaning or a workman?

Well hell, he thought, and got out and locked the Corvette. Let's just see who is in there, and he marched up the walk and punched the doorbell.

He stood patiently on the portico under an awning and waited, rang the bell several more times, and then felt for sure someone peeked through a corner of a drape from a side window.

Pissed, he held his finger on the bell and let it ring. A good five minutes went by and still no one answered. He finally gave up and went back down the street to the Corvette. And instead of driving by and showing his car, he turned around and went around the block and then parked again, out of sight from the house but where he could see it. He sat back again and waited. Something told him something was going on!

He'd taken a bottle of water along and he sipped on it and then lit up a cigarette. Goddamn, it tasted good to inhale the smoke but soon he would have to give it up. Seemed like no one smoked any more.

As he sat mulling that over, he suddenly glimpsed someone slide out a side door and then a vehicle that must have been parked in the alley somewhere close by speed off.

Goddamn, he growled and took off to follow. It was a late model grey Ford SUV. He couldn't get a clear view of the driver, but it looked like someone wearing a hat was at the wheel. He had seen Bobby Wilson once, or someone he now thought was him, when a man had opened the door at Rena's the day before. But now he hadn't gotten a good look at the person who had darted out of the Hovland house.

Whoever you are, let's see where you go, Reed muttered as he followed at a safe distance. Leaving Restless Waters, the SUV flew over the bridge and entered the expressway leading to the twin cities. Now Reed closed up the distance between them as the heavy traffic covered his surveillance. He was close enough now for him to get the license and he punched in a number on his cell-phone.

"Buddy, Reed Conners. Can you run this for me please?" He said to his friend Bernard, the computer whiz.

"Hey Conners," the guy answered, "Sure thing. Give me three minutes."

While Reed waited on his cell, he smoked another cigarette as he drove.

The landscape along the freeway had turned into a kaleidoscope of autumn for the travelers as the bushes, tress, and plantings took their last bow in a blazing crescendo of colors. Dozens of shades of red and yellow mixed with orange crowned the ditches along the way.

Reed had put his cell on speaker and laid it on the seat as he drove. Now Bernard came back on. "Conners, here's what I got," he said. "The license is registered to a Rose Jensen, and here's the address in Minneapolis."

"Thanks buddy," Reed said, "I'll stop by soon." Now he had something to start with.

Just who the hell was Bobby Wilson? And now a woman called Rose Jensen had entered the picture.

-22-

Lindy's tears slid down her cheeks as she sat in the Police Station in downtown Hilton Head that day. She had just found out where Mitzi Grover had disappeared to. She was buried, right there in the Lutheran Church cemetery.

"Miss Lewis, take this," Detective Mike Mann said as he handed her his hanky.

Lindy wiped at her tears. "When did this happen?" she asked brokenly as they stood together.

After a few minutes, the detective patted her on her shoulder and stepped back to his desk, where he checked some files. "Her body was found months ago. Early spring, in March, I have here."

My God. She felt her face pale. That would have been right at the time Mario was held in jail, just before his trial. She swallowed hard and clenched her hands together to hold back more of the shakes.

"But, she has a son and her mother lived here in Hilton Head too. Where are they?" Lindy managed to ask.

"Miss Lewis, remember we have had no idea who our Jane Doe was until you identified her."

Lindy sat up straighter. That's right, she thought now. But should she tell this man the whole story, and that she was sure Mitzi had been murdered by the D'Agustino Mafia?"

She choked back a sob and took a breath to settle her shakes. There was no doubt in her mind about who had killed Mitzi. She was sure it was ordered by Mario's dynasty. While she had been staying with Reed for protection until Mario's trial, Mitzi had been here alone.

What in the hell would she have known about the D'Agustino drug trade? Nothing, Lindy was sure, but they must have thought she did and they killed her for it!

She turned to go. "I have my car and I can find my way to the cemetery," she said to Mike Mann and fluffed her hair.

"Just to make sure, Miss Lewis, I will show you the way." And he took her elbow and led her through the front office and outside.

Lindy followed, still terribly heartsick at the news. "My car is over there," she said, and just then the heel of her sandal caught on a crack in the sidewalk. She started to fall but Detective Mann caught her.

"Whoa," he managed to say as she straightened up and apologized. "I better drive you over to the church." He guided her to his shiny black sedan standing at the curb and opened the passenger's car door and tucked her in.

By now, Lindy was a total wreck. She just couldn't fathom her good friend gone. Dead! But she'd seen her picture so she had to be!

She laid her head back against the seat in Detective Mann's car as he drove through the familiar streets of Hilton Head. Through Main Street, by the beautiful golf courses and gated communities, then to a snow white painted church, complete with a tall cross mounted on its roof in the middle of downtown.

Detective Mann drove into its parking lot. "I'll show you where our Jane Doe is buried, and then you can have some time." And he helped her out of the car.

The graveyard had a picket fence surrounding its grounds. He opened the latch and took Lindy' hand.

"I can't believe this," she whispered, then tiptoed softly over the grass as she followed.

They walked to a far corner and then he pointed to a small flat plaque in the ground that said Jane Doe and listed number 126.

Lindy sank to her knees and began to cry, great sobs that racked her body. Detective Mann stood off to the side. Finally after a few minutes, she stood up, horrified then as she realized she had been kneeling right on top of the grave.

"Do you want more time?" the detective asked. And he handed her another hanky to wipe her tears.

She stood up and brushed some grass clippings off her knees. "No, I'm okay and I just need to go home. Could you just take me back to my car please?"

He took her arm and helped her over the uneven ground again. "Are you going to be okay?" He asked then.

Lindy walked along back to the car, still in a fog about what she'd found out in the last hours about her friend and still couldn't believe it all. But there it was, seeing the proof in those 8x10 black and white pictures and now the small designated space in the cemetery.

Back at her condo, Lindy took off her dress and sandals and put on shorts and a tee-shirt and grabbing a sweat shirt ran down to the water. Here she could walk and cry and no one would pay any attention to her tears behind her sun glasses.

Silence

The tide had come in earlier and left behind a variety of shells and drift wood that had previously always aroused her curiosity, but today she didn't see them, lost as she was in pain.

Poor Mitzi. Had they tormented her first and then finally taken her life? She just knew the D'Agustino family had to be behind this. Then she remembered the bartender at Gloria's had said Mitzi had mentioned one time that she thought she was being followed.

Lindy walked and cried for her friend, terribly remorseful that she hadn't stayed in touch. After several miles, she turned and began the trek back to her condo.

Several days went by as she walked the beach. She had finally cried out her tears and now she picked up the phone. She needed to tell Reed.

As it rang in the north, the call went unanswered. She finally hung up, and then remembered he had a cell. She grabbed her purse and found that number she had tucked away just in case she really needed to get in touch with him again. Now all the hurt and anger she had felt for him when she left Birch Lake seemed unimportant compared to this.

As she punched in his cell-phone number though, just a little apprehension came over her and set her heartbeat charging through her body. Then his voice echoed over the lines.

"Conners," he bellowed.

She took a breath. "Reed," she said hurriedly, "It's me and something has happened. I need to tell you about it!"

"Lindy," he grumbled, "where the hell are you?"

"Reed," she said, "Don't yell and make me hang up. Now listen!"

A few seconds went by, and she could just see his face as he sobered his thoughts.

"Reed, remember my friend Mitzi Grover? Remember when she came with me to your lake?"

"Yeah, I remember. Why?"

Lindy swallowed hard to keep her voice steady. "She's dead!" She finally said.

"Dead! How did that happen?" Reed asked.

"Reed, she was found dead this spring, before Mario's trial." Lindy's voice choked up again.

"I'm so sorry, Lindy, I know she was a close friend."

"Reed, I never told you this, and I never told anyone that she dated Mario's brother for a while, Andre D'Agustino."

"Goddamn, you never told me that, Lindy!" He roared.

"Well, I never told anyone. I thought I could keep her out of that fiasco."

"Where the hell is this Andre now?" Reed asked.

'I don't know, but I got the impression that he was just along with Mario for company. I met him and he was very charming."

"The fucker never showed his face at Birch. You said Mitzi went out with him?"

"Yes, several times is all," she said defensively. "He more than likely lives in Monterrey, Mexico where the whole clan is. And Reed, I doubt he ever told her anything about their drug business. She never told me that he had. And my God, if we had known who they were, we wouldn't have continued in their company!"

"I take it then, you're in Hilton Head?" Reed commented.

"Yes, I am. I'm not sure for how long though. Reed, listen I know Mitzi was murdered. She was found dead from a gunshot and she had been left in an alley behind a bar."

"Goddamn," Reed growled again.

"Here's the mystery Reed. There never was a missing bulletin put out for a female fitting her description. She was buried as a Jane Doe. When I went to the police department, they finally showed me pictures of this Jane Doe. It was her, Reed! And her son and mother have disappeared too!"

"Lindy, take a breath and calm down!"

-23-

Reed had followed the silver SUV as the driver expertly slipped into the late afternoon traffic leading from Rena Hovland's house in Stillbrook to Minneapolis. Then to his dismay just as they were coming to a big intersection, the SUV sailed right on through on a red light and by the time Reed got through, he was long gone. Pissed, there was nothing Reed could do but give up the chase and go back to his hotel.

As he was studying the Hovland files, he thought again of the telephone call.

"Take a breath and calm down," he had said to Lindy as he tried to understand her.

"For God's sake Reed, how the hell can I do that!" She had wailed to him, "Mitzi was murdered!"

"And you think it happened just before the D'Agustino trial?" He asked.

"Yes, during that time I was staying at your house, remember?

Reed listen to me," she said again and told him of the trickling fear she had tried to push away. "I'm scared! I just know she was killed by someone from the D'Agustino clan. And they must have murdered her because they thought she knew something about their drug sales, and would testify for the FBI at that trial! And, now Reed," she whispered, "they could be after me, as we speak, now!"

"Lindy it's over. And Mario is dead!" Reed lit a cigarette.

"Yes, I know that but, his cousin Rio Prada is head of that clan now."

"Goddamn, that fucker would not dare start up something again. Lindy, he was escorted out of the country!"

"I know that," Lindy whispered again, "But I don't think that would stop him from coming back or sending someone to get me!"

"Why the hell would you think that?" Goddamn, he groaned to himself. Would this ever stop?

"Because, I'd met him before, when I lived there in Monterrey. At the time I sure didn't know he was a cousin of Mario's!"

"What do you mean? You'd met this Prada jerk before he showed up in Birch?" Reed growled over the line.

"Reed, he is the Mayor of Monterrey and I met him several times when I lived there." For God's sake, she wasn't about to tell Reed that after seeing a vision, she'd saved the man's life from a bullet, then ended up in his bed!

"I don't think you have to worry about him trying anything here in the US again, Lindy." Reed remarked, almost offhandedly she thought.

"Don't you understand Reed," she cried impatiently, "her son and her mother have disappeared! What if they were murdered too?" Now he could hear she was in tears.

"Lindy, goddamn it, now get yourself together. You said you went to the Police department. What did they have to say?"

"I went there and identified Mitzi from their photos. A Jane Doe they called her." He heard her voice tremble, "I went to her grave in a church cemetery."

"I'm so sorry," he said again. "Now, you told them then that her son and mother were missing too?"

"Yes, I did. This was the first they had anything to go on. And I gave them their addresses!"

"Well, Lindy that's all you can do. I'm so sorry." He sat down in the easy chair in his hotel room and blew the cigarette smoke up toward the ceiling smoke vents. He heard the stress in her voice.

"Don't you understand Reed? I'm really, really scared," she said to him. "I doubt Mario's family will ever give up on getting me for testifying against him. I'm sure they will find me sometime!"

He could actually hear her teeth chatter then and said to her. "Lindy, come back here. You'll be safe with me!"

He heard her hesitation, and then she said, "I don't know, Reed."

Well goddamn, he thought. Why not?

"Lindy," he said then, "I'm in Minneapolis and you could stay here with me while I work this case. We could catch some shows and you could shop!" He was sure that would get her there with bells on.

"Well, I'm not sure Reed," she said then, "I know he would look for me there too."

Well goddamn, if she didn't want his protection, what could he do? He muttered then and sat back and smoked his cigarette.

That night he had a hard time sleeping and he had to agree that the thought of Mario's family getting even probably had some merit. The mafia seldom forgot. He finally tossed the covers aside and stumbled into the shower. He let the water run cold to wake up and then hot to take the kinks out of his body. He stopped in the hotel restaurant and ate a healthy breakfast. It didn't come close to what he really liked to eat but he was suddenly intent on starting a health kick. And after lighting a cigarette after getting in the Corvette, he almost threw it away, but then decided to finish it with pleasure and think about that later.

Goddamn, he was still pissed at Lindy's refusal of his help so he was just in the mood, waiting for someone else to irritate him.

First off, he was headed to the address of the woman listed as the owner of the SUV Bobby Wilson was driving. The houseboy/boy toy he had seen sneak out the side door of Rena's Hovland's house.

The Calhoun neighborhood he drove into was old money with old homes. Not run down old, but lovely brick and stucco houses with sun porches and tall old trees. Pine, elm and weeping willows swayed in the early autumn breeze. Flower gardens perfumed the area as the morning sun warmed the gorgeous blooms.

As Reed drove into the area, he could smell the mossy bouquet from a lake. He drove slowly around the block until he found the address of Rose Jensen, the owner of the SUV Bobby Wilson drove. He parked down the block from the house for a few minutes and studied it from a distance.

It was a ranch style red brick with a huge garage that could easily house at least four cars. A bricked sidewalk led up to glistening black double doors which stood under a high canopy roof. The front yard was meticulously landscaped with shrubs and flower beds and a huge weeping willow took up most of the middle part of the yard. As Reed parked the Corvette, he jumped out and put the hood up on the car and pretended to study the insides, then put his cell phone to his ear. He figured he had thirty minutes before the cops would show up after being called by a resident. He was close enough to the house to see movement inside a huge bay window that looked out to the street. But, he was too far away to see if it was male or female.

Goddamn, he'd give big bucks if he could get a look in the garage. Was the gray SUV in there?

Time crawled by as the neighborhood awoke to another day. A lawn care company drove up to one house and two men began to mow the luxurious green grass. A young woman from another house came by pushing a baby carriage. Then suddenly, a UPS truck drove up to the house and the driver got out and carrying a box walked up and rang the bell.

Reed glanced over and as the door opened and he saw a slim blonde woman in the entrance. She was dressed in what looked like black jeans and a black tee-shirt.

After she took the package from the driver, she turned to a man who stood beside her. Was it Bobby Wilson? Had to be, he reasoned.

He slid the hood down and back in the Corvette, as the motor roared to life, he dialed Bernard.

"Hey buddy," he said as he drove away, "it's me again. Can you put the woman, Rose Jensen, through your computer and see what comes up?"

"Sure thing, Conners," the computer guy said. "I'll need a minute."

Reed tossed the cell in the passenger seat. He turned on the CD again and slipped in another recording. This time it was by another artist by the name of E.J Miller whom he hadn't had the time to listen to either. Dick and E.J. Miller were brothers and friends of his that were originally from Birch Lake before they went to Nashville and made it big. Soon the melodic strains of accordion music flowed again softly through the Corvette with the song, the Tennessee Waltz.

Goddamn, Reed grumbled. That song always haunted him and reminded him it was popular way back in his college days and one that he and Lindy would waltz together to around their small apartment and collapse in laughter and out of breath in each other's arms on their bed. He punched the dismiss bar and the next song came on.

He lit a cigarette as he drove, still pissed, but soon his cell rang and Bernard came on.

"Hey Conners, you won't believe what came up on this dame. Listen to this; she buried her old man a few years ago. They owned Jensen's; you've seen them, the trucking company? Its small, but she was the sole owner of the business!"

So what was the connection between this apparently well to do woman and the likes of this seemingly loser, Bobby Wilson?

-24-

Lindy hung up the phone after talking to Reed. Why did she ever call him? When most of the time he just got bossy and wanted to run her life. She went to the refrigerator for a bottle of water and sat down on the couch.

But as she sat, she let her thoughts wonder; she could get back on a plane and fly to Minneapolis and stay with him as he suggested, but then she'd be right back to being under his wing. She had been in love with him back in college and she still cared about him, and he had helped her out of some things over the years, but just now, she was not ready to run back into his arms. Although, she was scared as hell of revenge from the Mexican mafia, as she thought of them now, she would make doubly sure she was not being watched or followed. And she knew Detective Mann now.

Besides, there was something that she wanted to try to do. Ever since finding out Mitzi had been murdered, she wanted to try to contact her through a vision and find out who had taken her life. While she had been in Monterrey, she had had some really vivid images of happenings and that was one reason she had to stay and do it from right here in Hilton Head where it had all taken place. It would take time, preparation and concentration. This was something she had never tried and had no idea if it would even work. And right now, she felt was a good time to try it.

She went out to the balcony and stretched out in one of the chaise loungers. She set the water bottle down and closed her eyes and started a relaxation exercise. A simple one; where she had learned to totally relax and finally rid her body of all aches, and then erase all the thoughts that muddled her mind. This took many minutes of deep breathing and concentration and sometimes much longer before she could feel herself so relaxed she seemed to melt into the mattress of whatever she was lying on. This was as far as she had gone before.

Now she took some slow breaths and let the mellow breeze and the beat of the ocean waves consume her total being. She was totally relaxed now and time elapsed as she rested in this soft cocoon of safety. Then she brought Mitzi into focus and in a vision the two women smiled and hugged after exclaiming how they had missed each other. Lindy actually felt the emotional happiness they shared at that moment as she watched the picture of them.

"Girlfriend, you look good," she said as she studied Mitzi's new hair color. "When did you decide to be a brunette?"

Mitzi ran her hand through her new look and smiled, "I did it weeks ago. I've gotten so many compliments on it."

For a minute, the vision stayed, and then suddenly it blurred as Lindy thought of seeing those 8x10 pictures of Mitzi that the police department had shown her. That had been what was different about her, she realized now. Mitzi had had darker hair. Then the vision totally disappeared!

Lindy lay still and waited, then went through the self-hypnotic exercises again, but now to no avail. The images were gone and she could not bring them back. After some time, she sat up and realized several hours had gone by. She did feel rested, and most importantly, she had found a way to bring on her own psychic séance. She was thrilled and now maybe, with more practice she could find Mitzi again and learn just how she had died. But she'd wait and try it again later, at night maybe.

She went into the condo and made a sandwich, then took out a notebook and began to make notes. From her memory, she wrote down word for word how she had brought on the vision. How she needed to remember every word and every thought she had had. This was so exciting as previously she had had no control over the visions that would just appear out of the blue, most times at odd hours of the day or night. And lately, none had appeared at all. She'd had mixed emotions about that, glad to be rid of the haunted stirrings and the worrisome times when an awful event would follow. But she really missed having the ability and besides she had made a lot of money at this while living in Monterrey. In the back of her mind, she had had an idea of using this again soon, right here,

For a moment in her excitement, she thought of calling Reed back and telling him what she had been able to do. And why she couldn't rush back just now. Although he seemed to believe her psychic abilities when she had seen where that man they had called Wolf, had taken Murphy's wife that time, and then helped solve the mystery of who those two men were who were found in his lake there. She knew he just barely tolerated her gift, acknowledging only once or twice that it could have just been a lucky guess. That alone irritated her enough to put the whole idea aside for now and not explain to him why she had to stay here.

Silence

The phone rang just then, shattering her thoughts and glad of the diversion, she hurried to answer.

"Miss Lewis," a man's voice exclaimed in her ear, "this is Mike Mann. How are you? I'm wondering if we could meet this evening. I would like to go over some things with you."

"Possibly," she said.

"I can come by and pick you up at seven!" Mike Mann directed.

"Thank you," she answered coolly, to cover a sudden attack of nerves. "But I could meet you."

"Okay, how about Leon's. Do you know the place?" He asked.

"Very well," Lindy assured him. When she hung up, a chill went through her, just why did he want to meet her there, of all places? The place where all this trouble began with the D'Agustino brothers.

Would it be safe going there again?

However, she showered and dressed in her finest. She put on the new red dress that she had bought earlier at the Shops by the Ocean as it was called. This was a low-cut organza with a flared skirt that twirled around her knees. She'd had a mani-pedi earlier too, so her toes peeked out of the strappy high-heeled sandals. She fluffed and spiked her red tresses, then added a dab here and there of her new cologne called Creed and glancing in the mirror, she did have to admit she looked good!

But was she making a huge mistake by going back to that place, and would she be exposing herself to danger again?

Leon's was a popular restaurant in the Shelter Cove area on the water that housed a marina, boutiques and an assortment of eateries. She had been there many times before with Mitzi, and it was there that they had gotten on the yacht with Mario and Andre. Also, it was the same place that she had quickly exited off the boat after witnessing Mario kill that federal agent.

For God's sake she hadn't been here since! Was she nuts to go there now?

She parked the Lexus in the lot and walked past the huge statue of King Neptune who guarded the area with his spear ready to chase any and all marauders out of the large open area that faced the water. Her high heels tapped smartly on the pavement and turned heads as she walked purposely to her destination. Now she came to Leon's exclusive entrance and opened the frosted glass door. Just inside, soft guitar jazz floated around her as she came into the foyer, and then stepped into a cocktail lounge with a bar that ran along the far wall. She walked up and settled on a stool where all around her people were busily occupied with each other. Leon, the owner, being a connoisseur of good-looking single women did not miss her entrance into his hive of fun loving customers, and immediately took up space beside her stool.

"Well hello, Lindy Lewis. I haven't seen you for a good year or more," he said now as he took her hand and brushed his lips over her knuckles. "My dear, you're even more beautiful than before!"

Lindy smiled at the man. He was of Greek descent, over sixty with dyed black hair and mustache and loved all women.

"Leon," she whispered in his ear, playfully, "I couldn't stay away any longer."

"You will be my steady then won't you?" He asked and winked at her.

"I'll be near your side, noon and especially at night!" Lindy said as she leaned closer to the man and looked into his eyes.

"Yes, yes," Leon groaned, "I've found my soul-mate." This was a running joke between them and he kissed her cheek and laughed. "Hey Bruno," he said to the bartender just then who stood across the bar from them. "Bring this beautiful lady a glass of our best champagne!" And he went on to greet another female who had just come in.

Lindy sipped the champagne and looked around the room. She and Mitzi had enjoyed the place so much; they had had lunch out on the veranda by the water, danced to the music at night and now such a short time later, both Mitzi and Mario were dead and who knew, where the brother Andre was.

She sucked in a breath and wished for a cigarette as these thoughts saddened her. But just then someone tapped her on the shoulder and she turned to see Mike Mann, the handsome detective.

"Good evening Miss Lewis," he said. "Sorry, I got held up. I hope I didn't keep you waiting too long."

Glad for the interruption she smiled and said, "Hello. No, I just got here. Now should I call you Detective Mann, or Mike?" She asked.

"For you, I'm Mike." He said and sat down on the next stool.

Lindy gave him the once over. He was a good-looking man she'd seen before, when she'd met him at the police department. And this evening he was wearing an elegant black suit with a stark white shirt open at neck, which accentuated his graying hair. A quick peek and she saw he was wearing black tasseled loafers. She smiled her approval now as she loved when a man dressed with class.

"And may I call you Lindy, Miss Lewis?" he asked

"Sure," she said and adjusted the hem-line of her dress to just above her knees.

Not missing that, Mike Mann said then taking her breath away, "So now, I get to meet the infamous woman who brought down one of the biggest drug cartels in US history!"

-25-

Reed had been in the Lake Calhoun area for the last few hours after locating the address listed for the owner of the SUV Bobby Wilson was driving. Bernard, his computer guy, had found Rose Jensen owned the vehicle and apparently was the woman who had opened the door for a delivery from Ups. From a distance, all Reed could make out was that she was slim and had light hair. The man who had joined her at the doorway could have been this Wilson, but Reed had only seen him once before and he really hadn't paid too much attention to the guy at the time and could not be sure.

If, he was the one and the same, he was a very dangerous man out on the loose.

Would the DA decide this man should be prosecuted for attempted murder and arrest him again?

Reed left the area puzzling over who all these people were and how they were connected with Jonas Hovland's death and the twenty-five million dollars. According to Hovland's will, Reed read that it was to go the sons; precisely, to expand the building empire which Nigel and Aaron were to continue to run. It was stipulated that his daughter Rena was to get a yearly sum of one hundred thousand dollars to live on, since she was considered to be unlikely to be able to support herself. And according to the brothers Reed had seen, they let it be known that their sister was somewhat slow.

Well she hadn't looked slow the times he had met her. She looked well dressed and well- motivated.

Had Bobby Wilson been involved in her change? And what was his agenda?

By now, it was late afternoon and Reed was tired and cranky. He wanted a drink and good company so he drove to Gina's to see his friends.

"Conners, good to see you," Paul, the bartender greeted him.

"Hey buddy," Reed answered and took a stool at the bar. "How are you?"

"Great thanks. Your usual?" Paul asked and reached to the top shelf for the Crown Royal whiskey that Reed drank.

"Yup. Goddamn, I need to get away from these people for a while. The more I find out, the more complicated it gets!"

"If you're talking about that Hovland case you're working on, I overheard something a few nights ago that might be of interest to you." Paul commented as he poured the whiskey.

Surprised, Reed looked at him and asked, "What?"

Paul checked for new customers after he put the drink down on the bar for Reed, and then leaned across. "Listen to this," he said, "a group of people were in one night and they were talking about this guy that they called a sleaze-ball and a bigamist. That he was busy charming some older woman who was going to inherit millions!"

"Really?" Reed took another swallow of the whiskey, reached for his pack of Marlboros, and then muttered an expletive under his breath.

Seeing his frustration, Paul shook his head and added, "Sorry pal, I feel your pain."

Reed almost laughed, knowing Paul used to smoke like a locomotive before the new laws. After a minute he asked, "Did you get names?"

"Some, I heard the name Wilson mentioned I know. Then, I heard San Diego and the name

Hovland. It sounded like this Wilson was from out in California." Paul nodded to a new group of customers and went over to take their orders.

Reed thought about what Paul had told him, then picked up his cell again.

"Hey Bernard," he said, "Can you call up your buddy in San Diego, and see what he can tell you about a Bobby Wilson?" He asked his friend.

Then he sat and tried to piece together this mystery. Was he going out on a limb with this Wilson?

Then Gina sailed into the bar aglow in a blazing red cocktail suit. A low neckline under a diamond necklace revealed firm breasts. Her high-heels were red patent sling-backs.

"My darling detective, how are you?" And she bent over and gave Reed a kiss on a cheek.

Reed stood up and returned the friendly embrace, "Gina, you only get better!"

Gina sat down on the next stool and motioned for Paul to bring her a drink, then said, "thank you, but between you and me, it takes longer every day to get to this!" And she blinked her false eyelashes at Reed and laughed.

"It's the results that count," Reed returned and smiled.

"Seriously Reed, how is the investigation going?"

"Not good so far. Too many possibilities!"

"Well Reed my dear, I've got something that will make it easier for you!"

-26-

Bobby Wilson smiled slyly. God how he loved women! And, how they loved a well-dressed man! He slipped a silk shirt over his head and grabbed a cashmere jacket off the hanger. And it didn't matter much how clear your credentials were, just as long as you could keep them happy! There was Rose Jensen whom he lived with and then there was Rena Hovland. He had always liked to have his next venture in sight as you never knew when it became necessary to depart and start over. So he'd planned that down the road, he would continue living the life of luxury and means with Rena after she got her share of the inherited millions from her fathers will. But now, had he blown it or could she be swayed into being sympathetic about this rash reaction he'd had to her claim that he was no good?

Bobby Wilson had previously met and made arrangements with this clothing store salesman, and the young man had eagerly slipped the c-notes in his own pocket and agreed to look the other way, then make the call to the cops after a good thirty minutes had elapsed and claim a robbery had taken place. And now after one quick peek around the clothing store, Bobby saw the one and only salesman had ducked in the back as was arranged. He left the dressing room, picked up the rest of the prearranged bag of clothing and walked out of the store.

Now he finally had the look together he needed for this new venture, he thought as he swung down the street and got into the silver SUV. But was it too late?

Robert Ellis Wilson was past fifty years old but told acquaintances that he was forty. He had a wiry build and weighed around one hundred and fifty pounds, but more if he had a good scene going for himself. Like the regular meals he had now with Rose Jensen, the regular trips to the fitness center, massages and styled haircuts. This was not always possible for Bobby Wilson as he was a habitual liar and often found himself caught in his own fabrications. He did not have a real job, and hadn't had one for oh maybe, twenty years now. Not since that time years ago when that blonde broad he'd moved in with, threw him out until he brought home a paycheck. Christ almighty, he had never worked so goddamned hard. And for what in the end? She'd tossed him out anyway just because he liked to stop and have a drink with the boys. Never mind the cards and women; things evolved out there sometimes that you had no control over. At least that's how he looked at it.

He had flown into Minneapolis on somebody else's charge card a good year ago now after leaving California. He hadn't wanted to leave the state, but then when word out on the street reached him that the bedroom communities he had burgled were getting close to getting their man, he split.

Actually Bobby Wilson was not an unintelligent man. He'd started his second year of high school when his aged father died leaving him an orphan and penniless. He lived in their rented rooms until he was kicked out, and then he hit the streets. He quit school and took up with a group of rich young losers and learned how to lie, cheat and steal. At sixteen he had lost his virginity, and soon after got caught breaking into a liquor store and was sent to a correctional institution for wayward teens for a year. At legal age, he had been in prison three times, and married twice. And, he had learned a valuable lesson he thought, that almost always kept him in cash; and that was, the world was full of rich, vulnerable women.

But now you would think after years of living a somewhat loose life this man would be wrinkled, worn and sickly, but he was in splendid health and looked good. His dyed dark hair was high-lighted with gray and with the styled cut and the fine clothes he looked to be someone of importance. Now with thousands of dollars' worth of stolen clothes for his new wardrobe, he whistled a tune through his teeth.

On the way to the spacious home at Lake Calhoun where he lived with Rosie as he called her, he stopped and picked up a box of Godiva chocolates. She'd been a little testy when he left there this morning, but then UPS had conveniently shown up with the gift he'd bought. And she'd thrown her arms around him to thank him for the lovely mink jacket. Never mind that he'd charged it on one of her cards, but then he would pay that long before the bill came.

He blew out a relieved breath. He'd covered his ass over there and had a place to call home, but that welcome would wear out soon as they always did. But now, what about Rena? Christ, he'd lost it when she had told him to hit the streets yesterday, when she said she'd had him checked out. That he was not affiliated with any investment house, that he was a liar, a thief and a goddamn bum! And she didn't want to see his cheating ass ever again! And before he knew what he was doing he'd had his knife in his hand and stabbed her. Then ran!

Silence

Christ, now he'd probably blown his plan to cash in on her new status. He fumbled for his pack of Pall Malls and lit up as he drove. And after all he'd done for the old broad! He remembered seeing the pictures of her in the society pages and had looked her up. With a plan in mind he had taken her in hand and taught her how to dress and to act as a woman of means. He had spent an endless amount of time in her bed showing her how to enjoy his expertise in the art of love.

Christ, he loved living rich and he never minded the price he had to pay. After all, love was easy, but now would he have to start all over again and look for someone new?

-27-

Lindy gaped at Detective Mann's comment that he was "meeting the infamous woman who brought down the Mexican Mafia!"

"Well, I didn't--," she started to say and then clamed up. Apparently he had done some investigating since their last meeting. But what did he know?

"How long were you involved with the leader of that cartel?" He asked and looked pointedly at her.

"A very short time!" She exclaimed.

"Well, you were hanging around with some dangerous people!" He commented dryly. "Tell me, when you ran off to Mexico, were you going there to join up with D'Agustino and his drug business?"

Lindy glared at him. "No," she whispered. "And I didn't know he lived there, I left as soon as I found that out!"

"Where did you go?"

"I came back here to the US and stayed with a friend." She took a sip of the champagne. For God's sake, why was he questioning her?

"Was that friend named Reed Conners?" He asked.

Now Lindy lost her patience and said, "I presume you've read the reports on the whole episode. I don't want to talk about this anymore."

"Understandable," he said, "but there are just some things I want to know. For instance, did you ever give back the million dollars that you defrauded that insurance company out of?"

Lindy slid of her bar stool. Now he had crossed the line. "Am I on trial here?" she whispered angrily. "Frankly, Detective, it's none of your business!" And she started for the door. The nerve of the jerk, she mumbled under her breath as she slammed out and hurried to her car. As she neared the Lexus, he caught up with her.

"Lindy," he said, "I'm sorry, I just needed some more details."

"Well, I'd advise you to do some more detecting then!" She got in her car and sped out of the parking lot and left him standing in the dust. She wiped tears of distress off her cheeks as she drove through the streets of Hilton Head.

It was a Friday evening and the small resort town was filling up with tourists and the week-end residents. The air was festive with the array of colored vehicles and heavy with humidity as the temp lazily stayed at a plus ninety degrees inland. But if you visited anywhere on the beaches, the ocean breezes cooled you immediately.

Lindy went back to the Adventure Inn, to her condo and changed clothes. She put on one of her new bikinis and tied the flimsy skirt around her waist, found her flip-flops and went down to the beach and the water. Here she walked until finally she felt she'd walked off the distress of the past and she came back to the Inn and stopped at the ocean side lounge. She bought a pina-colada and then fell into a chaise amongst a crowd. Two sun-tanned young men were providing guitar music and all eyes were turned to the ocean as the setting sun sent its kaleidoscope of colors across the waves.

As many times as she had seen it, she still sat spell-bound and watched the scene before her, only taking her eyes away from the developing panorama to sip her drink.

The sun had colored her to a beautiful golden tan too, and she was well on her way into the fourth decade of her life, but she just could not think of the fifty year mark lurking ahead. A family was sitting close by and she watched the exchange of whispers as parents and youngsters sat enthralled by the sight of the setting sun. Of course, she'd never had any children, but she wondered how it felt to have someone totally dependent on you?

Then her thoughts went back again to her friend Mitzi. Now, she was gone and would miss seeing her son grow into a young man.

But where was she and her son? Had the two of them gone into hiding when she noticed she was being followed! Were they still alive?

Lindy sat smoking and sipping on her drink and then heard a familiar voice call her name across the mass of people gathered at the Adventure Inn beach bar. She studied the crowd and found her friend Mila, who lived just down over the dunes.

"Lindy," she called out again, then stood up and waved over the heads of the crowd. "Over here," she said.

Lindy got up and carried her drink over to her table. Mila, her friend was seated with a group of people, all of which were visiting from her native country of Peru, she said happily.

"Join us," Mila said motioning Lindy to an empty seat. "These are my cousins," she said and ran off their names in one long string of unintelligible words.

Lindy nodded and smiled at the handsome group. There were two women and three men and they were tanned and beautiful, and all of them were wearing skimpy bathing suits and loads of jewelry. Pitchers of frosty margueritas stood on their table.

"A special party?" Lindy asked and stretched out on a chaise.

Mila laughed. "Nothing but," she said and hugged her nearest cousin. "They are staying at the Hilton and will be here for a month."

"Really?" Lindy smiled. "You're so lucky Mila to have so many relatives!"

"Don't I know it?" Mila added and then murmured under her breath, "And they're all rich!" She shook her mane of dark hair and her brown eyes sparkled.

Lindy looked them over; that changed her interest. She loved to be around people who were in the money. "Okay, now let's go over your names again. And go slow?

And let's start with you," and she pointed to the man who was sitting next to her, knowing he was appraising her behind his dark glasses.

"Emilio," he said taking off his glasses, and then pointing to each one introduced them and then blew her a kiss.

She laughed, "Happy to meet you all. Let's have some fun!" And she raised her glass and Mila filled it from their margarita pitcher.

The sun was going down and the waiters were lighting the torches that lined the gated deck. And now the atmosphere changed to romance and dancing. And before Lindy knew what was happening, she was pulled to her feet by Emilio and to the portable dance floor that reached out over the water.

"You are so beautiful," he whispered in her ear, "I'm in love already!" He added then and continued murmuring in Spanish.

Lindy felt the heat from his hand on her bare back and then his attempt to clutch her close.

Oh, for God's sake, she groaned to herself and pulled away from his hot body. She just wasn't up to playing this game, especially so soon after leaving Reed and his needs. But then after a moment she changed her mind. You just never knew when you might need a man around, she thought, so she smiled at the man and danced, enjoying the spectacular Hilton Head evening scene.

-28-

Reed had stopped in at Gina's Bar and Restaurant to take a break from the Hovland case, where Gina and Paul the bartender, were two of his best friends. Gina had bustled in after closing her dining room and exclaimed she had something of interest to tell Reed.

"What could help me?" He asked curiously.

"Listen to this," she said now, "I had lunch with my girlfriends yesterday and I heard something from one, Reed. Now, she has worked for the Hovland family for years as their housekeeper. And she moved along with the old man over to the daughter's place to live awhile back."

"Yeah?" Reed leaned over.

Gina went on, "Rena was a recluse all her life, then this man came along and suddenly she had a make-over, started shopping for classy clothes and began doing the town with him. Then her father died and she suddenly started working next to the brothers in the business too. She also told my friend, the housekeeper, she was in love with this guy.

"Let me guess. His name is Bobby Wilson, right?" Reed commented dryly.

"That's him," Gina said."

"Yeah, the same asshole that stabbed her and put me in jail!" Reed whipped a hand through his hair.

"I know Reed, but let me tell you the rest. My friend said Rena had him investigated and found he was wanted in California for fraud and burglary. And get this, for bigamy too!"

"I knew it!" Reed growled.

"She was there, back when Jonas Hovland sailed over the banister. And she said Rena was at home that day, and Rena's boy-friend was over and they were out at the pool and she was not with her brothers as they claimed earlier. And Reed, there's more. My friend said Rena Hovland just received the report a few days ago that her lover was a wanted man!" Gina sat back and nodded her head.

"And yesterday when Wilson came to see Rena in the office," Reed went on, "and she told him what she had found out, that's when he stabbed her and ran, and I had the misfortune of finding her!" Reed shook his head and took a long swallow of the Crown Royal. "And get this," he added, "Today she said she won't press charges against him either!"

"Oh, for God's sake. Why not?" Gina exclaimed.

"I'm not sure, but I'd bet he got to her and talked her out of it sometime during the night." Reed said.

"Well, this Wilson bum knew he had a lot to lose if she booted him out." Gina leaned over for a napkin and wiped at a spot on the bar.

"Yeah, and I know it was him I found today over at her house. He ducked out a side door and then, goddamn, I lost him on the freeway." Reed blew out a tired breath.

"Reed my darling, you look pretty peaked." Gina exclaimed out of the blue as she gazed at him. "I'm going to get a nice big steak for you!"

"Yeah, maybe that's what I need, some real red meat!"

"Now just relax and a waiter will set you up right here at the bar!" Gina ordered then left to check on her people in the kitchen.

Both Paul and Reed watched her provocative walk as she left and she glanced back at them and winked.

"I've known her since my college days," Reed commented, "and she can still make me smile."

Paul laughed. "She does that!"

Later after eating a large porterhouse steak and a baked potato, Reed went back to his hotel. This time when he checked the invisible scotch tape he'd taken to attaching to the bottom of the door, it was gone!

He reached for the .38 he'd started to carry since this first happened. He tried the doorknob then slipped his key in and quietly opened the door. Then kicked it wide open and raised the gun. Not seeing anyone he edged into the room and scanned it quickly, then dropped to his knees and looked under the bed, then got to his feet and checked the bathroom. No one!

Goddamn, he said as he slipped the safety on the .38 and tried to slow down his pounding heart. Who the hell was it who had broken into his room twice now?

Since the last break in, he had changed rooms but still kept this one and intently left some files naming the case, but actually not giving anything away. But he did hint that he was getting close to catching the person, the murderer, who had pitched Hovland over the banister in his daughter's house in Restless Waters.

He tried to calm down. Although it was going on midnight, he knew he couldn't go to sleep now, even after the good steak and whiskeys he'd had at Gina's. He had a gut feeling this was not over for the night, and he was right on most times. He rolled up the covers and plumped up the pillows to make it look like he was there in bed and then hurried out of the room. There was a sitting area just down the hallway,

Silence

off to the side from the elevators, and he sat down and pulled a silk tree close for cover. From there he had a clear view of the door to his old room.

He was wide awake now, and as he waited he went over the case in his head. The Hovland kids were fighting. Rena wanted equal shares in the family business and her two brothers were trying to keep her out.

Were the brothers responsible for their father's death? Had Rena and her boyfriend planned it? The three Hovland's had said they were together when their father died, and had each other's alibi, but the housekeeper said Rena and Wilson were home and out at the swimming pool that day when Jonas Hovland died. One or both could have crept into the house and tossed the old man to his death.

He was almost sure Bobby Wilson was behind the whole affair. But the two brothers looked pretty good for it too.

He waited, and then waited some more. Goddamn, he wished he had some coffee, and glancing at his watch, he saw it was going on two am. But after all this time of sitting there, he wasn't ready to give it up yet. He had this feeling! A few people had hurried by through the hallway to their respected rooms but no one looked suspicious so far or paid any attention to him. He rested his eyes for a moment, and then something happened! He opened them suddenly and then realized it was the door to the elevator closing with a swish that awakened him. And goddamn, he'd fallen asleep!

He tossed his files under the couch and ran to the stairs. Thank God, he was only on the second floor and when he got downstairs he ran to the elevator door just as it was opening, and it was empty!

The lobby was quiet and he went to the front entrance and ran out the double doors. The downtown streets were lit up and a few stragglers about but no one who looked suspicious.

He stood for a few minutes as several cars sped by. Who had been after him? Then, swearing under his breath he went back up on the elevator to his room.

He drew his .38 again and cautiously opened his door, then kicked it wide and stepped in, ready to shoot. The room was clear!

Then he saw them, the bullet holes in his bed! Two in the pillows and two in the roll of bed clothes he'd made earlier. The asshole had gotten by him, sometime during the time he had nodded off as he sat waiting in the hallway!

Goddamn, now he was pissed!

-29-

Lindy danced the night away with Emilio and Mila's cousins from Peru.

It was close to two in the morning when he insisted on walking her back to her condo.

"Good night," Lindy said after unlocking her door, "And thank you for seeing me home."

Emilio pulled her into a tight embrace and his lips claimed hers in a hot kiss. "De nada Senorita," he whispered, but she pulled back. "Don't you want me to come in?" He asked with a feverish look on his face.

"Not tonight," she said firmly, "I've got an early appointment."

"Senorita, I won't stay long!" He trailed his fingers down her arm and then raised her hand to his lips and kissed her palm.

"Emilio," Lindy said, "I had a good time tonight, but I'll catch up with you all later." She just wasn't going to get involved again, especially with a foreigner! Although he sure is charming, she had to admit.

Crestfallen, he turned. "I'll stop over later then," he said as he waved and reluctantly left. Relieved he hadn't become too insistent, Lindy closed the door and went to her bedroom where she dropped her bikini and skirt on the floor and collapsed in bed. She slept soundly until the bright South Carolina sun awakened her as it shone through the window and in her bedroom. She sat up in bed with the worst headache she'd had for a long time and put her head in her hands.

Lordy, how many margaritas did I drink last night? She wondered.

She finally got up enough energy to locate the bottle of aspirin and swallowed three with some water, then on trembling legs closed the shade on the window and sank back down in her bed. She closed her eyes and did some relaxation exercises, and then lay in limbo waiting for relief from the headache. The soft swish of the ocean outside lulled her into a cocoon of wellbeing as she lay under the down filled blanket. She fell into a restful slumber, and then a vision floated before her eyes. She saw her friend Mitzi again. She was running, out of breath, running as fast as she could. Then Lindy heard a door slam, and she saw Mitzi bracing against it and fumbling to lock it. Her breathing echoed in the room, and Lindy recognized it as her kitchen. It seemed to be nighttime as the curtains were closed. She saw Mitzi frantically grab the phone and dial for help.

Then the vision wavered, and Lindy concentrated for more, and then instead got a sudden glimpse of the person out front. She saw it was a slightly built man and she watched as he crept around to the side of Mitzi's house and looked in the windows, which she saw were tightly closed and shaded. Then the man turned for just an instant and she saw his face. She did not recognize him, but she had time to memorize it. Then her vision trailed off and she slid into a restful nap.

Hours later, she awoke and outside of having an awful taste in her mouth, the headache was gone. As she lay in bed the memory of her vision came back and she remembered the man's face. My God, this was important, she whispered and she jumped up and found her sketching tablet and pencil and began to draw. She wasn't a trained artist but she could sketch pretty well. And she needed to get this man's face down on paper before she forgot his features. So she drew and erased and sat for a long time working on a picture until she had a pretty good copy of the man's features. As she studied it now, she could see he looked to be of foreign ancestry. And an idea had begun taking form in the back of her mind.

She picked up her cell phone and dialed her friend Monica in Monterrey. "Hey girlfriend, I need a quick favor."

"Lola Lindy, where the hell are you?" Monica asked, first off.

"Monica, I'm back at my favorite place." Lindy answered and went back to the bed and stretched out.

"Let me guess, Hilton Head?"

"Where else. I got here a few days ago. But I'll catch you up on those things later. Right now I need your help!"

"Okay. What's up?"

"Monica, this is important. I'm going to send a picture on an e-mail to you and I need you to study it and see if you recognize the man!" Lindy sat up now and tossed the covers to the floor as she explained

"Okay," Monica said again. "Shoot it down here and give me an hour. I'll get it right back to you."

"Thanks," Lindy said. She showered and dressed then and went down to the complex offices to use the computers they supplied there for their guests use.

That done she went back to her condo and waited. She made a pot of coffee and toasted some cinnamon bread which she took out to the deck and sat down in one of the chaise lounges.

The day was beautiful. The sun was almost right overhead and the tide was out. The wide expanse of beach was crowded with sunbathers and colorful umbrellas and a gentle breeze brought the hushed bits of music and conversations across the dunes to her on the balcony. She brushed her hair back off her face as she ate her breakfast.

She thought again of the man she'd seen in her vision stalking Mitzi. Could Monica identify him as someone from the D'Agustino/Mercado clan? But then again there were a lot of foreign tourists always on the island and it could be someone entirely different.

She stretched out on the chaise after finishing eating and let her mind wander.

If Monica was able to identify the man from the picture what could she do about it anyway? Tell Detective Mann? Probably not, not just on that kind of evidence. He'd laugh at her. But to get him interested in the case she'd have to tell him about her visions and she just wasn't about to tell anyone about that, that is not just yet!

She'd gotten the money back from the bank in Newport Rhode Island, where the original five hundred thousand she'd gotten for the sale of her house in Monterrey Mexico, she'd put into short term investments. That had netted her another ten thousand, and she'd add that to the million plus she had stashed, and she would soon be ready to go ahead with her plan. She'd spotted several possibilities.

Checking her watch Lindy saw an hour had passed and she hurried back down to the complex offices again and turned on one of the computers. She opened up her e-mail site and there was the message from Monica.

Not wasting any time, she'd written, "Lola Lindy, that face belongs to one of the D'Agustino sons!"

Lindy's breath caught in her throat. Just what she'd feared; the mafia family! Mitzi had been dating Andre D'Agustino, Mario's brother those months last summer when Mario had killed that Federal agent!

Lindy walked back to her condo, but now a creepy feeling bit at her heels. She looked around. The Adventure Inn complex was gated to keep out the non-residents, but if you wanted to come in all you had to do was walk the beach and come in that way. It was a busy place with three large buildings facing the ocean, then quite a few buildings sitting further back, first and second tier as they were called. Then it had a building that housed the business offices, a restaurant and lounge, a small convenience store and a ballroom where parties and meetings were held.

She had stayed there enough times in one of the ocean side condos and always felt safe, but now she had a feeling of unease. She hurried into her place and locked the door.

Now what should she do, call Reed?

-30-

After finding the bullet holes in the bed, Reed went across the hallway to the room he had moved into at the hotel after the first break-in. He opened the door of the second room and had the .38 ready as he went in just to be sure no one was in there.

He sat down and pulled out his smokes. He lit up and puffed hard on the Marlboro. It was after two AM in the morning and he needed to calm down before he could hope to get some sleep. He turned on the television and found an original Hawaii Five O show and watched Jack Lord bring peace to his city again. After an hour or so, he was finally able to climb into the bed and sleep.

The next morning as he showered, he planned the day. First of all, he wanted to visit the Hovland boys again. He took his time and ate a leisurely breakfast and read the Star Tribune papers giving the brothers time to get in to their offices. On the way over to Saint Paul, he held back on the gas pedal on the Corvette and cruised at a moderate sixty-five miles an hour. And as he drove, he listened to the purr of the motor and loved the hum of the machine.

He parked in the underground lot at the Hovland building and took the elevator up to the floor occupied by Hovland Builders and their assorted architects and planners. The front office was decorated now with a brunette who had apparently taken the post vacated by Rena Hovland. She asked Reed's business and seemed duly perturbed that he did not have an appointment to see her important employers.

"You do understand you will have to wait without one, don't you?" She admonished.

"Of course," Reed said politely. "I stand corrected!" He added and grinned.

However, within five minutes he was ushered into the Hovland offices. Nigel, the oldest of the Hovland siblings was sitting at his huge desk, leaning back, with his feet in Cole Haan tasseled loafers propped up on the corner. His polished good looks reminded Reed of someone from the silent movies. Aaron was lounging on a leather couch; his dress today was jeans, a t-shirt under a tan cashmere jacket and boots. His rugged good looks were accentuated by his unruly golden brown hair which reached his shoulders.

"What the hell do you want? You got all the information you need from the files!" Nigel Hovland tossed at Reed as he stood waiting for an invitation to take a seat.

"Good morning to you too," Reed said, "So sorry to interrupt your busy meeting. I just need some questions answered."

Aaron Hovland sat up and pulled out a cigar. "What the hell? That goddamn case is closed; you got all the answers you need!" He lit a cabana and blew the smoke in Reed's direction.

Reed took his time as he said, "Seems someone has come forward and will testify that your sister was not with you two when your father died, that she was at her home with her boy-toy Bobby Wilson." Reed went on, "Fellows, sorry that blows your alibi that you three were all together."

Nigel sat up and his feet hit the floor. "Look, asshole," he said, "We were here working as usual. You can check with our staff. They will vouch for us!"

Biting down a sarcastic reply Reed asked, "Were any of them in here with you at the time?"

"We are each other's witnesses," Aaron growled. "It's in the files!"

"Sorry. Like I said, this leaves a big hole in your claim for your father's insurance. We're not ready to hand over our millions at this point!" Reed almost smiled when he laid this info on the boys, and then added, "Well, since you haven't invited me to take a seat, guess I'll leave. But I might add, don't leave town!"

Nigel stood up and his face turned red with rage as he yelled, "Fuck off, Conners!"

Reed walked out leaving the door open, then took his time as he sauntered through the hallway to the front office. He smiled at the brunette at the front and said. "Thank you for arranging my meeting with the guys. You must be new here. I haven't seen you before?"

"I am, I just started last week," she gushed.

"I can see you are a real asset to their company. Have you met everyone?" Reed asked.

"Oh yes. It's sure a big place." She shifted some papers on her desk importantly as she talked.

Reed looked around innocently. "Is this the only entrance/exit?"

The receptionist laughed. "Oh no," she said, "There is one in the back. And I have the hardest time keeping track of my bosses!"

Reed smiled at her. She had a lot to learn about being discrete, as she had inadvertently told him the brothers had a back entrance where they could come and go as they pleased!

He left the Hovland offices and next he wanted to catch up with Rena Hovland. When he had called the hospital earlier where she had been taken the other day after being stabbed, he was informed that she had gone home to recover, with a trained nurse at her side. So he retraced his route back to her house in Restless Waters and parked again in the bricked circular driveway. He had been there the day before and had seen Bobby Wilson duck out a side door and that's when he had lost the fucker on the freeway. Now Reed had a chance and peeked in the garage as he walked up to the house and sure enough; saw the silver SUV Wilson had hidden in the garage that belonged to his other girl-friend. How the hell was this bum Bobby Wilson keeping all this straight? The guy had to be a real fucking charmer!

He stood on the portico and heard the doorbell chime inside several times before he heard footsteps approaching from the inside and the double doors were flung open.

None other than Bobby Wilson stood in the doorway with a surprised look on his face.

"Fuck, I thought you were the delivery man." He hissed.

"And I thought you were the hired help when I ran into you last time opening this same door!" Reed sized him up and down. He was a scrawny man, not very good-looking. His perfect hair-cut and expensive clothes saved him from being plain and ordinary, Reed thought.

"What do you want?" Wilson growled.

"I came to see Rena. Do you mind?" And he elbowed Wilson out of the way and stepped into the foyer.

"Who is it?" He heard Rena's voice.

"Reed Conners, Miss Hovland. I stopped in to check on you. How are you?"

As Reed was talking, he marched further into the house and found her in the living room on the couch.

Bobby Wilson trailed behind and when they got to the living room, he hurried over to her and protectively fluffed some pillows and sat down on the edge of the sofa.

"The asshole forced his way in. Should I call the police? Or should I just shoot him?" Wilson said and they laughed together at his apparent joke, and then she took his hand.

Again today, Rena was without make-up and a professional hair-do and she really did show her plain looks. And being in her late forties, she did have quite a few wrinkles and bulges. A loose blue robe covered whatever bandages covered the wound that Bobby Wilson had inflicted her with.

However now today, they gave off the look of two love-birds. Just like Reed had suspected, Wilson had gotten to her and filled her with more lies.

Silence

"I don't believe this, Miss Hovland," Reed exclaimed, "This man tried to kill you and you still allow him near you and in your home! Incredible!"

Rena sat up and smiled at her man. "It was all a mistake and I have forgiven him!"

"For coming at you with a knife! Are you insane? I'm sure the state hasn't!" Reed said, coming closer in the room.

"But I have already told them, I will not testify for them! They can't do anything, they don't have a case!" Rena ended in a whisper and laid back and Wilson moved closer and kissed her cheek.

"For Christ's sake, I can't believe the stupidity of you two," Reed exclaimed, totally disgusted. "I'll see myself out, thank you." And he retraced his steps and slammed the door.

It was going on noon as he drove back to Minneapolis. He stopped at his hotel to check the room, his first room, and again, the tape on the bottom of the door was missing. He had gone in earlier and unrolled the bed linens purposely leaving it obvious to the shooter that he had not been in that bed that he'd shot full of holes. That it was a ruse. He took a minute to steady his hand now as he reached for the .38, then he opened the door slowly at first, then flung it wide and flew in. Nothing, no one! But right off, he saw the shooter had been there again as the bed linens were full of bullet holes and tossed on the floor. And of course, the shooter was using a silencer.

Now, just as Reed wanted, the asshole would know he'd been suckered! And Reed would be right there and ready for him!

-31-

The more Lindy thought about calling Reed in Minneapolis, the more she leaned toward not rushing into doing anything rash. After all, what could he do about anything anyway?

After seeing this young man in a vision, Lindy had sketched the face from memory and e-mailed the picture to Monica.

"That face belongs to one of Rio Prada's sons," Monica had e-mailed back. "Remember the mayor of Monterrey? He has three sons!"

The Mexican Mafia, as Lindy called them now, had apparently sent one of their sons to tie up any loose ends they felt might have influenced the courts in Mario's trial. And poor Mitzi was killed just in case she might have known something about the world wide drug trade the D'Agustino/Mercado/Prada family owned. So now Lindy had guessed who and then why Mitzi had met her demise, but what had happened to her son and her mother? Where were they? And, would someone soon show up looking for her?

She came back to her condo and went out on the balcony. She sat down on the chaise, put her head back and tried to relax and forget her fears about that old situation. She gazed out at the water and soon felt her eyelids droop. Then, something flashed through her thoughts. A house! A house that was for sale that she'd seen along the beach on her walks and one she'd gazed at longingly time and again. She'd had a quick peek in the vision and she'd seen herself living in it!

A niggling plan had been forming in the back of her mind for some time, and now could it be time to buy that special house and get on with her life? Yes, she murmured in her dream, it was.

Bright and early the next day she called the real estate friend she had met awhile back. Joyce Mills was her name and they set a time to meet at the house several hours later. Lindy repaired her make-up and fluffed her hair and hurried over to the place to get a good look around the neighborhood. To her excitement, moss-draped water oaks leaned in over the bricked sidewalk that led to the front of the house. The lawn was lush and green with three perfect palms standing gracefully in the middle. Smaller versions were mixed with pink blooming azalea bushes along the front of the white stucco, one story home. Until the realtor got there, she studied the place carefully from her car, and just then the lady pulled up.

"Hey," Lindy said as she hurried over. "I'm so anxious to see inside of this place!"

"Hello Miss Lewis," Joyce Mills said from her car as she gathered her files and got out.

"I've had an eye on this place for some time, Miss Mills," Lindy said, "And I remember this was for sale earlier!"

"It was sold. But the buyer died suddenly right after moving in and it just came back on the market!" Joyce Mills looked up the combination to the lock box as they stood there.

As they walked closer to the building Lindy could see white seashells were embedded in the white stucco of the outside walls. She loved it already!

Joyce Mills opened the door and they walked into a foyer with marbled floors and where a round table stood laden with a huge flower arrangement. Like a lot of places in the south, the furniture came with the homes and Lindy could see this was filled with contemporary high-end furnishings. The prevalent color scheme was pastel green, blue and cream. Stainless steel and granite gleamed in the kitchen, beautiful plantation blinds in the on-suite bedrooms. Stuffed sofas and chairs and soft lighting filled the living room and colorful art graced the walls. Whole walls of sliding glass opened out to a lanai on the dunes and the ocean was right there. It was totally breathtaking!

Lindy stood gazing at the scene, listening to the constant swish and roll of the water. It had a lolling effect and she loved it.

Was she ready to ask the price? Yes!

"The price is exactly one million one hundred thousand dollars," Joyce Mills said.

Lindy's heart did a leap. Could she spend that much of her money? She'd grown used to having her pile of greenbacks, but after thinking about it she figured she'd still have close to another million left.

"Tell me about this house. What did the last owner die from?" she asked then.

Joyce began, "I heard he was a bachelor and had a sudden heart attack. But it happened when he was out on a walk, and not in here." Joyce Mills hastened to add. "Now this home has three thousand square feet. It was built ten years ago by a family who lived here. They sold and moved away, and the next owner was here a week only and it has stood vacant now for a good year. Upkeep inside and out has been done by a professional company so you can see it's spotless and ready to move into."

Silence

All the while Joyce Mills was talking; she followed Lindy as she retraced their steps through the rooms again. The three bedrooms had their own bath; one of them a beautiful master. It also had a library and a pantry. Not that Lindy was a planning on cooking, but she'd never had one of those, not even in that mansion she and her husband had renovated a lifetime ago back in Minneapolis.

She fluffed her hair as she stood out on the lanai. The room was huge with a bricked floor and sliding walls and held bright blue and green padded/rattan furniture.

With her red hair, coral sundress and matching sandals she made a colorful picture as she stood weighing her options.

"I need to think about this." Lindy exclaimed then.

"This is a hot property, Miss Lewis. I wouldn't advise waiting too long." Joyce Mills exclaimed. "I have several other people wanting to see it!"

"I need twenty four hours." Dam, she wasn't going to be pushed.

"May I ask what type of financing you will need Miss Lewis?" The realtor asked then, apparently wanting to know first how she was going to pay for this huge undertaking.

"If I decide to buy this, I will be paying cash!" Lindy remarked.

"It's over a million dollars!" Joyce Mills exclaimed totally surprised.

"I know; No problem!" Lindy said. She loved to say things like that.

"You don't need financing?" The realtor asked again, and then must have realized what her take would be on a cash deal. "Wow," she remarked and gave Lindy a new look.

"I'll try to hold off for twenty four hours, however, I can't promise. My other people are very anxious too!" Miss Mills said then.

Lindy turned to the door and ran her hands over the silk covered chairs. Excitement curled in her stomach as she went to her car and drove back to her condo. She just knew that house was meant to be hers! Later as she walked the beach, she studied the area she would have if she bought that beautiful house. A huge tree trunk had washed up on the beach and overtime had become a popular place to sit and rest if a person got tired on a walk. She had used it many times in her treks and sat down on it now.

It was a sunny glorious day and she was feeling wonderful. She decided she would put her friend Mitzi to rest and not worry about any more repercussions of the past. She gazed lovingly at the place that could finally provide solace and warmth. But as she peered at this magnificent home that might soon be hers, she sat up and wondered, was that a shadow she thought she saw move by one of the bedroom windows?

-32-

Reed went back to his room and had his .38 ready as he had become used to doing. Of course by now, the asshole shooter had become wise to his trick move after he found he had only shot rolled up bed clothes. Reed quickly packed his belongings and took off back down to the front desk to register for another room. His third one since coming here. He didn't want to go to another hotel and possibly lose the connection, since he was so close to the bastard now. But he had to be careful to not disrupt his friend's hotel business.

He unpacked his things again in the new room and sat down to think and study the situation. He needed to see the maid, the friend of Gina's, who had come forward and made the statement that Rena had been at home, cozy with her boy-friend when her father Jonas Hovland had gone over the balcony there. And not with her brothers as formally stated. That blew the previous statement that had been made to the police investigator. Now it definitely looked like the two brothers could have been behind the death of their father, but then again there was Rena and or Bobby Wilson.

Reed picked up the cell and looked for the telephone number of the maid, the friend of Gina's. He listened now as the phone on the other end rang and rang and after the fifth, the receiver was picked up.

"Hello," an out of breath voice whispered.

Looking at his watch, Reed quickly apologized seeing the time was going on ten. "Miss Barnes, I'm sorry to call so late. My name is Reed Conners and I'm a friend of Gina's."

"Yes, yes, I know you."

"I'm wondering if I could come over in the morning. I would like to talk to you about that day Jonas Hovland died."

"Oh my goodness yes, Mr. Conners. You can come over tonight if you want. This is my night off. I'm a night-owl and will be up for hours."

"You don't mind?" he asked, "I'm sort of one myself!"

Silence

The woman laughed. "Well, then we must meet, Mr. Conners!" And she gave him her address and clunked down receiver.

Anxious now to see the woman, Reed combed his hair and brushed his teeth, then tucking the .38 in his shoulder holster he put the strip of tape on the bottom of the door here at his new room as he had become used to doing. He checked the faces of the people in the elevator and in the lobby as he went through for anyone who might look suspicious, and also in the parking ramp as he walked to the Corvette. It was ten twenty as he circled down the ramp and out into the street. Apparently the theaters had just let out as the area was stop and go. Then as he got deeper into the city on the way out, he saw the stadium had opened its doors also and the cascading crowds suddenly sprawled everywhere including the street he was on. Now he was forced to stop as the cheering mass walked in front of his car.

Goddamn. Get the hell out of my way! He swore, but they kept coming. He lit a cigarette and tried to calm down. Then a police car appeared and a cop jumped out and soon his whistle pierced the air as he directed the people. Finally Reed was out of there and cruising to his destination.

Miss Barnes lived in an end unit town house in the suburb of Oak Grove. On the first ring of the bell, the door was flung open and he was greeted with a firm hand-shake.

"Hello, Mr. Conners," she said, "I was about to give up on you!" She stood a good six feet tall in a red kimono. Her hair was also a fierce red and her face was shiny with crème and devoid of any make-up.

"I'm so sorry to keep you waiting Miss Barnes. I got caught in the late night exodus downtown and couldn't move. Should I come back tomorrow, after all?" Reed stood uncertainly in the doorway.

"Oh for God's sake. Come in and don't worry about it!" Miss Barnes took his arm and motioned him in and closed the door.

"If you're sure," he said and followed her into a living room.

"Mr. Conners, sit down. I'm having a nip of whiskey. Can I pour you some?" And she indicated a side chair for him as she sat on the couch and presided over a bucket of ice and a gleaming bottle of Crown Royal.

A woman who knows what's good! Reed thought to himself as he nodded yes to her questioning look. He saw now that she could be in her eighties, and well preserved.

Soon they were sitting savoring the mellow warmth of the whiskey and after some small talk, Miss Barnes said, "Okay, you want my take on the day my friend Jonas died. Let me tell you this. I came to work for that man when I was a young girl. You see I fell in love with him." She took a hefty swallow of the drink and daintily wiped her lips on napkin. "No sir, I never wanted to marry him, and he asked me many times. You see his wife had run off and left him to raise those three kids. He divorced her years ago," she added.

Reed sat back and put his ankle over his knee. He looked around as Gina talked and noted all her furnishings were top-end and the room was beautifully put together.

"I loved those kids but they were a handful," Miss Barnes went on to say, then took a minute to wipe a tear. "Jonas spoiled them rotten. They had everything and soon the boys were running around. Rena now was another story. She was sort of slow." Miss Barnes nodded her head and sat for a minute. "She went to a special school but never really excelled in anything. But her dad gave her a job in the business and she did that for twenty years."

"When did Bobby Wilson come into the picture?" Reed asked. He could see she was getting teary eyed talking and changed the subject.

Miss Barnes sucked in her breath and took another hefty nip of her whiskey.

"Oh, him. That was the day," she exclaimed then. "Rena came home from work absolutely beaming because this man had literally bumped into her on the elevator when she was going out to lunch. She said he apologized and invited her out for a sandwich.

Well, of course she went and it seemed like every day he would appear somewhere. Soon she was going out on dates with him, and soon in the whirl-wind, she was shopping and wearing make-up. Then she said she was in love with the man and suddenly he moved in with her."

As Miss Barnes talked, she suddenly fumbled in a pocket and took out a pack of Pall Malls. "Do you mind?" she asked.

"Not at all, but do you mind if I indulge too?" Reed commented, and took out his Marlboros.

Soon the air was blue with smoke as they puffed and sipped their good whiskey.

Miss Barnes sat up straighter on the couch. "Well, you see I'd been living over there at Rena's place to be near Jonas. Then he died and she asked me to stay on and take care of her house. Well, that's what I do, so I've been over there now for quite a while."

"So what do you think of this guy, Bobby Wilson?" Reed asked then.

"For God's sake, right away I could tell he was no good. Well, I finally convinced her to call an investigator and have him checked out. I was there with her in the kitchen that morning when the investigator came over and gave her the news. Bobby was still upstairs in bed!"

"Did she go up there then?"

"No, she ran out to her car, yelling for me to throw him out!" Miss Barnes mumbled under her

Silence

breath, something like God almighty and took another sip of the whiskey. "Well, I marched up there and threw the covers off that snake. There he was sleeping without a stitch on. Well, I told him what I thought of that, and what we had found out about him. It wasn't more than five minutes and I saw him rush out the door. That's when he went directly down to the office and Rena told him what she had found out about him. That's when he stabbed her!" She huffed out a breath now.

Reed nodded as he listened.

"Now the snake has got her believing all those things are untrue and he was so beside himself that she would think that of him he just lost it and hurt her. And now she's fallen for that BS again!" Miss Barnes finally sat back and rolled her eyes.

"I know I just left them at her house." Reed said and blew out a smoke ring. "Getting back to the day Mr. Hovland died, Miss Barnes, where was Wilson when that happened?"

She chewed on her lip for a moment. "You know, I've thought this over and over in my mind and I know the fucker did it!" Miss Barnes nodded her head and stared at him for a minute then went on. "They were out in the pool and I heard him say something about getting more towels. He was the one who found Jonas, you know. He was inside the house alone with him. I was busy cooking on the grill out there for them and didn't pay close attention, but the more I think about it, I'd swear I glimpsed him through the upstairs window as he pushed Jonas over the balcony railing to his death." She sat back and poured another nip in her glass. "In fact I'm sure!"

"Miss Barnes, would you be willing to stand up in court and swear to that?" Reed asked then.

"You can count on it!" She said then.

-33-

Lindy got up from the washed up log she had been sitting on at the beach and finished her walk back to her condo. She was so happy and finally free of all her previous worries now that she had made up her mind to let go and get on with her life.

The days sped by as she indulged herself in sun and fun. She met Mila and her cousins again and they proceeded to dance, party, and laugh and partake of Mila's teas, both iced and hot. Enzio kept up his ardent advances but she managed to keep him at arm's length when he became too feverish.

Mila asked when she would be moving into her new home as they sat in lounge chairs by the water today and Lindy remarked, "I'm packed and ready to go in the first of the week, just as soon as I can sign the final papers."

"We'll have a party for you then!" Mila waved her arm at the groups of people sunning themselves by the water. "We have so many friends."

"Sounds good to me," Lindy smiled. "Mila, I want to take another look at the place from this side, will you come with me?" She got up and tucked a towel over her red bikini and brushed sand off her legs. Her tousled red hair shimmered in the sunshine.

The women got up and walked down the beach. The house was down six beach markers and would probably be around six blocks from the Adventure Inn where Lindy was living.

"I am so excited, Mila," Lindy said to her friend. "I can't wait to have you see the inside. I don't have to do a thing as it comes with everything. It even has towels and pots and pans!"

"You do cook then?" Mila asked.

"Nope," Lindy answered. "Oh, I used to a million years ago," she added, "but I gave it up!"

"Never?" Mila asked and laughed.

"Nope," Lindy repeated.

"Well, okay then, I guess, you don't have to." Mila's bracelets rattled on her wrists as she walked and talked. Her long black hair was tied up in a ponytail and her suit today was a one piece white number that hugged her generous curves.

Silence

Minutes later, perched on the log in front of the place, they gazed at Lindy's dream house.

The snow white stucco rambler gleamed in the afternoon sunshine and faced east to the Atlantic Ocean. The roof was the usual coral tile bricks which was common in the south and which Lindy loved. A huge magnolia tree decorated one side of the house and pines and landscaped flower beds on the other. A long board walk led over the sea oats covered dunes and on to more beach and then to the lanai that led into the home.

"It sort of looks like a mini-mansion," Lindy remarked as they both stared at the place. It did somewhat with its huge windows.

"Hmm-yes, yes," Mila said, "but look, does it have an upstairs, a loft maybe?"

They were both quiet then as they crooked their heads and studied the expanse between the top of those huge windows and the roof.

"No," Lindy said. "I didn't notice it before, but it looks like there could be wasted space up there!"

"Maybe eet's big to make another guest room," Mila exclaimed, "when people come, you know."

They sat engrossed in their own thoughts and then Mila sat up suddenly and gasped. "Lindey, the sun plays beautifully peectures in your house!" Whenever Mila got excited, she reverted back to a heavy Spanish accent in her language. She pointed and exclaimed, "I just saw in the window, eets's an angel!"

Lindy jerked to attention. "A what?" She exclaimed.

"Lindey, it's a special one!" Mila clapped her hands together and laughed. "You will be happy!"

But Lindy didn't see anything. She didn't know about angels but said to her friend, "Mila if that is so, that is good then!"

After a few more minutes studying the handsome place that would soon be hers, Lindy and her friend went back down the beach to their group of friends and turned their attention to the water and the play of waves.

The week-end passed and Lindy got ready for another meeting with her realtor. She had offered nine hundred thousand dollars for the house, down from one million, one hundred thousand. Today she would find out if the seller had agreed to come down two hundred thousand dollars. She always loved to do a little dickering.

She got in the Lexus and drove downtown Hilton Head to the realty office of Joyce Mills.

Greeting each other, they sat and shared a cup of coffee, then got down to business.

"So did the executors of the deceased owner agree to my offer Miss Mills?" Lindy asked.

The woman leaned in. "They made a counter offer of one million, firm."

Silence

Well, Lindy liked a good fight. "Okay, I'll counter offer again. Nine hundred thousand, five hundred is my final offer, and then I walk!" She picked up her purse and stood. "Thank you Miss Mills. I appreciate your work, but that's my final offer. You can reach me on my cell if we can do any further business."

And she left the offices in the Wexford plantation and drove to the famous Hilton Head Diner for a leisurely brunch. As she sat there, she remembered the time so long ago it seemed, but actually only a year, when the man who had been stalking her sat down at her table right there, and who turned out to be an agent from the FBI. The same man Mario later shot to death while she had been out on that infamous yacht with him for an evening out on the water.

Lordy, what a lot of time and travel had evolved since then. She'd been in jail, traveled back up north to Reed, lived in the south, the east, then Mexico, became psychic and then a successful palm reader. And here she was right back in the south. Well, she loved it here! She ordered a crab salad with toast points and a glass of iced tea and sat back to relax. Not much had changed in the place except now she couldn't enjoy a cigarette.

The Diner was a long building, an up-scale establishment that had booths up one side and down the other, with windows on both sides. It still bussed with tourists and locals, she saw, sporting sun tans and new burns from too much sun. Everybody looked well dressed and bejeweled. Lindy smoothed the white linen dress she'd slipped on, and then checked to make sure her diamond and ruby earrings were safely clasped. These were from her mom, and the only thing she had of hers.

As she finished her lunch and still sipped the tea, her cell-phone chirped in her purse.

"Hello," she said.

"Miss Lewis, this is Joyce Mills, and I have good news. The seller has agreed to your offer of nine hundred thousand five for the sale price of the house."

Lindy smiled and nodded her head, then said, "Let's meet tomorrow and I will bring an inspector to check over the structure. I'll also bring an attorney with me to the closing to go over the papers. I would like to complete this by the end of the week, if possible."

"I'm sure that will be achievable. Say tomorrow at ten o'clock?" Joyce Mills offered.

"Wonderful," Lindy said and clicked off. And after paying her check, she left the Diner and went to her bank. Over time she had been taking cash out of her safe deposit box and buying travelers checks at various banks and now gathered the stack from the box and also took a few thousand in cash for run around money.

The closing went through without a hitch a few days later and Lindy was finally handed the key to her

Silence

paradise. On flying feet she grabbed her things at the Adventure Inn and took the Lexus over to her house. 10 Beach Road was her address and even that sounded exclusive to her ears. She opened up the lanai to the beach and collapsed in one of the chaises and sat enveloped in her space as the ocean breeze filled her new home. She then stood up and raised her arms joyously and shouted; this is mine!

Later, after she had taken her time walking through her rooms again and sitting here and there, she took her time and unpacked. She found fresh linens and changed the king-sized bed, set out fresh towels and soaps. In the kitchen she made a list of foods she needed to get. Coffee, juice and bagels, primarily morning foods. Later in the day, she liked to go out.

By nine o'clock that first night she was totally beat and looked forward to climbing into her new bed. After she showered and moisturized she did just that, and inside of five minutes, was asleep. It wasn't until late in the black night as the ocean moaned a sorrowful mantra of incoming rain, that a shadow entered her bedroom and stood for a minute at her bedside and gazed at her sleeping face, then reached out and curiously touched her shining red hair.

Lindy shifted in her sleep then and the shadow immediately disappeared in a tailspin leaving only a small shift of fog. Then the house on 10 Beach Road settled down again and slept.

-34-

Reed walked out to his car in the suburb of Oak Grove, where he had visited Miss Barnes, the housekeeper and friend of Jonas Hovland. Now he had a witness who would swear in court she saw Bobby Wilson force the old man over the railing balcony to his death. All Reed had to do was meet with the DA and convince him to swear out a warrant for the asshole's arrest. Attempted murder! Of course when Wilson was found guilty of this murder at a trial, it would mean Reed would have saved his company a ton of money, which of course meant he would get a hefty bonus.

Relieved at last to be making progress, he lit a cigarette as he drove back to his hotel and parked in the underground lot. As he got out of the Corvette and stepped into the elevator, he didn't notice the two masked men who suddenly came out of nowhere and followed him in. As soon as the door closed, one hit him over the head with the butt of a gun, stunning him. He fell to his knees. The other man grabbed him and held his arms as blows landed on his face. Blood flew on both the assailants as Reed's nose cracked.

"Fuck," one muttered as he glanced down at his jacket. Reed was spun around and this time a bat appeared. He didn't have time to yell, or reach for his .38 as one started to practice batting on his person. He literally saw stars as he felt it crack on his head and then felt his warm blood soak through his hair. He felt himself falling and he welcomed darkness. It all took about sixty seconds and when the elevator stopped on Reed's floor, the masked men disappeared.

He was out cold when the medics arrived, and didn't come to on the ride to the hospital, or feel when they sewed up his head in ER and fixed his nose. After several more hours he was put upstairs in the trauma center of the hospital for further study. His friend who owned the hotel had contacted Murphy at the downtown police department and Murphy sat by his bed now.

"Come on, open your eyes buddy," he repeated again. "The doc put you back together. Wake up now and tell me what the hell happened?"

"Goddamn, quit yelling at me," Reed finally mumbled through swollen lips.

"Jesus, you've had us pretty worried," Murphy said and stood up by the bed.

"Where the hell am I?" Reed whispered and tried to sit up.

"Whoa buddy, you've got to take it easy."

Reed touched his face and head and felt the bandages. "What the--," he mumbled. "I'm in a hospital?"

"Someone found you in the elevator at your hotel. Casey over there rang me after they took you away. Do you want me to call someone?" Murphy asked. "I called my wife and she's on her way down here."

"Goddamn, Annie is coming here?" Reed whispered again through swollen lips."

"Yup, she's on her way." Murphy said, as he straightened his tie. "Can you remember anything? The cameras were evidently covered with something so we got zilch. You've been mumbling but I can't make it out."

Reed tried to run his tongue over his split lips and groaned. Murphy wet a towel and handed it to him. "Here," he said, "Hold this on your mouth for a while."

Just then the door flew open and Ann Murphy tiptoed into the room.

"Is he awake yet?" she asked her husband as she came over to the bed.

"He came to a few minutes ago," Murphy said.

Reed opened his eyes when he felt a cool hand stroke his forehead. He looked up at those blue eyes and red hair and for a minute almost felt like crying at her motherly touch. He blinked fast several times.

"Annie, you shouldn't be here," he managed to say.

"Of course, I should. Now I'm going to find your nurse and get some answers, then I'll be back! Keep a good eye on him," she ordered her husband and bustled off back down the hall.

As Reed watched her go out the door, he felt better.

"You'd best listen to her when she gets back here too," Murphy advised.

"Now can you remember anything?" He asked again.

Taking the cloth off his mouth Reed said, "Two in masks. They had a baseball bat," he managed to say.

"Any idea who they were?" Murphy asked.

Reed groaned. "Fuck, no." He sat up and swung his feet over the edge of the bed. "I've got to get out of here," he said then.

Murphy put a restraining hand on his shoulder. "Buddy, hold on. Let's see what Annie finds out first. Just cool it!"

Reed lay back down and groaned. After a few minutes Annie came back. "Here's the deal," she stated, "You have a concussion so you have to stay overnight, then you're coming home with us."

"No--, I can't do that. I'll be okay." Reed said.

"You can't be alone man," Murphy said. "We got room."

For once Reed didn't have an answer. Goddamn, he hurt all over and just wanted to shut his eyes and sleep. And, for once he let his friends take over and take care of him. And maybe just for a day it wouldn't hurt to lie around.

"Jesus," he swore as he looked at himself in the mirror when he got up to put on his clothes to leave the next day. Both his eyes were swollen and purple, a bandage covered his nose and another one the side of his head.

"Yeah, they almost got you, buddy," Murphy said as he helped Reed to a wheelchair.

"I don't need that. I can walk," Reed grumbled.

"Humor me," Murphy said and gently pushed him into it.

At the Murphy household, as it was a school holiday, the three little girls were home with a nanny and when Murph and Annie brought their houseguest home, their eyes widened with alarm at his bandages. He'd borrowed Murphy's sunglasses to cover his eyes and kept them on now.

"Hello, my beauties," he managed to say as he tried to stand up straight.

The three girls ranging in age from four to seven were his god-children and they loved to see him.

"Girls, remember what we told you. Uncle Reed has been in an accident and needs to rest. We have to let him lie down now. Come on and I'll help you to the guest room," Annie said and took Reed's arm.

"I'll need some kisses soon, girls." He said to them as they stood there holding their dolls and blankets, their red hair done up in French braids and bright colored ribbons.

In the guest room, Annie bustled around with an extra blanket and covered him up to his chin. "Now, sleep but remember I'll be waking you up every few hours to check on you." Which he did, without any more protests.

Twenty four hours later, he awoke from another nap to whispers and felt the bed move. He cocked one eye open and saw three little faces staring at his black eyes.

"Mama said we could come in," the tallest one said. "Uncle Reed, does it hurt?" She reached over and gently touched his face. "Can we come up," she asked then and when Reed nodded his head, all three clamored up in his bed. "Mama said, maybe we could read you a story while she makes you something to eat."

Then the three Murphy girls busily arranged themselves by his side under the blankets and began to read the story of the Three Bears to him.

Silence

Today, Reed felt better, still hurt like hell, but now he lay content and wondered at having all this concern, from all these little lives.

Why didn't he have something like this of his own? Immediately his feelings plummeted and he felt sorry for himself. Why, why indeed? Then a nagging thought surfaced. Could it be because he never seriously took the time to find the right partner?

As the story of the Three Bears enfolded, the smallest girl found his hand and lays her tender dainty one in his. Reed looked at the difference in them and closed his protectively over hers and turned to smile at her.

"Uncle Reed," she lisped, "can I feel your sore eye?"

He leaned over and felt her little hand brush over his black eye. "See it doesn't hurt. It just looks scary."

Just then Ann came in the room carrying a tray and set it on the bedside table. "They didn't wear you out, did they?" She asked and then nodding at her girls said, "Now you have to come out and let our guest eat. Come on girls!"

During the night Murph had helped him into a pair of his p.j.s and Reed sat up now. "You don't have to do this, Annie." He protested as she handed him a cup of soup.

"Oh yes I do, my friend! I owe you my life for finding me after that certain episode." She raised her eyebrows and nodded toward the girls. "We are forever in you debt Reed and don't you forget it!"

The next day, he tossed the bandages and showered as best as he could and dressed, then made it into the kitchen as the family sat around the table having breakfast. He still hurt like hell and looked worse, but amidst greetings, Ann directed him to a chair and handed him a plate of scrambled eggs and toast. After a hearty breakfast, and amongst numerous protests, Murphy gave him a ride back to his hotel.

"Now take it easy for a few days," Murphy directed to which he answered, "for sure."

"And let me know if you come across anything new. We need to catch those fuckers," Murph added before letting Reed out of his car.

Reed took the same elevator up to his room and when he checked the tape on the bottom of his door, again it was gone!

Goddamn, he swore under his breath and again threw his things in a bag and left. He'd had enough of this bullshit. He went out to the Corvette in the ramp and as he came closer, he saw it! The front windshield lay in shards on the front seat, along with the windows on both sides. He stopped in his tracks. Goddamn, he knew it was done by the same assholes that had beaten him up the day before. He took out his cell and called the cops, and made another report, then called a tow truck.

Silence

This all took a couple of hours and when the Corvette had been loaded, he asked the driver. "Mind if I ride down to Morrie's Garage with you?" He pushed his sunglasses up over his black eyes and remarked, "I was in an accident."

By the end of the day, the windows had been replaced in the Corvette. And he needed to check in with his boss at First Federated Insurance.

"Hey Ed," he said then. "I've run into a little trouble, but I'm making headway on the case."

"What kind of trouble?" Ed barked.

"Just a little skirmish," Reed answered evasively.

"Conners, just don't get yourself killed out there!" he said. Of course he didn't tell Ed about the gun shots in the hotel room or getting beaten. Or that someone had smashed the windows on the Corvette. It wasn't his nature to complain about any of it either. It came with the territory, was how he felt about it.

He had purposely driven back to the hotel and checked out, and knew more than likely he would be followed. So this time he drove to the north side of Minneapolis where he rented two rooms in a motel, a side by side suite. He parked in front of one door. Now he had a sure fire plan.

Let the fuckers come! He growled.

-35-

Lindy awoke in her new home with the ocean crashing outside the windows that she had left open overnight. She lay in her king-sized bed and watched the sheer window treatments blow out over the shiny bamboo bedroom floor.

How she loved it. She finally had a home again. And this time for good! The bedroom was a soft sage and had the same accents of a mellow blue and cream as the rest of the house. This area of the on-suite bedroom housed a walk-in closet with a mirrored dressing room, a Jacuzzi bath and rain-vented shower, and a finish steam room. Lordy, she could spend all day in there just getting ready for it!

But today, she wanted to really check out her new home again and excitedly slipped on a robe. In the kitchen she gazed lovingly at the cream and oak cupboards, stainless steel appliances and marble topped counters and once again saw they were top of the line, especially the six burner gas stove. She stopped and looked at that for a minute again. Maybe she would cook again, but then thought, for whom? And she instantly felt sad and alone.

Well hell, she murmured, then forced her thoughts to her life now. She made a pot of coffee and while that was perking merrily, she opened the back door to the green lawn. Then, breathed in the lovely aroma from the magnolia tree that leaned in close in the side yard. Sitting later at the counter in her kitchen drinking her coffee, she worked on her next plan.

It took a few days for her then to put it together, but finally she had it. She would call it LOLITA'S, just "LOLITA'S" And she would continue the same psychic business she had made so much money with in Monterrey, Mexico. She had put out discreet signs and notes around town especially in the tourist's shops and eateries that read LOLITA'S. And today, bright and early she put out the two small signs outside her house, one in front and one in back. She'd gotten a license from South Carolina to operate as a small and in home jewelry business. Of course, she wouldn't have any, but if someone checked, she would have just conveniently sold out. She knew there were all kinds of avenues to proceed down if she were questioned. One thing she could not do was advertise a charge, but she would take her chances, knowing if her predictions were good, people were more than generous with their money.

She had told Mila about her endeavor and Mila had promised to put out the word to her great abundance of friends and acquaintances. There was a large population of Spanish residents in the area too that Mila had connections with, and from what she had told Lindy they were truly anxious to hear their destiny from such a gifted clairvoyant.

The date Lindy had set for opening was today and she rushed to shower and get ready. She figured she would open the doors at 9:00, and precisely at that time someone rang her doorbell. It chimed merrily to the tune of The William Tell Overture.

Lordy, what is that all about, she shuddered and shook her head. She had dressed in a long flowing brightly colored caftan. Brushed her red hair to stand up with loads hair spray, and put on some dark lipstick and lots eye make-up. She'd cleared one bedroom and furnished it with a clothed table and chairs, then put her CD player under it and lowered the window shades. She found the crystal ball that Margaret Ames, the millionaire artist in Monterrey, had given her and she put that squarely on the table. She stopped in there now and turned the CD on to set the scene as she went to the door. As she swung the door open, to her amazement there was a number of people lined up.

"Good morning," she uttered under her breath to a chorus of Buenos Dias! And hellos." And for a minute, she wondered what in the world she would do with all these people. But she had had the foresight to put out the lawn furniture she had found in the garage earlier so now they had something to sit on while they waited.

"Wonderful to see you all," she said now and cleared her throat, as she gained her composure. "Have a seat," she offered them and nodded to the first in line. A beautiful young girl stepped up and followed Lindy through the door to the magic room.

"Please sit," Lindy indicated and they both sat down. "May I ask your name?" Lindy asked then and reached for her hand.

"Violet," the girl offered.

Lindy had no qualms about starting out again as a psychic as all along she had been getting bits and pieces of info and assorted visions about the people she would meet around town. Some was good, but then again some was horrible!

Now as she sat in the magic room holding this girls hand, the strains of Enya played softly from under the table. The blinds were lowered, and the air was perfumed with jasmine from a scented plug-in she had hidden behind one drape. She believed these

Silence

little extras were essential to her business and it did really sound and smell good in there.

Violet's hand was small and delicate, but right away Lindy saw the lines in her palm were broken.

"Violet, are you in love with someone who is unavailable?" This had popped into Lindy's head suddenly.

Violet looked askew momentarily, then whispered, "How do you know?"

Then as Lindy traced her finger over Violet's palm, she felt turmoil, and then a picture flashed before her eyes of a bullet exploding into this girl's heart!

For God's sake, she sat back for a minute and sucked in her breath at this God awful vision. What the hell would she do now? Was this true? Whatever it was, she couldn't tell the poor girl that she was going to be killed. But she had to warn her. She took a breath.

"Violet," she said then swallowing hard. "I see danger ahead for you if you continue this relationship!"

"But I love him," Violet said through tears. "Won't he leave home and marry me like he promised?"

"I'm sorry Violet. I don't see that for you," Lindy remarked sincerely. "But wait," she said and stared into the crystal ball for a minute. "Violet, I see you at a piano somewhere in a big room, I hear thundering applause! Does that mean something?"

The young girl wiped her eyes and sat up straight. "Yes, yes," she murmured, "I will do it!" Then Violet smiled. And after heaping the girl with positives that Lindy felt she needed to hear to make her visit worthwhile, Violet stood up and thanked her. "Gracias. Muchas gracias." Violet said and pressed bills in Lindy's hand.

The days flew by and one day a customer, a middle-aged woman wearing a worried frown came in. She said her name was Elsa and that she had lived on the island all her life.

"I need to know," she said, "before I do something I can't take back!" She exclaimed as she followed Lindy to the magic room, as Lindy had grown used to thinking of the space.

"Please have a seat and relax," Lindy said as they arranged themselves at the table.

Elsa sat down but immediately glanced around the room until she found the picture Lindy had placed on one wall. It was a gift she had received from her friend, the artist Margaret Ames, in Monterrey, Mexico. A lovely watercolor of an old crippled woman struggling to carry a basket of wet clothes to a clothesline strung between some trees.

"That's her," Elsa exclaimed now as she stared at the painting.

"Who," Lindy asked alarmed.

Silence

"She's the one!" The woman hissed and raised a clenched fist in the air and pointed at the picture.

Lindy followed her indication. "Are you talking about that picture?"

"Si, si," Elsa whispered. "That woman!"

"Who, the artist, the woman in the picture?" Lindy asked totally flabbergasted at her outburst.

"I was told you had this, and that is my mother in the picture. That woman, she stole it!" Elsa sat with a thunderous look on her face. "I want it!" She exclaimed.

Lindy looked askew at her customer. What the hell was she talking about?

Elsa wanted her painting? She stumbled for an appropriate answer. "Wait a minute Elsa; let's see what's in your future before we make such a decision!" Good Lord, the woman wanted her painting! Had she heard right?

"But don't you see, that woman took a picture of my mother and then put it in paint!" Elsa wrung her hands.

"Elsa, let's just see what your destiny says." That seemed to calm her down, but, sweat glistened on her round Latin face and her unruly gray hair seemed to curl tighter on her head.

Lindy took her time as she studied her palm, then she turned to the crystal ball on her table and looked deep into its bottomless space. Then needing more time, she closed her eyes and sat very still.

Elsa started to say something but Lindy hastily raised her hand to still any and all conversation. For God's sake, now when she needed help to get out of this fix, she was not getting a thing and she couldn't keep the woman under her spell much longer!

Well hell, she decided she'd have to go out on a limb here on her own. She opened her eyes and took both Elsa's hands and spoke slowly, "Elsa, my dear woman," Lindy said, "Your mother spoke to me, and she said do not disturb her home. She wants to stay right here, but she wants to see you often!"

Elsa's face paled. "You mean you talked to my mother?" She pulled a hand back and pulled a hanky out of her sleeve and wiped her eyes.

"Oh yes, she was right here. She looked you over, too." Lindy exclaimed. Now a fine line of perspiration glistened on Lindy's upper lip. Lordy, this was a first. The first time she had gotten into a situation and had to struggle to get out.

Elsa stood up then and gasped, "Lolita, I am sorry. I will tell my family she is happy being here after all!" And she thrust a bunch of bills in Lindy's hand and rushed out of the house.

Lindy closed and locked her door. She was done for the day and maybe she would take tomorrow off too! For the first time she had worked hard for her money.

That night as she slept soundly in her big bed, the same shadow appeared out of the dark and stood silently and peered at her as she slept. This time it reached out and laid its cool hand on her brow. Lindy stirred but soon was still. But that morning when she awoke she had a dreadful headache.

Later she met Mila and her cousins at the beach, and Emilio came and sat next to her in one of the chaises.

"Lindy," he said now, "I would like to take you to dinner tonight."

She had been ducking his invitations for days and for some reason it sounded rather interesting this morning. Also she needed a diversion from the aching in her head. "Emilio that would be fun!" She remarked casually and surprised him. "Let's plan at five o'clock if that's okay?"

"Magnifeek!" he exclaimed and reached over and took her hand and kissed it.

Lindy did not put her signs out this day and took a long nap in the afternoon and took her time getting ready for her date. Tonight she would wear the new white dress and her white four inch sling back sandals. Her red hair shimmered and her eyes were a deep brown tonight and set off her lovely golden tan.

Enzio rang her bell promptly at five and as she opened the door, she stood aside and admired his look as he came in. Previously, she had only seen him in beach attire and flip-flops. Now she sucked in her breath and his cologne as she let him into her house. He had on a hand-tailored beige suit with a snow white shirt open at the neck. His feet were bare in his brown tasseled loafers. His dark hair and eyes glistened against his tanned skin. A gold Rolex adorned his wrist.

"You are beautiful," he enthused as he looked her up and down. "Ready to do the town?" he asked.

"Ready and waiting," Lindy chimed in equaling his energy. "Where should we go?" She asked now.

"How about we check out your friend Shirley's place?" Emilio offered and took her arm as they stepped out of her house and she locked up.

"Good, I haven't been there for a few weeks. She's from my home town you know."

"I remember, you told us about her awhile back." And Emilio led her out the door to a black limo that stood in her driveway.

"Way to go," Lindy remarked as he helped her inside. At Shirley's, the late afternoon lunchers and the early evening diners were crowded around the piano bar where the owner, Shirley was charming her followers with her rendition of the song called Misty. As soon as she saw Lindy come in the door, she got ready to take a break and stood up after reassuring her friends she'd be back shortly.

"Shirley," Lindy greeted her with a hug and said, "I want you to meet Emilio. He's here from Peru."

"Emilio," Shirley gushed, "Come here, my handsome stranger," she said and pulled him into a close hug. And he didn't mind as he wrapped his arms around her too and stood with a big smile on his face.

They were escorted to a table where all three sat down and soon a bottle of champagne arrived in an iced bucket with glasses.

"My treat," Shirley exclaimed and tasted the first pour as she said, 'It's a special night now that you're here Lindy, and I already know Emilio."

Lindy chocked on her champagne. "You know each other?" She looked askew.

Shirley sat back and gave Emilio a once over. "You clean up pretty good Emilio, but have you cleaned up your act?"

And he just smiled at her and took Lindy's hand.

-36-

Reed threw his briefcase and suitcase on the shabby bed in this new motel room and sat down on the one chair. A poor excuse for one, he grumbled. The 59 Motel it was called and had seen its better days. He had rented two rooms that could adjoin, and had parked the Corvette in front of room four, but actually he was in five. He had gone into four and turned on the TV and lights and closed the door that connected them. He still hurt like hell after someone had attacked him several days before, and he knew goddamn well, since they hadn't gotten him the first time, they would be back! When they had broken the windows in his car, well, that was it. He had to admit, sometimes he got really pissed, and this was sometime! He would be ready for the fuckers now and get the assholes cold!

He opened and set the blinds just right in his room now so he had a clear view of the parking lot. The Corvette was visible from the freeway and set right in front of the adjoining room. He was sure he had been followed leaving the hotel downtown, to the garage where he'd had the windows replaced on the Corvette and then to this motel. But it was still daylight and he was almost sure whoever his attackers were wouldn't hit this place until after dark. So right now he needed lots of coffee and food to get him through the night. After that well, he'd figure it out then.

He called Speedy pizza and ordered and asked them to deliver to room number four, then sat back, turned the television in room five to low and waited.

The early evening news was on and as usual covered murders, accidents, unemployment and ended on one single piece of positive news and that was that it had been a beautiful autumn day and the next would be just as glorious.

Reed shook his head at this load of negatives that he had just sat still for. Although he was raised in the small Midwest town of Williston, he had spent six years in Minneapolis working on his law degree and he was familiar with the never ending news of the day. Now he just shook his head and mumbled; people are nuts to watch this stuff, and switched to

Silence

the channel that ran the old classics and settled in then to an old Gunsmoke rerun.

As he sat smoking, alone in the late night, his thoughts went to Lindy. He thought back to weeks ago when they had been together at his home on Birch Lake and the complete feeling he would get at night when he could reach over and put an arm over her hip and draw her close. Goddamn, he had taken that feeling for granted. And now look where he was again!

His pizza order came and he had finished the whole thing and now at one AM he began on the coffee. A small microwave sat on a wobbly table and served its purpose when his eyelids became heavy and he heated up the second container. He'd almost given in and said to hell with staying up, but then, caught himself in time.

Each room had a door and a window and he had opened the window about an inch earlier so he could hear if and when anybody crept close. He stood to the side now and peered outside. The hot day had cooled and now humidity hung like ghostly ragged cloaks amongst the car filled spaces. Then suddenly as he watched, the parking lot lights went out, one by one. The place went dark. He sucked in his breath. Had the electricity failed or had he heard bullets hum through a silencer as they were just shot out? A chill marched up his spine.

He had the .38 ready in his hand as he stood silently, watching. He shifted his stance after a few minutes, and then suddenly, he was sure he had just seen a figure dart behind a semi-truck parked on the edge of the space. He blinked to see better and tightened the hold on his gun. Did he just imagine seeing things? Sure enough, after a few minutes he saw a lone figure creep silently between the parked vehicles edging closer. He strained to see better. The creeper slouched but looked to be tall and was dressed in black with a mask over his face. Reed watched as the stalker crept silently to door number four, then reached out and tried the doorknob. He was just several feet away at the door, and so close Reed could hear him breathing hard, smell his breath. Guessing it would take several minutes at least for him to break the lock with his tools; Reed went over and quietly opened the door to the adjoining room and stood ready for the asshole to make his entrance.

His breath was burning in his already beat up chest as he stood inside room four, just behind the door. Then the outside door opened silently and the stalker stepped in with his gun aimed and ready. He quickly spun around in the room looking for his target.

The instant his back was turned Reed stepped out from behind the door and yelled in a deadly voice, "Drop it or your dead!"

Silence

The gunman froze and stood stock still for a second, then turned and fired. Reed ducked just in time. He got a shot off then at the assailant's knees and suddenly the fucker fell with a groan and dropped the gun. Reed took a step closer and kicked the gun out of the way, then with his .38 still pointed he edged over to the person who was clutching his knees and crying out in pain.

"Who the hell are you?" He yelled again as he stood over him with the gun pointed at his head.

"Fuck off," the person lying on the floor hissed.

"Yeah, look who's talking." Reed said, and with his foot again he pushed the mask off his pursuer's face. The cap slid off with the mask exposing bright red hair. Stunned he exclaimed, "Miss Barnes, "I can't believe it's you!"

"Let me up, you arrogant fool," she hissed again, raising up and leaning on an elbow.

"Goddamn, Miss Barnes. So it was you who killed Jonas Hovland?" Reed exclaimed!

-37-

Lindy looked at her friend Shirley in surprise when Shirley told her she was already acquainted with Emilio.

"Well, you two better tell me how that is?" She said irritated that Emilio had not told her of this when he recommended going to Shirley's to spend the evening.

He winked at her now and took her hand. "My darling Lindy, I wanted you to be happy. See!"

"I am happy, Emilio, and I don't understand your intentions." Lindy did not like when people were not straight with her, although she was guilty of it time and again. But that was different, she thought now.

"I appreciate your business, Emilio," Shirley said and passed around the glasses of champagne, "But don't get my friend mixed up in any of your ventures." Then she gave him a glaring look.

Lindy did not miss the electricity that bounced between them. And then in an instant a vision flashed through her thoughts of the two of them in an embrace, and it left her speechless for the moment.

Emilio went on with a grin, "I can see the two of you beautiful ladies can break a man's heart."

Lindy regrouped. "We did many times over," she remarked acidly. "And soon I might break yours!" She was pissed at him. It was a stressful moment and to break it Shirley got up saying, "I'll be back shortly," and left the table. Lindy sat there in a huff. How dare he play some kind of a joke on her and her friend!

"But Lindy, don't be angry, my romance with Shirley was over a long time ago. It meant nothing!" Emilio tried to take her hand but she pulled it away.

And that really made her mad. "You can't talk about my friend like that, you, you gigolo!" And she took a sip from the glass of champagne and tossed the rest in his face. She stood up then and left him sitting there with it dripping down his beautiful attire. She walked outside and found the limo still waiting at the curb with the motor running. And without missing a beat, she climbed in.

"Emilio has been detained but I need to get home please," Lindy declared. And the limo swung into action.

Serves you right, she said to herself as she rode home in style. Emilio had certainly brought about an uncalled for situation. Back in her house, Lindy undressed and curled up on her couch with the television. Then her cell rang and she saw it was Shirley on the phone.

"Lindy," Shirley said to her, "I saw you leave and I need to talk to you. I'm in my office now so it's quiet. Lindy, I'm sorry about this. Listen, I need to tell you this. I made a mistake a few years ago and cheated on my husband. I thought Emilio was charming and sexy and I fell for his BS."

"It lasted only a few weeks and then I saw through all his talk. Now listen," she went on, "there was something about that man that I couldn't put a finger on. He's bad news Lindy, so please don't get mixed up with him!"

"Shirley, I'm sorry too for being put in this situation. I'm okay with you, my dear friend. And I don't have any intention of being caught up in a cheap affair."

"You're sure we're okay?" Shirley asked.

"Definitely, and let's have lunch next week." And Lindy put the cell down and again it rang and thinking Shirley forgot something she answered without checking the incoming call. And it was Emilio.

"Lindy," he said, "my heart is broken, my love, can I come over and have you fix it?"

"In your dreams," Lindy remarked, "and don't call me again." She dropped the phone to the floor. Later in the evening as she sat, still upset, another picture flashed across her thoughts; a picture of Emilio and a man who looked just like someone from the D'Agustino family. The resemblance was there. Stunned, she fell back against the couch.

Oh my god! Oh my god, she whispered. How could that be? How could Emilio know the D'Agustino's in Mexico when he lived in Peru? Lindy jumped up and ran to make sure her doors and windows were all locked and the shades drawn. Then she turned off the TV and the lights and sat in the dark. In silence! She got an afghan and covered up and sat there, just sat there in the dark as her thoughts went wild.

That's why Shirley had gotten bad vibes about the guy, she guessed. If Emilio knew the D'Agustino family, did that mean that he was in the drug business too? Well of course, Lindy whispered to the walls, the drug worlds were all connected. And that would mean that he also knew that she had been involved with Mario and his death, and the FBI!

Silence

She picked up the phone and called Mila; her beachfront friend who was entertaining her cousins, one of which was Emilio.

"Hello Mila," Lindy greeted her, knowing she was a night-owl. "Sorry to bother you so late, but I just want to know Emilio's family name," she said.

"Eet is fine," Mila answered. "Is like mine. Okay? His mama's name is Ramirez. A big family, big, big family."

"Thanks my friend. I'll see you at the beach." Lindy hung up the phone and clutched a corner of the afghan to her chest. Then looked over at the lap-top computer she had bought a few days ago. She had read the instruction book and got it hooked up to the internet, and then put it aside. But now would be a good time to see what it could do.

Personally, she didn't exactly think it would interest her too much, but she liked to stay up on things. She reached for it and settled in again on the couch.

After numerous mistakes in the operation, she opened up the internet and typed in Ramirez family in Mexico. Her eyes widened and she leaned in closer as it immediately sprang into action with pages of links. When she settled in to read, her breath caught at the innuendoes in some of the articles that implied that they were part of the drug world. It even showed newspaper pictures of family events. Then as Lindy sat in the dark and read on, a small clipping of a group of people at a gathering caught her eye and she read, a family reunion had taken place a few years back, and it had included members from the Prada family, the D'Agustino, the Mercado's and the Ramirez clan.

Oh god, Lindy whispered in the dark. Emilio was one of them! Now what? Her thoughts raced and panicked, she found her Marlboros and lit up. Damn, she wasn't going to smoke in her new house, but this was different. This was an emergency!

She finished one and lit another, and soon her lovely new living room turned blue with smoke.

After several hours of panic and tears, she got pissed and in anger she made up her mind. She opened the lanai doors and let the ocean breezes clear out the smoke in her house. Nothing or nobody, was going to take away her peace and enjoyment now of the ocean, or her home and her money. She would get a gun and carry that and if anyone tried to get in her face she would shoot to kill. Damn, this time she would be ready.

With that situation settled, and after closing up the house again, Lindy went to bed and finally slept. Again the ghost-like shadow in a wisp of a flowing robe came to her bed and watched. And then leaned over and touched her heart and felt its beat. It studied Lindy's golden skin and timidly touched her lustrous red hair and then settled in for the night on the edge of her bed to watch and keep her safe.

-38-

Reed had stood stock still and waited for the assailant to step in. Then he'd been forced to shoot in self-defense after a bullet whizzed by his head. He'd purposely aimed below the intruder's knees.

Now, he stood in complete surprise in room five at the 59 Motel, as instead of discovering the assailant was one of the Hovland boys or that gigolo, Bobby Wilson, he saw it was the red-haired, nursemaid and housekeeper, Miss Barnes.

Reed asked her again, "Why did you push your old boyfriend over the railing?"

Miss Barnes sat up. "Put that fricking pea-shooter away," she yelled at him. "And I never said I did!"

She attempted to straighten her clothes and pulled her black sweater down to cover her bare stomach.

Reed still held the .38 on her. "Before I call the cops, Miss Barnes, here's your chance to tell me your story and I might even help you!" He circled around her and opened the outside door to room five so the police could see which room they were needed in when he called.

"Help me?" she growled. "You've only caused trouble since you've come here!"

"'If there's no crime, then no one needs to worry!" Reed answered. "Now get up off the floor and sit in that chair," he ordered. "And don't try anything or I will shoot again and this time it will be at a direct target!"

"Look what you did to me," Miss Barnes said indignantly as she clasped her hand over her bleeding knee. "Help me, you fool," she struggled to stand, then limped over to a chair and collapsed on its hard surface, and then took a deep breath.

"Okay, start talking Miss Barnes," Reed said again.

"I didn't try to kill the old man," she repeated. "And why the hell did you come here and nose around in our business! Everything was going along just fine!"

"Maybe you thought so, but my company didn't. Who do you think sent me?"

Silence

Miss Barnes was silent. Her face was glaringly pale against her tangled fiery red hair and now as she slumped in the straight backed chair, her former stature of a large and domineering woman had diminished and she looked just like an old homeless drifter.

She drew herself up then and smoothed her hair. "Mr. Conners," she said, "I repeat, I did not push Jonas over the railing!"

"Well, it looks like someone tried and succeeded. If you didn't who did?"

Reed asked again patiently. He still held the gun pointed at her. "I'll give you two minutes, Miss Barnes, and then I am calling in the cops, starting now!" And he held his wrist out that had the watch.

Miss Barnes bent over and clasped her left knee. It had stopped bleeding but the bullet had torn the material of her trousers.

'Oh, cut the crap Conners," she mumbled as she tried to cover her bare leg. "There was no murder. It was an accident!" She finally said. They had sat there as the two minutes seemed to tick out loud and Reed hadn't taken his eyes of her.

Miss Barnes had a defiant look on her face all the while. Finally, after what Reed thought had to be two minutes, he declared, "times up!" And then took his cell out of his pocket with his other hand.

"Wait, wait," Miss Barnes whined then. "Alright, I'll tell you. I went in the house that day and as I went upstairs to get towels for Rena and that fucker Bobby Wilson, just as I came to the cat-walk and the stairway; that's that ungodly upstairs balcony over the living room, twenty feet below. I found Jonas standing there and seeming to hover over the top of the railing. I hollered for him to get back and ran toward him." Her voice faltered then, and she whispered, "He just seemed to float over the top. I was too late!"

Reed studied her face as she was retelling the event and he didn't see any anguish in her face or hear any sadness in her voice.

Just then sirens blared out front of the 59 Motel and within seconds two cops blew through the open door with guns drawn.

"Put it down," they yelled, and immediately Reed dropped his .38 to the floor.

"And you're both under arrest!" They said in the next breath and within another few seconds both he and Miss Barnes were handcuffed.

"Wait a minute," Reed growled, "I'm a detective for an insurance company and this woman is guilty of a murder!" He nodded at the gun lying on the floor. "That's her gun that she just tried to kill me with!"

"Yeah, yeah, tell it to the judge," The skinny one of the pair said, trying to look tall next to his giant-sized partner.

And then Reed recognized them. They were the same pair of cops that had been involved the night before at the hotel downtown.

Goddamn, this case was nothing but trouble. This would be the second time he would have to go downtown, wasting time again just when he thought he could close the case. But it would be useless to try to talk his way out of this situation, so he went with them out to the squad car and let them shove him into the back seat. He saw Miss Barnes in the other squad car and then saw her drop her head in her hands.

It was a hot steamy night in the north side of Minneapolis. A low slung Mercedes with dark windows roared by and the beat of a base guitar echoed, taunting the two cop guys to take notice. Lightning flashed across the sky then lighting up the early morning causing an almost instant stoppage of activity while everyone waited breathlessly for the first crack of thunder before continuing on their journey.

Reed swallowed over the taste of stale coffee on his breath, and then sat back as much as he could with the goddamn cuffs killing his hands, as the roar of thunder echoed through the streets.

"Okay, this time we've got you. Why were you trying to hurt that nice old lady?" The skinny one of the pair asked with a sly look on his pock-marked face as the two cops got in the vehicle.

"When you broke down that door into her room, were you trying to rob her? We got a call that gun shots were heard and then loud voices." The partner added.

Reed just shook his head. Goddamn, did the police force really hire these clods with their pea-sized brains and actually pay them? He sucked in his breath and forced himself to be still and not let them get him pissed. When they got downtown to the precinct he'd have his chance to make his one phone call. He'd call his buddy Murphy, for the second time! Hopefully Murphy could get the facts straightened out in time before Miss Barnes was released and probably take off for parts unknown!

Finally, after all the same old paper work, Reed was put in a cell. And goddamn, this time they were trying to pin him with robbery and attempted murder. In the morning he would go before a judge and then would see if he would be charged. In the meantime, he was granted his one phone call.

He rubbed circulation back into his wrists as he sat on the hard bench seat in the jail cell. He was still mad as hell at the circumstances that brought him back into this hell-hole. He looked at his wrist for the time; where his silver Rolex watch should have been, but of course, that had been taken too. By God, that better be with his wallet and his .38 revolver when he checked out.

Silence

Just then an officer banged on the bars and opened his cell door.

"Okay, you got ten minutes," he said and stood aside as Reed stepped out. "The phones are over on the wall," and he pointed down the hallway.

Reed hadn't wanted to call Murphy at home and upset the family so he had waited and called his precinct, which was just down the street.

"Hey buddy," he said taking a relieved breath, "I'm in trouble again with this goddamn case. Can you make another trip down here?"

"What's going on?" Murphy asked.

"I'm sitting in jail after being arrested for attempted robbery and get this murder!"

"For Christ's sake Conners, give me ten minutes and I'll be over. Sit tight and I'll see what's up!"

Reed put down the phone and ran a hand over his day-old whiskers and through his hair. Goddamn, he didn't even have a comb and his mouth tasted like road-kill.

As he sat impatiently waiting to get out, he wondered what was happening with Barnes. Would she be hospitalized for the gun-shot to her knees? For Christ sake, if what she said was true, and old man Hovland had just accidentally fallen over the railing to his death, then his company would have to pay out the twenty-five million bucks to the kids after all! And, it would mean goodbye to his getting that hefty bonus!

Well, if that was it. That was it! The company had been good to him over the years and he would get a pretty nice check anyway.

But, as he sat in the cell thinking about things something about good old Miss Barnes just didn't sit right to him.

When she claimed Jonas Hovland had asked for her hand in marriage countless times years ago, just why wouldn't a struggling, hard-working young girl jump at the chance of marriage and riches? It just didn't ring true that she had turned his marriage proposal down!

And now his gut told him she had helped him over that railing. And, it had never let him down yet!

-39-

The next morning the sunshine awoke Lindy and she got up and slid open the floor length sliding doors of the lanai for the cool breeze. The ocean was calm with only its rolling caps reaching for shore. The tide had been in again and she could see the sand was littered with its usual array of conch shells. She stretched and slipped a long t-shirt over her bronzed body and tip-toed to the kitchen to start her coffee.

Then she remembered last night and the heart stopping revelation she'd found that Emilio was part of the drug world too. She shivered now and wrapped her arms around herself as she stood in the kitchen.

Should she confront him for not telling her who he was? That he was a relative of the infamous D'Agustino family? Her thoughts went around in circles.

Was he sent by the families to watch her or even kill her?

Well, her face hardened at that thought. The first thing she would do today was buy that gun and she would shoot to kill.

For God's sake, would she ever get free of those blood sucking drug dealers that she had been so unlucky to get involved with when she dated Mario and saw him kill that Federal agent?

Well, now they knew where she was. And Hilton Head had always been her special secret island. Now what should she do? And she'd just bought her home and started her business!

As her coffee perked, several ideas were taking up residence in her thoughts.

Maybe she'd hire a bodyguard. Someone who would be at her side at all times! Or should she call that good-looking chief of police she'd met earlier when she'd been looking for Mitzi, and ask for his advice.

Later, as she stepped outside she looked around warily as she got in her Lexus. She had looked up the address of a local gun dealer and was on her way to a shop right off main street.

Silence

There were no buildings higher than one floor in downtown Hilton Head and there were no billboards or advertising signs. The streets and sidewalks were not laid out in grids either. Discreet small signs listed the businesses on the street corners and the whole downtown area was located in and amongst huge water oak trees laden with moss. Lindy loved the maze of it all.

But this day she walked purposely into a place called Guns and Red Roses! When she opened the door, the stunning smell of metal and oils hit her nostrils and she covered her nose. Then a man's voice said, "Good morning," in a low sexy drawl and stepped from behind a glass covered table. He reached out a hand and clasped hers. "My name is Joe Brown."

"Hello," Lindy said and without thinking she said, "Lola Lang."

"Well, Lola Lang what can I do for you?"

Lindy sucked in her breath as she felt a surge of heat shoot through her limbs as they clasped hands. The man was tall and slim, with black hair, piercing brown eyes and olive skin. She'd been so taken by his handsome appearance that she'd lost her cool, and now she felt him take in her appearance. She was glad she had worn her new yellow sundress and matching sling back sandals

"Well," she murmured, momentarily tongue-tied, and worried why she'd let one of her favorite aliases slip out. Then she got herself together and said, "I need a gun. Something I can carry in my pocket or purse."

"Okay, but what are you going to shoot at?" Joe Brown stood back and smiled, "A bear, a buffalo, a husband or what?" He had perfect teeth.

Lindy wasn't sure just how to take him. Was he making fun of her?

If he was, then she would play along with him and his absurdity and she replied, "Well, it might be one of those!"

"Okay, let me show you some of these little gems. Just perfect for someone like you," and he hustled back behind the glass shelves.

Lindy had never seen so many guns in her life. Her dad and brothers had had some on the farm way back when. Now the man carefully laid out models on a felt cover for her to see. And after standing there amazed at them all she asked, "What would you suggest for me?"

He handed her a small silver and blue gun which fit perfectly in her hand. "This is a derringer Lola, and I can see you carrying this."

Lindy quickly made up her mind and said, "I'll take it but I need you to show me how to use it."

"No problem, may I call you Lola? And, we have some papers to fill out first, and I'll need to see some ID."

"Of course, Joe," she said and hastily found the two forms which she kept in a secret pocket in her purse.

And after the paperwork was done, he said, "I have a shooting range downstairs for you to practice on. Do you want to do that now, or do you want to come back?"

Good Lord, she didn't have time for that now. A killer could be after her right this minute. And how could she concentrate on that with this man so near? It had been a long time since a man had set her heart to thumping. "I," she stammered, "why don't you show me how to put the bullets in and I'll come back for that." She was embarrassed at her nervous actions.

"Well, okay then. These little beauties are easy to handle and great for a woman."

"It will kill, then?" Lindy asked.

"Oh sure, if your aim is on and you're close to your target!" He laughed.

"I'll make sure of that!" She smiled as she laid out the cash.

"Lola," he said then, "I'd like to have a cup of coffee with you. There's a café next door."

And even though she was interested, she needed to get back home and open her doors for her people. She said, "I'm sorry I can't now, but how about meeting for a glass of wine this evening?"

"Better yet," Joe Brown said. "I'll look forward to that." And he took her hand and kissed her palm. "And I'll meet you at six, if that's alright?"

Lindy swallowed then sucked in her breath. Lordy, who was this man?

She turned and hurried out of the gun shop to her Lexus. The locks on the doors clicked on as she drove off. Back home she put the bullets back in the gun as Joe Brown had shown her and held it this way and that. Lordy, she didn't need any instructions; all she had to do was point and pull the trigger.

And she might as well get used to carrying it now so she slipped it in a pocket of her dress and got ready for her customers.

This morning her first customer was a local Latino old man who said his name was Eb. He walked slow and painfully. He had a ring of white fuzz around his bald head, and his face was so full of wrinkles they seemed to crisscross. He wore a muscle shirt and cut-off shorts and his skin was so tanned and old it looked like rich leather. His eyes were brown and looked to be dimmed with cataracts.

"Just Eb. I don't remember if I had more," he repeated as he sat down in Lindy's magic room and looked around curiously.

"I'll be a ninety years now Missy. I want to know when I'll be going up yonder to that place in the sky. When should I get ready to go?"

Silence

Lindy hid a surprised smile, and then took his wrinkled hand and could see nothing but broken lines. Well, this was a new one for her. She stared into the glass ball and closed her eyes but she wasn't getting a thing there today either. Oh Lord, she'd have to embellish for him too. So just for effect she sat quietly as if in a vision, then she started to hum, actually it was the so-hum mantra she used for her own meditation. And after a few minutes she opened her eyes and whispered, "Eb, I see you are not leaving here for a long, long time. I see you having many more birthdays and I see a beautiful lady with gleaming golden hair at your side. I see you two happy and holding hands." She let some time go by as they sat silently inhaling the aroma of Jasmine coming from the plug-in under the table along with the soft strains of Enya. Then Lindy unclasped their hands and exclaimed, "That was good Eb you'll be around for a long time yet!" And she went on to tell him of things that were in his future, a letter that would come containing money, that he would soon see tall buildings and soon have that new love.

Then he stood up and pushed some bills in her hand and walked out of her house, and now, with a definite lift in his stride. But after he left, Lindy was struck, with the reminder that she hadn't felt a thing or saw anything in a vision about his actual wish, about when he would be going to die and go to heaven. Sure, she'd been able to override his actual question by flattering him to forget, but she'd have to think about this.

The day flew by and by late afternoon she saw her last customer, but today she'd had to embellish more than usual and she was worn out and, somewhat worried. But she had collected a large amount of money, which she counted and put rubber bands around each bundle, then went to her secret place and put it away. She'd go to the bank again at the end of the week.

Even though she was tired, it was time to get ready for that glass of wine with Joe Brown. She showered and perfumed, took her time with her make-up and chose another of her new dresses. This one was a black sleeveless figure fitting sheath. Her black high-heeled sandals looked good on her gold toned legs. She'd spiked her red hair as was the fashion, her stylist had assured her. And again as she went out to her car, she glanced around anxiously. But now, she had the cute little derringer right beside her.

The café where she was to meet Joe Brown was under a grove of trees with gray moss hanging like lace curtains to soften its brick exterior. Huge sage palms stood on each side of the entrance. As Lindy walked up and opened the door, the strains of southern jazz hit her full blast as a sultry clarinet and a melodious accordion rang out.

Silence

She walked in and stood a minute to let her eyes adjust to the dark interior. And that didn't help much, as she jumped when a huge black man appeared out of the gloom.

"Hello little lady, come in and join the party!" And he looked her up and down.

Not one to turn and run under this, Lindy grinned "I'm meeting someone here, Joe Brown. Do you know him?"

"Aha, you mean Joey? Yeah sure, he's here!"

Just then Joe Brown came over and took her arm. "Hey Lola Lang. Glad you made it," he said and led her to a table in the darkened room.

"For God's sake, did they forget to pay the light bill?" She murmured jokingly, as she tried not to stumble as she followed him through the crowd, and then as her eyes adjusted somewhat to the gloom, she could make out its dim interior.

Actually everywhere she looked she saw dark wood; floors, walls and ceiling. Garish colored framed art of Picasso like posters adorned the walls and the quaint candle burning in a wine bottle stood on each table. She saw the room was filled with locals as well as tourists, and the noise level deafening.

"I've got a bottle of wine cooling for us," Joe Brown said above the din as he pulled out her chair. Lindy sat down and adjusted the skirt of her dress. Of course she crossed her legs and put one out there to be seen, even though it was dark as dawn in there.

"Sounds wonderful," she murmured. "I've had a busy day!"

"I hope you like champagne," Joe Brown said and poured a glass and handed it to her. Then refilled his and pulled his chair in closer to the table.

"Tell me, what keeps you busy Lola Lang?" He smiled then and checked out her cleavage.

And not one to pretend ignorance she smiled demurely at his obvious interest as she said, "Hmm—my days are full!"

"May I ask, are you here on holiday?" She didn't miss a note of shrewdness in his voice.

"That too," she answered. And to change the subject she said, "Tell me about yourself Joe, have you lived here long?"

"Sure, all my life," he said as he played with his mustache and then added, "But I travel."

"Where do you like to travel to?" Lindy asked then to keep the conversation going and away from herself.

And when Mexico was in his listing of exotic countries, she abruptly put the glass of champagne down and left Joe Brown sitting at the table.

-40-

As Reed Conners sat in the cell in downtown Minneapolis, the jail resonated with the sounds of cussing from some and drunken ramblings from others. He'd managed to get a few hours of sleep and as morning dawned, he called Murphy's cell. So all he could do now was wait for Murphy and his company, First Federated, to get him out of this mess.

As he had lain awake all these hours, he had come to the conclusion good old Miss Barnes had shoved Jonas Hovland over the railing. He felt it for sure, and his gut feeling never failed him. Now, if he could just get the hell out of here fast and work on her some more. He had been close. She had been pissed, and when people got pissed they usually got careless with their story.

The air in the jail was humid and stale and he brushed at his hair and threw water on his face at the steel sink. He felt like crap after losing most of his night's sleep and still wearing the same old clothes from yesterday. They'd taken his boots so he was in his stocking feet; apparently they thought he might be hiding something in them. Which sometimes he did!

He thought of Lindy and how she must have felt that time the FBI had tossed her in jail to threaten a further sentence if she didn't testify for them against that scum D'Agustino. In his instance, he knew people who had influence and could get him out fast, but she must have been petrified alone in there for those weeks. He stood up and stretched his aching back.

"Hey bro, what they got you on?" the guy in the next cell asked.

Reed looked over and saw a young man who looked like he couldn't be much over eighteen. "Nothing they can prove," he said. "What about you?"

"The fuckers got me for dealin!" Now the man came to the bars separating them and Reed could see he was young but had an old wary look in his eyes. He was thin and his clothes were dirty and ragged.

"Can you get me outta here?" he asked. "I'll pay you back, soon!"

"Hey buddy," Reed said and shook his head, "Sorry, I can't." And then Reed went to his cot and lay down. Goddamn, he hated drugs and dealers and everything about it. He closed his eyes and thankfully the guy turned away and was quiet and Reed drifted. Then suddenly he sat up as he heard his cell door open and Murphy and one of the company lawyers from First Federated Insurance came in.

"Thanks guys, you got these charges dropped, didn't you?" Reed asked.

"Yeah, yeah, Conners you're free to go," the attorney said. "Jesus, close this case so I don't have to come down here again!"

"Thank you, I appreciate it and it won't be long now!" Reed shook his hand. Then looked at Murphy and asked, "Do you know where the Barnes woman is right now?"

"She was released for lack of enough evidence to hold her."

"For Christ's sake, listen to this Murph. I want to bring her back in for further questioning. I know she killed Jonas Hovland!"

"You sure?" Murphy asked then.

"Yup, I had her. She was just about to spill it!"

"Let's talk about this, Conners, in my office." And they went over everything again. "I'm going to call the DA and get a warrant for her arrest!" Murphy exclaimed a short time later, and picked up the phone.

"Great and I know exactly where she lives." Reed brushed an impatient hand over his hair.

"Okay, it's going to take thirty to forty-five minutes in this traffic to get there, so I'm going to send a black and white from that suburb over right now to contain her so she doesn't run. Hold her until we get there. Where's your car?"

"At a motel over north and I need to get it out of there."

"Why the hell were you over there in one of those roach hotels? Jesus man, there's nothing but trouble over there. You'll be lucky if it's still there."

They hurried out of the downtown precinct and stopped at a new shiny LTD sedan at the curb.

"Cool ride," Reed said as they got in.

"New ones for all the detectives. Cost the department a fortune though," Murphy grinned as he put the key in the ignition and the motor purred. He turned on the red lights.

"Murph, goddamn, I had a perfect setup and it went to hell when some outsider called in the cops. I almost had her then for the murder; she was ready to talk!" Reed exclaimed in frustration as they raced along. Arriving at the motel, the Corvette was still standing safely in one piece.

"Okay, I'll meet you at the Barnes address," Murphy said and sped off.

Silence

Speeding through the streets on the way to Miss Barnes who lived in Oak Grove, Reed lit a Marlboro and inhaled the fragrant smoke.

As he got to the suburb and close to her neighborhood, a black and white came screeching around the corner with sirens blasting. Then another siren seemed to scream from another direction and he was forced to the side of the streets to let the emergency vehicle by. Another few minutes went by before he could get on his way again. By now he was pissed and he began to speed, but as he got into the residential area he had to slow down. He jammed on the brakes at the apartment where Barnes lived and parked. Murphy was nowhere to be seen.

"What's going on," he yelled over to a group of people standing gawking at the building as he hurried toward the door. Another vehicle came in then and double parked and he saw it was the paramedics.

"We heard someone is threatening to blow a cops brains out!" A woman said.

Miss Barnes lived in the big building of co-op apartments and a uniformed doorman stood at the door as Reed ran up, and two cops were at his side.

"No one is allowed in!" They said.

"Is it true, a resident is holding a gun to a cop's head?" Reed asked.

"Sorry man, we got orders!"

Reed leaned in the door and tried to see whatever was going on.

"Like I said, we got orders!" The doorman replied and nodded toward the cops.

Reed walked back to the sidewalk in front of the building and stood.

Could that resident be Miss Barnes? His breath caught at the thought.

Just then he saw a blue LTD spin right over the manicured lawn and stop inches from the door. Murphy jumped out.

"Hey buddy," Reed said.

"I got caught in a jam coming over the bridge. I just got the call; we got a hostage situation here too?" Murphy said. "This is the same address!"

"Murph, this is the same building I was in just a few nights ago having a whiskey with Barnes. She lives here." Reed said as they hurried up to the cops at the door.

Murphy identified himself and they were told to go to the fourth floor. They ran to the elevators. When they got to that floor and hurried down the hallway, residents peeked out of their own doors curiously. Several cops stood guarding one, and it was the same door Reed remembered going into.

"What do we have here?" Murphy asked.

"It's one of our men. This old broad has a gun to his head, says she'll blow his brains out unless we get the DA to clear her name."

"Do we have confirmation on this woman's identity?" Murphy asked.

Silence

"Her name is Barnes." One said. Reed and Murphy exchanged looks.

"Goddamn Murph, I know her. I'll go in. I can talk her out of it!" Reed brushed at his hair again.

But, just then they heard shots and both men barged through the door into the Barnes apartment.

Right off, the smell of gunpowder hit their nostrils in the enclosed rooms. And then Reed's stomach heaved in rebellion at the scene he was thrust into.

The policeman was on the floor and still, and on the same couch that Miss Barnes had sat on when he had been there several days ago; now, her crumpled body remained except minus most of her head. Behind her, the shelves of a bookcase containing hundreds of hard cover books were splattered with blood and gray matter. Everywhere! A piece of fiery red dyed hair clung to one and now the smell of blood and urine permeated the air. The whole scene seemed to be hanging suspended in silence. Murphy yelled for the paramedics and rushed to the still policeman. He pressed for a pulse and found one.

Reed suddenly clamped a hand over his mouth and raced to a bathroom and slammed the door and got sick. Goddamn, he growled after hanging over the toilet bowl and puking. Minutes later, he rinsed out his mouth and splashed cold water over his face, then combed his hair. The stench was heavier yet when he came out.

"My prints are on the flusher and the faucets in the room," he said to Murphy who held a sheet of paper. "She left a note?" He asked then.

"She did and she addressed it to you. Here read it! Apparently she had a plan in mind when our man showed up." He held the edges of it for Reed to read. Then nodded to the cop on the floor, who had been shot in the hip. The paramedics had administered their emergency procedures and he was talking.

"She tricked me, got my gun, and I went down." The cop's name was Bristle, Reed noticed on his badge. Bristle took a shuttering breath and closed his eyes, then whispered, "The last thing I remember, I saw her holding it to her head. Then it sounded liked an explosion. Jesus! I must have passed out then."

Murphy had crouched down closer now as the wounded man tried to talk.

"I told her the DA had signed a warrant for her arrest and we were there to take her in. She got pissed, feigned shock, and she got my gun!" He took another shuttering breath. We got here just in time, she was leaving town." The wounded man added faintly, as apparently the drugs started working for the pain from his wound. "She said she had written a note and was going to disappear."

"We got it." Murphy said. And then the room became crowded with the BCA and officials. After Murphy brought the men up to date, they left and went to their own cars.

Silence

"I'll meet you at your office," Reed said then.

As he drove downtown to the Minneapolis Police Department, his throat was still sore from the violent upset he'd had. After all his years of dealing with humanity and their frailties, he thought he'd seen it all. He chewed furiously on Listerine tabs to soothe and freshen his breath and tried to wipe the scene from his thoughts.

Back at the precinct Murphy had put the letter in a plastic sleeve. "I've got to turn this over to the BCA, but here take another look before I send it to them!"

The letter was addressed to Reed: Dear Mr. Conners, it read, I'm sure you will find out before long, that I pushed that bastard, Jonas Hovland over the railing. However, I am not going to rot in prison for doing it." It was signed, Agatha Barnes.

He read it over several times and ran a hand through his hair as he stood there with the confession addressed to him in hand. He almost got sick again.

Was he responsible for her taking her life?

It was the first time he had been named in a case. And he realized it would soon be closed. And as always, he was somewhat stunned when it came to an end, most of the time abruptly.

Murphy ran off a copy of the note for him and Reed turned to go. "I've got to see Ed over at the office now to wrap this up but I'll get in touch with you before I leave town."

"Hey, buddy I haven't asked. How are you feeling?"

By now, the bruises on Reed face had faded to yellow and the path of the bullet that had graced the side of his head had only left a small scab under his hair.

"I'll be better when I get back to Birch and spend a few days out in my boat," Reed commented and raised his hand in leaving. And over at the First Federated Insurance Company, he drawled, "Hello beautiful!"

Surprised, Mona stood and slipped her arms around him and their lips met in a warm kiss. "Well now, that's the way I like to be greeted," he smiled.

"Sorry, I haven't been in touch. How are you?" Reed stepped back and looked her up and down and as usual Mona was decked out. Her black hair was shiny and short, still not fully grown out from losing it from the chemo months back, but it curled and framed her face. She was clad in a rose colored dress with a slim skirt. Low cut and revealing.

Reed did a double take, as there they were; both her breasts. He knew she had lost one in the mastectomy surgery.

Mona noticed his obvious interest and pointed to her chest. "Isn't it marvelous? I had reconstructive surgery and I have a matched set again." She laughed, "Outside of a small scar, I don't think anyone would know!"

"Well," Reed grinned, "for sure I won't tell anyone!"

They laughed together like the old friends they were. "First off though, I better tend to business. Is he in?" Reed asked and nodded towards the CEO's door.

"Yes, he's here and he already knows. The chief just called him!" Mona sat back down at her desk and adjusted her dress. "Go ahead and go in," she added.

"Conners, I just heard. So we have a signed confession. She did the old man!" Ed said and reached out for Reed's hand.

"I've got a copy of it right here," Reed said as they shook. "The official one will be here later." Reed shook hands with his boss. "She was ready to put it into words at the last minute there too."

"Okay, Jesus, you saved my company a lot of money. You know what five percent of twenty-five million is, don't you?"

Reed grinned and admitted, "The number has been circling around in my head!"

"Yeah, yeah," Ed said, "like they say, the check is in the mail!"

Silence

-41-

Lindy ran out of the bar where she had met Joe Brown for a glass of wine. He was the gunsmith and owner of the shop called Guns and Red Roses, where she'd bought the cute little derringer. The gun, that weighed down her purse now as she sidestepped the liquor guzzling patrons of the place in her haste.

Lordy, were they purposely standing in her path?

Nearing the Lexus outside and close to safety, the scene inside replayed in her head. Joe Brown was the local gunsmith here in Hilton Head and she had recognized his face on the Mexican Mafia family picture.

She slammed the door of the Lexus and the gravel spew out from under the wheels as she flew out of the parking lot. She was not in a good mood as she left the area, but instead of going back to her house she aimed her car to the other side of the island to a new place called The House of Blue Lights. She had planned to go over and meet the owners and since she was dressed up this evening and no place to go, she didn't want all the preparation to go to waste. Besides she needed to eat something.

A valet in a tux stood ready to park her car when she drove up to the door. Then another escorted her in the door.

Well, now she was impressed. She had heard talk that this was a new up-scale eatery and bar that catered to the upper echelon, which of course included her.

When the doorman ushered her into the place, it didn't have blue lights anywhere, she noticed, but she remembered a popular song called that from years back. She carried her cell phone along with her at all times now, and that with her latest purchase really loaded down her purse. Now she heard the phone chirping away faintly but she wasn't going to answer it. Lordy, she was tired of it all. From now on she just wanted to concentrate on her home and her business.

The House of Blue Lights was located on the beach and right of Lindy was impressed. A jazz trio was playing soft music and the lights were low. Blue linen dressed tables with individual lamps filled the middle of the room with booths on one side. A long mahogany bar graced another. Hanging crystal chandeliers sparkled over the booths and a huge one dominated a dance floor off to the side.

As Lindy stood in the foyer in her yellow dress and blonde tresses, her entrance into the packed dining room turned heads.

"Good afternoon," the tuxedo clad host greeted her. "Will you be dining alone with us?"

"Yes," she said and followed him into the dining room where he pulled out a chair for her.

She sat down and placed her purse on the table. When the server came over she ordered a glass of their best wine and asked to see their menu. As she sat relaxing, she casually looked around the room at the crowded tables of customers. She didn't know a soul. But after a few more minutes, she happened to glance over to a big round table in the corner of the room, and her eyes bugged at the sight. There at the center of the table sat Rio Prada, the Mayor of Monterrey, Mexico, surrounded by what must be members of his family. She quickly turned her head.

What the hell was Prada doing here in Hilton Head? For God's sake, were they all related? Did their tentacles reach out in all directions?

As Lindy sat in the ritzy dining room sipping her expensive wine she forced herself to remain calm. Had Rio Prada recognized her from across the crowded room? Then she remembered she had been a redhead months ago when his two nephews had drowned in Birch Lake in northern Minnesota and he'd shown up with his entourage and claimed foul play. And had shown up again, and threatened her when she'd been hospitalized later after being shot by Mario.

Months and months ago, but she didn't think Prada would have missed a single thing. But she made up her mind, she wasn't going to run and hide from these murdering, drug lords. She was going to continue enjoying her life here at the beach and if anyone threatened her, she would just use her new shooter!

She ordered fresh mussels and a spinach salad and took her time eating her dinner. Then she sat and enjoyed a liqueur and coffee. When the Prada family began its exit, thank God, they went out a side door and didn't come near her table.

The next day, Lindy made a call to the Hilton Head Police Department and asked for Detective Mike Mann, whom she had met a few weeks ago, when she had identified the Jane Doe they had found as her friend, Mitzi Grover. A pang of grief shot through her chest again as she remembered her friend!

As Lindy sat this next morning in her ultra modern kitchen, the sun gleamed on the stainless steel appliances, and caught the sparkles in the granite counter tops. She took a breath as he answered, "Detective Mike Mann," then said gruffly, "what can I do for you?"

"Hello," she said, "Lindy Lewis, do you remember me?"

"Miss Lewis, of course I remember you."

"There's something I need to talk to you about Detective."

"All right, do you want to come down?" He asked. She had forgotten he had such a sexy voice, but she didn't feel like going down to that hellish place. It brought back too many bad memories just thinking about a police department.

"Can you meet me at my house?" She asked then on the spur of the moment.

"I can do that, Miss Lewis, when?"

And they agreed that later that morning would be fine. And besides, that gave her enough time to get ready for her afternoon business.

She hung up the phone and hurried to shower and got ready for the day. She slipped on a long dress with a halter top, a vibrant pink. Then, a pair of silver backless heels. Her make-up was sheer since her complexion had darkened to a lovely golden color. She brushed her silver tresses into a spiky look and then spritzed on her daytime cologne. She stepped back and checked herself in the floor-length mirror in the dressing room and liked the results.

For a middle-aged broad, you're not too bad she said to her reflection. Then, blew a kiss to herself. Just then the door-bell chimed and she hurried to the front of the house.

"Hello, detective," she said. "Come on in."

Detective Mann stepped into the foyer. "Beautiful," he said as he looked around.

"Thank you." Lindy said, "I just made a pot of coffee, why don't you come into the kitchen."

"Sounds good, I haven't had my caffeine yet today." He followed Lindy and took a stool at the counter. "You got quite a spread here; did you win a lottery or something?" As he smiled, Lindy noticed his full lips under the mustache.

"Or something," she said then. Be darned if she had to explain her financial worth. "Detective," she said then, "I need to ask you about someone I saw on the island last night."

"Okay," he said, "but first, call me Mike. Can I call you Lindy?"

"Of course." And as they talked she noticed he was wearing a tailor made beige suit with a black t-shirt underneath. His shoes were black tasseled loafers. She felt his appraising eyes go over her as well. And as she poured the coffee she had to pause a minute between cups to steady her hands that held the pot.

"Mike," she said as she passed him a cup and saucer. "Here's what I want to know, does Rio Prada have a residence here?" She settled on a stool then and sipped her coffee.

"Who?" He asked.

"Rio Prada, do you know him?" She asked.

Detective Mike Mann shook his head. "No, but several million tourists come through this island in a year's time." Lindy watched him stir sugar in his coffee. "But who is he and why are you interested in him?" He asked.

Lindy could feel his eyes on her. "I just heard some talk about the Prada family living here." She said.

"Beats the hell out of me!" Mike Mann answered. He put a foot over a knee and sat back and looked at her appraisingly.

Lindy suddenly felt something wasn't right about his off-hand remark. But, wouldn't he be surprised if I told him I had saved Rio Prada's life when I lived in Mexico. And, in thanks the man raped me.

She sipped her coffee. Someday she would make Prada pay for what he had done to her. But today, this man was making her heart thump and her breath heavy.

"What do you do here in Hilton Head," Mike asked.

"Not too much," she answered. "I just enjoy the water and the sun."

He looked at her almost slyly then. "Oh, but I hear you've got quite the business going for yourself." He said then, startling her.

Lindy did a double take but asked innocently. "Whatever do you mean? Are you talking about my jewelry business?"

"Is that what you call it?" He laughed. "I did check on you when I heard you were running some kind of business out of your home."

Lindy returned a smile. "Oh Mike, it's nothing, I just play with stones and wire and make jewelry for people. Sometimes they give me a few dollars for my work. It's strictly a craft."

"Hmm--, I see," he said.

Then chills suddenly raced down her back. She had just had a vision where she'd seen Detective Mike Mann standing arm and arm with Joe Brown, in that same picture of the D'Agustino's, Mercodo and Prada families in Mexico.

My lord, he was one of them too! But how much did he really know about her? Then she remembered he hadn't asked for her address earlier when she'd called, which meant, he knew exactly where she lived! Apparently Mike Mann, the detective, knew more about her then she thought.

Had the Mexican tentacles followed her to her island too?

-42-

"I guess you will be heading out now," Ed, Reed's boss at First Federated said as they stood together in the office the next day after wrapping up the paperwork. The Jonas Hovland case was closed, and since Hovland had been murdered by the Barnes woman and not died from a natural death, the family could not collect the twenty-five million dollars insurance on him.

"You're right. I'll tie up some loose ends and then get on the road." Reed said and grinned.

"Reed, you saved my company millions. I promise now this time, you can have a nice long retirement." They shook hands and then Reed left his office.

"Hey Mona, want to have a cocktail," he asked Ed's secretary as he came up beside her.

"Are you buying dinner too, or do I have to go home hungry?" Mona laughed.

"I might spring for a burger!" Reed grinned and went on, "but it might cost you?"

"Why don't I meet you at Gina's around five-thirty?"

"Perfect," Reed said. "Gives me time to take care of some things."

At Nordstrom's he did some power shopping and bought slacks, shirts, boots and underwear. He tossed his shopping bags in the trunk of the Corvette and had just enough time to meet Mona. At the hotel earlier, he had taken time to shower for the second time in the day and change into fresh clothes. And added an extra spritz of Armani cologne.

As he spun up to Gina's, the parking attendant and doorman were standing ready to greet him. Brothers and friends of Gina's, Reed had known them for years. He remembered that she had taken them in off the streets, cleaned them up and offered them a job if they stayed that way, when she had first opened her business decades ago, and they had remained dedicated to her ever since.

"Good to see you again Reed," they said and came up and shook hands.

"Same here guys," he said to both of them. "Been doing any fishing lately here on the river?" Reed had invited them up to Birch Lake last year to spend a few days. Since he had had a guest house built several years ago, he could accommodate 6-8 people at a time. It even had a kitchen if anyone wanted to cook.

"Yup, we got a few "pan fish" last week." One said, then got in the Corvette and drove it away to a safe spot in the lot.

"Look at some dates when you both can get away and come on up!" Reed said then to the other who opened the door into the restaurant for him. "Just give me a call," he said.

Gina herself was standing at her desk busily studying her reservations. It was a Friday night and soon her place would be bursting with patrons enjoying her offerings.

The mouth-watering aroma of grilled steaks hit him as he stood for a minute, then he stepped up to Gina and surprised her in a hug.

"Reed Conners," she said then laughing and returning his hug. "How long have you been in town this time?"

"A few weeks," he answered. "Sorry, I've been so busy with this case I just couldn't get away."

Gina was dressed as usual in her silver and diamonds. Her blond hair was piled high on her head and her make-up was perfect. Tonight she had on white silk pants and top, with a silver gray linen jacket. Her nails gleamed in scarlet.

"Goddamn, you just get better looking," Reed grinned.

"Well, thanks darling. I'll tell my stylist that." She matched his grin and took his arm. "Come on in, there's a good looking dame waiting for you at the bar." And she led him over to where Mona was sitting with a glass in her hand.

"Hello beautiful," Reed said to Mona and climbed on the next stool. "I see you started without me."

"Well, how can you sit at a bar and not have a tall one. Actually," and she smiled, "I just ordered some plain soda water."

"So what would you like?"

"A Stolys martini with two olives," she remarked easily.

Paul, the bartender came over then "Hey buddy," he said, "good to see you." He reached over the bar and shook hands with Reed.

"How have you been Paul?" Reed had known Paul too for years and counted him as a close friend. "It's been awhile again."

"Yeah, on a case again?"

"Yes, this one ended abruptly yesterday, so I'm free for a while. Can't wait to get back and out on my boat."

"What can I bring you folks?" Paul asked then.

Reed ordered and as they waited, he looked Mona up and down and grinned. "Goddamn, lady you look good!"

And Mona winked with a come hither look on her face. She'd had on a red business suit earlier when he seen her at the office and now she had taken off the jacket and in its place had a low cut black top that exposed her smooth shoulders and rather sumptuous chest.

"Thank you my dear," she said. "I love it, and it helps that you live up there in the woods too."

"And time only makes you better." Reed leaned over and kissed her on her lips. And then Paul was back with their drinks.

As Mona sipped her Stolys and Reed his Crown Royal, their eyes met over their drinks. "I guess you will be retreating to your island soon, now that you wrapped up your case," she murmured.

"You guessed right, Mona, why don't you take off some time and come on up?"

Mona picked up an olive and ate it slowly. Then said, "Maybe I can sometime later."

"Why not sooner? You haven't been back since last year, after your chemo treatments."

"I know. But now is not a good time."

"Why not Mona, is something wrong?" Reed asked anxiously.

"No, no it's something else. Reed, I'm planning on going to Europe for a month and see some friends."

"I didn't know you had friends there. When are you planning on going?" Reed asked.

"In a couple of weeks." Mona answered.

"You mean Ed can get along without you for all that time?"

Mona smiled. "I trained my file clerk to fill in for me."

"Well, who do you know over there?" Reed asked again, curiously.

"Reed, you don't know him. It's a friend I've known just about as long as I've known you.

"A man huh?" Reed commented dryly. "Well, I didn't know I had competition!"

Mona laughed. "No competition there. He's a good friend!"

Just then, Gina came over. "I've got one of your favorite tables ready," she said.

"Wonderful," Reed mumbled as Gina took their glasses and nodded for Mona to follow. He was trying to digest the fact that she had other plans that didn't include him.

Well hell, he guessed he had some that didn't include her either. Some went through his head in the short time they were making their way to that table.

"There you are my dear friends." Gina said in her husky voice and handed them the menus. "Now take your time and enjoy your dinner!" She left them then and stopped at tables throughout the room to see that all her customers were happy and content.

"What would you like to order?" Reed asked. He put his jealous streak aside, realizing again, they both had their own lives and that's what made their friendship special.

Mona studied the menu for a few minutes then said, "Let's have the filet dinner for two. I feel like some red meat tonight."

"Sounds good to me." When the waiter came over, Reed ordered their dinner and also asked for another martini for her and a whiskey for him.

"What are your plans now?" Mona asked.

Reed grinned. "I'm looking forward to getting back to the lake, I've been gone almost a month."

"Do you still have your neighbors looking after things?"

"Sure. I have a service that takes care of the lawn and the greenery." Reed took a drink of his whiskey.

"Are you going to do some shopping with the million plus you just collected?"

She asked then.

Reed grinned. "I've been thinking about a bigger boat!"

"I wondered about that," Mona laughed and playfully tapped his hand.

"Just how much bigger do you need?"

"I'll know it when I see it!" Reed grinned.

Mona delicately sipped her martini and just then the waiter brought their steaks.

"Yumm--, she whispered as she eyed the steak. The 16 oz piece of meat had been cooked rare, sliced and laid out steaming and ready on their plates. Along with red-skin potatoes sautéed with golden scallions, and fresh red and green peppers. Spring grown asparagus with hollandaise sauce claimed another corner of the plate.

"This is always so lovely, isn't it" Mona murmured as they began to eat. "I haven't had a good steak for weeks." And they ate in comfortable silence and then sat back and asked for coffee and a liqueur.

A baby grand piano stood off to the side in the room and earlier a lady had come in and began to play some golden oldies as the dinner crowd enjoyed their repast. Reed looked up suddenly as she wound up her set with the Tennessee Waltz.

Goddamn, that song always tugged at his heart as Lindy's face came back to haunt him. He remembered how they used to dance to that song. An old one they had both grown up hearing in their homes. He wondered where she was and if she was safe. And on the drive back to Birch Lake the next day, he couldn't get her out of his mind.

-43-

Lindy refilled their coffee cups as Detective Mike Mann sat at the counter in her kitchen. The late morning sun sparkled on the highly waxed stone floors that edged its way throughout the house. Fluffy rugs softened the open rooms with hues that matched the mellow greens and soft blue of the décor.

Mike Mann looked around himself appreciatively. "Did you do the decorating in here?" He asked curiously. "If you did, it's a great job."

"Most of it," Lindy fibbed. Right now she was too perturbed to think straight. The vision that she'd just had showed him as being another member of the infamous Mexican drug family. Her blood ran cold.

What was the connection between him and Emilio? Joe Brown, the gun salesman and the rest of Mila's cousins? Were they all connected in the drug world?

Lindy's thought were going a mile a minute as she sat there in her kitchen with Detective Mann. She had to get rid of him, but to stay safe she couldn't let him know that she knew who he was. And when she got nervous she smoked.

"Mike, let's take our coffee out to the lanai." She said and her silver sandals clicked on the stone floors.

"Have a seat," she invited taking one of the rattan chairs in the glass and screen covered room.

Detective Mann followed and looked around and then out to the vast expanse of ocean.

"Christ, what a view to have in your back yard!" He said and took a seat.

"This must have cost you a bundle. Do you live here alone?" He asked then.

A little warning sign went up and Lindy answered, "Most of the time," evasively.

"Well, are you attached?" He persisted.

Lindy turned it around and laughed, "Well, are you?" She wasn't about to tell him anything about her private life either. But she had the sense to know she had to stay on his good side. Thank God, she'd learned of his family ties now, and not gotten involved with him.

Detective Mann took out his Merits and offered her one.

"Thanks, I've got my own," she remarked taking a pack out of her pocket. "But I'll take a light." And as she lowered her head to the lighter another thought sprang into action in her thoughts. So quick and so brutal, she sucked in her breath and choked on the smoke. She saw this same man, the detective, bending over her dead friend Mitzi. It seemed to be in a car, as there looked to be a dashboard in the background.

Lindy stood up and coughed suddenly and tears ran down her face.

"Are you okay?" the detective asked. "Do you need some water?"

She had to get away from the man. And fast!

"I'm sorry," she managed to say as a stunning wave of nausea suddenly came over her. "Do you mind seeing yourself out?"

She ran out of the lanai, into the great room and then to the bathroom on the other side of the house. After a minute she heard his car start and she peeked out the window to make sure he was leaving her driveway. The nauseous sensation left then.

For God's sake, she had landed right in the middle of these rattlesnakes. All part of the Mexican Mafia family that she feared. First, there was Emilio; Mila's cousin, then Joe Brown the gun-shop owner, and now Detective Mike Mann. For sure, they all knew she had testified for the FBI that their brother and uncle, Mario D'Agustino, had killed a federal agent!

She glanced at the time then and saw several people waiting on the patio to see her today. She had to get rid of them.

She stepped outside and sucked in her breath. The sun glistened on her pink halter dress and her silver tresses. "I'm sorry, I can't see you today," Lindy said. "I have an emergency." But an old woman stood up.

"Miss Lindy, I need to see you!" She whispered.

Lindy looked at her. "Maybe tomorrow," she said.

The woman stepped up to her and took her hands. "Miss Lindy, I'm afraid it'll be too late then."

"Too late? For what?" Lindy gaped at her.

"I have to tell you." The woman whispered again.

"Very well then," Lindy said and the woman followed her back inside the house, and then into the magic room. She walked slowly, almost painfully. Beforehand, as usual Lindy had quickly turned on the soothing strains of Enya and the air was gently scented with jasmine. They settled on comfortable chairs. Lindy's glass ball stood to one side on the black silk covered table and she took a minute and stared into its depths, then sucked in her breath as a scene floated there for just a second.

The lady was of Spanish decent and said her name was Leta and had come to the island to visit and had stayed on. Her stature was slight and her hair was salt and pepper. Her complexion was creamy, but lined in wrinkles. Her colorful dress draped around her body and fell to floor length and a matching scarf held her flowing hair back.

"I needed to see you," Leta exclaimed then as she twisted a hanky in her hands.

Lindy looked at her questioningly.

"Miss Lindy," the woman said, "I don't know what this means, but I keep seeing this picture of you in my dreams." The tissue lay in shreds in her gnarled hands now.

"Have we met Leta? I'm sorry I don't remember." Lindy exclaimed.

"No, I have never been introduced to you. But I know who you are?" Leta dabbed at her eyes.

"Did you say you see me in your dreams, Leta?" Lindy asked curiously.

"That's why I've come, Miss Lindy, I see you're in danger!"

Lindy sat up straighter and stared at her. She swallowed hard before she could get any more words out. Then asked, "What do you see me doing in your dream Leta?"

Leta put her arms securely around her chest and whispered, "I'm so sorry, but I had to come. You see, sometimes I see pictures in my dreams, maybe like you." Leta's brown eyes saddened as she breathed deeply.

Lindy reached for her hand. "Tell me, what have you seen that troubles you Leta?"

Leta dabbed at her eyes again. "Miss Lindy," she said, "I see you dead!"

Lindy gaped at the stranger and Leta apologized again profusely.

"I am so sorry," she whispered, "but you see, I had to come!"

Lindy managed to send Leta on her way shortly after, then told the other waiting people that she had to close for the day and locked her doors.

Leta's vision most certainly meant one of the men here would kill her to avenge Mario's death? There was Emilio, Joe Brown and the detective?"

She had to get away fast, but she needed her money and the bank wouldn't open for hours, till morning. She hurriedly packed her suitcases and sat down on her bed. The clock on her bedside table chimed softly and reminded her it was only going on midnight. Maybe a glass of milk would help the knots of panic in her stomach and she padded out to the kitchen. Then taking it with her she went out to the lanai and settled down on a couch in the darkness to wait for morning.

A full moon had spread its silver dress over the ocean, as it hummed its hushing midnight song. And sitting there half asleep, sometime later, she had a dream, or was it a vision. And she too, saw herself dead, lying in an alley. At the exact same place where she had seen Mitzi. And again, Detective Mann was hovering.

Later, Lindy wasn't sure when she thought back on it, if it was a dream or another vision, but a friendly ghost had come to her then and whispered, "Lindy, hurry!" She immediately awoke fully and clutched her suitcases and locked up her house! But as she drove away, a shadow in the house brushed at a tear.

She waited downtown for hours for the bank to open and then frantically gathered all her money. Now days later, after the long journey from Hilton Head Island, as she drove the last few miles nearing Birch Lake, she felt as if she was finally coming home after a long, long journey.

The end

Watch for another adventure soon called
Moonbeams on my Shoulders

Watch for
Moonbeams Coming soon---

TO ORDER COPIES OF
THIS BOOK
Please feel free to contact me through
my e-mail at
lindylewis1@msn.com
or my website at
**Mystery- Novels- Lyn Miller
LaCoursiere.com**
You can find my books in soft cover
or e-books on
Amazon.com and
NightwritersBooks.com

Lyn Miller LaCoursiere is an avid reader and loves to travel. She has a large loving family and joyfully jumps on a plane when an invitation arrives to visit. She lives in Minnesota but also spends as much time as possible by the ocean in the south. Her passion is relaxing by water anywhere, ocean, pond or puddle. Lyn has published numerous newspaper articles dealing with life and life's challenges. This is her sixth novel in her adventures featuring Lindy Lewis and Reed Conners set in the Midwest.
Watch for Moonbeams coming soon----